A KI

Pamela Haines was ... educated at a conv... read English at Cambridge. As a child she wrote prolifically but she did not take up writing as an adult until her late thirties, by which time she was married with five children. In 1971 she won the *Spectator* New Writing Prize with a short story and in 1973 completed her first novel, *Tea at Gunter's*. Acclaimed by the critics, it was joint winner of the first Yorkshire Arts Association Award for Young Writers. It was followed by *A Kind of War* in 1976, *Men On White Horses* in 1978, *The Kissing Gate* in 1981, *The Diamond Waterfall* in 1984, *The Golden Lion* in 1986 and *Daughter of the Northern Fields* in 1987.

PAMELA HAINES

A Kind of War

FONTANA/Collins

First published in Great Britain by William Heinemann Ltd 1976
First issued in Fontana Paperbacks 1989

Copyright © Pamela Haines 1976

Printed and bound in Great Britain by
William Collins Sons & Co. Ltd, Glasgow

For my parents
Muriel and Harry Burrows

A KIND OF WAR

PART ONE

Love is a kind of warre; Hence those who feare,
No cowards must his royall Ensignes beare:

Robert Herrick, 'On Love'

Chapter 1

'Your teeth are like the stars – they come out at night . . .' A joke of Christopher's, his half-term greeting; and she supposed, at eleven, a satisfying remark to make to a grandmother.

A milk float outside whined. Its whine had been part of her dream then it had woken her sharply, painfully. That was what she hated about old age, this sudden total waking. Any day was too long that began at six with the delivery of someone else's milk (or was it just – any day was too long?). Now there was the sound of a dog barking, throaty, persistent, on and on. Someone else's dog.

This is London, she thought, in the dusty pointless year of 1973. She felt, feared, the tightening of her right leg, about to cramp. Quinine – had she taken it the night before? Both legs felt knotted, nowadays looked knotted. Legs that had once been perfect (she'd been glad, was still glad, of the return to long skirts. She had gone into them at once). The whole of her now a disaster area. Only good bonework, that remained. And at least she was not fat: so many slim beauties ended their days plump cushions – billowy not willowy. Her hair too. In a way that had been preserved. She was put in mind suddenly of the mammoth's mane in the museum in St Petersburg – held for how many millennia in frozen Siberian earth? It had captured her imagination as a child.

Ah then, she thought, why didn't I go to St Petersburg that time – when I had the chance – that time in 1912, when the Harcourts invited us? Four weeks: every sort of introduction. Unbelievable that I said 'no'. But it would have been in Theo's company – how *tedious*, I thought then. It would be even more so now. We cannot choose our brothers (and if we could, would I have chosen Con?). But I thought at the time: I have hundreds more chances. I was immortal then.

Milk bottles rattled, a crate clattered, then the whine again as the float started up. She tried to lie still but she had lost the art. Knew too that ahead of her lay the slow painful un-

3

stiffening of her hip. Soon she would have to get out. Her bladder no longer waited these days. She tried once more, forced herself to lie still.

But she had become obsessed with St Petersburg, with the road not taken. It would be with her now in the bed until nine, until her daughter-in-law brought up her breakfast. (And what sort of treat is that? she asked herself. Teresa is quite insensitive to my wants, needs, my constantly patiently explained requirements.) She would not even see Polly today: Polly is my life line, she thought; she is more than Teresa or Barney deserved. (She is certainly all they have managed.) Christopher is a pleasant enough little boy – but with an adopted child one can't know.

The dog started up yet again and she drummed her fingers furiously on the eiderdown. Her legs knotted – with rage it seemed. Her bursts of anger these days frightened her. It was as if some controlling agent had gone, some censor no longer at the gate.

And if I had gone to Russia – then that would have been four weeks less with Con. Was I not perhaps thinking of that, even then? Now, I don't want really to go – I want only the choice again ...

A frustrated cry, too late? Time seemed to be accelerating: all those years in between – gone, raced by. Why then do my days drag so? How in God's name can there be *two* sorts of time?

I used to be such a doer, for so much of my life – after everything went wrong. Margaret Willingham, alias Muff: a woman of action. In those Yorkshire days – what ever got done that I hadn't a hand in? It was always I who organized.

Someone was trying to start up a motorbike: the engine just about to turn, then not making it.

What shall I do with today? Oh my God, *how shall I pass the day*?

∞

When the alarm went Polly turned it off without moving her head, without really opening her eyes. A crammer's – or coach-

4

ing establishment as they liked to call it – was nothing to wake up for, not an excitement to make her leap forth.

Her bed was too small – or she was too long. When she woke up her feet were always pushed out at the end or her hair up against the headboard. A restless sleeper (dormitory days and the bed all churned up, 'look at Polly's bed', tangled sheets as if there'd been sexy fun and games all night).

Probably it was stupid anxieties about tests. Thursday was always test day at Hatter's. What made it such a fucking thorough crammer's was the thoroughness of the tests. I don't get enough daylight, she thought suddenly, I'm like one of those plants, my face all white. I wouldn't like their bill for fluorescent tubes – you'd think a place like that, and Knightsbridge too, could have something up at ground level. And what a name . . . Hatter's. (Was there ever a hatter's there? Or even an Earl Hatter, Lord Hatter, *Mr* Hatter? They picked the name out of a hat, Patrick said . . . and that's about the standard of his jokes.)

Still, if you want 'A's and your school have had enough of you – then it'll do as well as anywhere. It's having to keep going till six though . . . and at the pace they set. We get to live for lunch time. Patrick and I must be known in The Grove. And then at four, that feeling desperate and shooting out for espressos and Danish pastries – all right for me who's so spindly. Some though . . . But I haven't really made friends there, except for the beautiful Patrick. What would I do without him?

Just a little more sleep, she thought. Turn over a little. Too much thinking about Hatter's, so drifting, dozing: into a dream. She is late; it's night and the place is empty – all the lights burning. Papers, books everywhere. She and Patrick sit at desks far far away from each other. She said to him then, 'I wish I loved you, I'd love to love you.' He said airily, 'All it needs is a little effort . . .' But in the dream she was tired, tired, tired of it all. She said, in the dream: 'I think I'm going to have to wake up.'

She sat up suddenly and saw that it was seven forty-five. 'O God – I'm going to be *late* . . .'

∞

Today was the day she was going to get it right: she, Tessie Willingham, would by nine a.m. have tasks, one, two, three, all done.

But a lot of time always got wasted arranging to save it. The paradox was: to get it all done in order, some sort of order was necessary first.

The first step was to leave Muff's breakfast tray almost complete before going upstairs. Then she'd only to see to the coffee and smooth *The Times*; fear of her mother-in-law was worse than carrying out any foolish chore.

She would make the bed first. When she left it and then guiltily covered it over at five in the afternoon, it was a temptation all day. It cried out to offer more sleep. Everything about me, she thought, is like that: just one more cake, just another five minutes, just have a cigarette . . . She thought now, I won't smoke till I've got it all done. But without a cigarette she felt not a complete person, almost a limb missing. Twenty years ago and newly married and suddenly finding herself even more socially inadequate than she'd realized – what do I do with my hands? Then at some party trying that and, surprise, it helped. Now it was just a thirst, all the time.

She lit up. My God it's all hopeless. She saw herself at turned forty-three, not yet pulled into recognizable shape – physically, emotionally, morally, intellectually. The lot. As she climbed the stairs, she thought, I'd move more quickly if I lost some weight. She went off to weigh herself, just to see how bad it was.

It was very bad. And already she'd wasted time. When she thought how many women worked, had a full time career; and all she had to do was take up her mother-in-law's tray, do some cleaning and cooking (and not too much of either), work for some 'O' levels, and care for a daughter and a son and a husband who departed early for the City and didn't appear again till seven.

She made the bed, rinsed the basin and bath, tidied the towels. She remembered then a sports jacket which – a week ago, a month ago? – Barney had said should be cleaned; also some shoes he wanted repaired. She got them both out ready to take in the afternoon.

Before tidying any further she went to fetch the transistor.

6

It was always easier to do dull repetitive work (what else was she capable of?) with noise in the background. She twisted the dial and got a Waldteufel waltz; it sounded sickly and far away – then fading into fuzz it was interfered with by speech. German. It seemed to be a quiz of sorts but she couldn't make out any of the questions. There was a lot of chattering and laughing; the programme was over. '*Wie Sexy sind Sie?*' said the announcer. 'Not very,' she replied sadly, glad she hadn't been in the quiz.

Then she caught sight of the bedroom clock. Ten minutes later she knocked on Muff's door.

A peremptory 'one moment, please.' She knew what it was. It might have been better to stand outside and wait for the ormolu clock to strike nine. Yet she'd set the kitchen clock by Radio One.

'I think your clock is a little in advance, Teresa.' Enlarged knuckles beat on the linen sheet. Her own fine linen was not all she'd brought. The room – originally a second drawing-room – had once seemed enormous: in far-off days Tessie'd thought of making a studio of it. She was going to learn sculpture, learn oils; let other people use it. A music room for Polly and friends. Now it looked tiny. Crowded. Odd in someone like Muff who must in her time, as all her generation, have reacted against Victorian fussiness and excess. It was as if faced with x amount of space and y amount of goods there had been no choice.

Hardly an inch of spare wall. Photographs, portraits, water-colours – many of them of Lough Corrib (always referred to by Muff as 'Corrib' – never the name of the house or village) where she'd spent so much of her childhood. Tiered miniatures of her grandparents, her father – killed in a railway accident – her plain, kind mother. Photographs of herself throughout her seven ages; of her husband Cecil, young then growing older; of her daughter Prue, and of Barney; Polly at all stages; people Tessie had never identified; one only of Muff's brother Theo (tall pinched impossibly dry Theo, who had given them the house). An enormous portrait, dwarfing everything else, of her younger brother Con. Solemn brooding thirteen-year-old, he seemed to Tessie never to see her as she came into the room.

Occasional tables crammed with ornaments; the huge brass-horned gramophone which was never played – except for Polly as a child; the pole screen with its Berlin-work panels; the giant tallboy, its lower drawers full of clothes no longer worn, and higher up, of letters, programmes, brochures, private treasures. The davenport at which straight-backed she sat to write letters of complaint to Harrods (alas that she seemed to have no friends left now, or had offended those she did have).

'It looks cold – but quite clear,' Tessie said, drawing the curtains back. She brought the tray over: 'What did you think of doing today?'

Muff froze. 'What concern is it of yours how I spend my time? I *cannot* – Such intolerable intrusions – Have I no right to a private life?' The ormolu clock struck nine. 'You have surely been to your service?' she said suddenly.

Tessie searched wildly: the day, the month, the date?

'To Mass, Teresa. Today. I have always had an excellent memory for these things. The first of November – All Saints' '

Answer her with spirit at least. 'I can't, don't want to go running half across London. I've homework to catch up with – '

This was ignored. It was not in any case, she knew, taken seriously. How could it be? ('Little Teresa, not very clever, but such a pleasant gel. Yes . . . delighted . . . Barney has chosen well – what would be more inappropriate than a blue stocking? Barney is well able to do any *thinking* required . . .')

'I hold no brief for your religion, Teresa, but at least the one thing I respect about it – respected your family for – was fidelity to obligation. A holiday of obligation as I think you call it – it *obliges* you, Teresa. An evening service?'

'Polly and I were going to hear Barney sing – this choral thing, concert. I mentioned it – '

'I shall happily use your ticket, Teresa. I think that is the end of the matter.'

She had begun eating. 'These grapefruit are extraordinarily acid, Teresa. Are you using *barrows* to buy your fruit?'

'It's that chain place, I forget its name. They're South African.'

'Thin skinned are preferable. The Florida pink, if in season of course. Perhaps you could remember when next shopping?'

∞

'Christ, awful, Polly. I mean – *buried alive*. How's that for a nightmare?'

'I don't want to hear about it, not when I'm eating, it's *lunch*, Patrick. Anyway I get dreams too, I dreamed about you.'

'There's hope then. But this, it could have been real, it *felt* real. Knocking like that on the box. I mean if you came round and knocked and no one heard – '

'Terrible thing *I* read ages ago – a girl dying having a baby, it was a very hot climate so they buried her quick – it was a sort of crypt place and when they looked in it later she'd been running round, tearing at things, frantic ... I'd rather be finished off properly. Chopped up in little bits – '

'You do talk crap. *Little bits* ... What about some more grub?'

'Not hungry. I wish it was summer again – I like sitting out in Beauchamp Palace watching the world go by.'

'When that happens we'll be nearly through. Know what? Hatter's may be one of those places parents pay fees by results – not that I'm going to let it get me down. School didn't. I'm a failure of the public school system. Unlike you and your convent – '

'They didn't rattle me. I won every round. I left before they discovered I was laughing at them.'

'It doesn't seem to have had much effect on you. Except that I can't get you into bed.'

'Someone's listening – '

'So what. If their own conversation's so bloody boring they have to tune in to ours.'

'Oh – you. I feel all spaghetti when I've sat with you.'

'I'll finish your beer. Free tonight? Any night?'

'I've this concert – the one my father's in the choir.'

'Let me imagine a merchant banker singing. Very upright and correct – I've this idea for an operetta, no, a musical number, all to the tune of "We're a Couple of Tramps" – "Cornhill Bankers are *we*, Debasing the currency, In November, December and – " '

'Stuff it – they'll have you for slander. Anyway he's got a gorgeous voice.'

'May you enjoy it all then. Sounds to me more Bach than bite.'

'*Patrick*.'

'OK, OK. Read any good graffiti lately?'

'That means you have – '

'Yes, just now, in here – it's castration day. "Stand a little closer it's shorter than you think . . ." '

'Patrick, Christ, get a bend on it – look at the *time* . . .'

∞

Tessie's afternoons (if she could keep awake) were set aside for working at 'O's. It had seemed to her that, as she'd missed out, this was the minimum luggage she would need before embarking afresh. Or rather that was what she'd been told. 'Get yourself something on paper,' Barney had said, 'and then we can discuss, possibly, the faint probability of your actually being able to do something . . .'

She had not dared aim earlier than a year this December although she had begun classes already. Five subjects: and she wasn't sure which she was worst at. She thought that what she would really like to do was teach adult illiterates to read and write. And when all this is over, I will.

She set the ringer for forty minutes to do history. She had a list of Congresses after 1815 – what they had achieved: she would read it carefully again and then try to jot down what she remembered because at classes that was how they'd told her to study. After that she would have a German session (thirty years ago, she'd been second in class for that).

Three minutes into the Congress of Vienna and she was wondering if she wouldn't have been better to do some cleaning. Plainly Sandy wasn't coming. Help from Sandy was anyway a fluid arrangement, although usually they cleaned together, mornings or afternoons – as and when.

Life without Sandy was unthinkable. As they sat chain smoking together she thought that often. 'Sandy the Sin' as Barney called her. 'She wasn't born,' he'd suggested. 'She just dropped off the back of a lorry . . .' Everything had become if not easier at least possible since her arrival, miraculously almost, eleven years ago: when adopting Christopher had thrown everything out of gear.

Appearing from nowhere it seemed – standing in the doorway of the kitchen, cigarette in mouth, mousy hair flopping, face like a small boy's. Outside up on the pavement, an ancient pram with her baby – the father had made off or he was around and didn't want to know: Tessie hadn't heard which at the time. Terry, nine months, was sitting up making 'Mum mum' sounds. Looking at Christopher – lying awkwardly in Tessie's arms, spluttering over the bottle teat – Sandy had said, 'If I'd known, my love. He only just come off last month – I'm all flat again, look. I'd have nursed that one. Plenty for two. A quid a day – I'd have done it. Or ten bob and my grub . . .'

'Nowadays Tessie often asked herself why Sandy – she lived with her mum and Terry was at school all day – didn't get some more definite job. But Sandy said, 'Well, I like to be free, old dear.' She worked as a barmaid five evenings a week, otherwise she came and went at Tessie's more or less as she liked; often disappearing for days at a time. ('One might have guessed you would be unable to choose or discipline staff, Teresa,' Muff had said. Barney had been unexpectedly tolerant.)

Although Sandy had got through a rough patch between about fourteen and eighteen – with court appearances and her widowed mother tearing her hair out – she was now an, almost, law-abiding citizen. Lots of her mental energy though went into getting something (often just anything) for nothing. Tessie would have left her own jewels lying about, and indeed never expected anything to go; nor had it; but chain stores, Marks and Spencer's particularly, had not been so fortunate.

That first time sitting down at the table, 'I like lots of nooky,' Sandy had said. 'Need it really. You see . . .' And they had begun to talk. It seemed to Tessie they had been talking ever since. Confessing to failure in bed, she took advice from Sandy – which never worked. Got advice too on her fruitless womb. That hadn't worked either. (And thank God, she thought sometimes: because in those early days she had been religious. Religion, which had slipped away, not through any grand crisis of faith but rather through a lukewarm wilting; she wore it still like a warm overcoat – an outward observance – knowing that in any emergency it would have little to say.)

11

Barren as I am, she thought now, at least I've been saved from all those charts and thermometers and knicker gazing. But what good had it done her? Polly, conceived with such ease; then swiftly after (Barney in search of a son) not one but two miscarriages. And then – nothing. Since the blame could be laid nowhere she felt obscurely that it must be her. 'No reason at all why you shouldn't have a large healthy brood,' the last of the consultants had said. 'Be patient.' After six or more years she had ceased to be that. 'If you can't make a son,' Barney had said, 'we shall have to settle for one of someone else's making.' So, Christopher: who from babyhood up had never been a moment's trouble – and soon had been taken from her. ('Why away to school?' she had said. 'Why *not*?' Barney had asked, surprised. And as usual, no smart answer – in fact no answer at all – had come to her.)

The ringer went off loudly. She'd dreamed away almost all of the history. Setting it again for the German, she remembered suddenly her resolution about the sports jacket. The shop shut at four-thirty.

Upstairs, she tried quickly to do something about her appearance. Some days it was better not to look in the glass. Except for an abundance of slightly waving dark hair (it wasn't she who'd given Polly her pre-Raphaelite frizz, often cursed and now suddenly so fashionable), she'd very little going for her, she thought.

But you can't lose what you never had. Muff now – she must surely mourn her beauty? After all, when people praised Muff nowadays, told her she was fabulous – they meant only: fabulous for her age.

She turned on the transistor, listening vaguely as she routinely emptied the sports jacket pockets. One handkerchief, two library tickets, a notice about his Bach society, and a crumpled piece of blue paper. She uncrumpled it idly.

'I shouldn't ever have said it, I shouldn't ever have said *anything*, you know that, don't you. What have you done, Baba, I want to laugh and shout when I should be working quietly – and I can *feel* you all the time you know – where you were – what about that? Isn't that lovely, I'll ask you to come again, and again and *again*! Your not-so-serious-any-more-I-love-you, M. I love you!'

She stood absolutely still. Only the hand holding the paper went up and down, like a pump. She thought her heart had stopped – until a violent thudding began. She could feel her blood draining. My life blood is running away.

She didn't know what to do: just went on standing, clutching the paper as if it would leave with every shake. She sat down on the edge of the bed, his side. The note had made sense when she read it, now it no longer did. She wanted to go backwards, into a state of innocence – when it had existed but she hadn't known about it.

She stared at it. It stared back at her like the cliché it was. Jealousy was what she should be feeling now. But knees trembling she could sense only a primitive terror. Such a mess as she was, had she not marvelled often that so far he had not looked seriously anywhere else? But to feel jealous was at least to be alive: she could summon up nothing so real now. It is the ground beneath my feet, she thought.

Who'd said (who in her life and when)? 'There are only three sorts of women: "Used, kept, and not wanted on voyage." '

Oh my God, she thought. My God, I know which I am.

Chapter 2

She'd been named Teresa not after Teresa of Avila (big St Teresa) but after Thérèse of Lisieux, the Little Flower. Beside the holy water stoup, on a low shelf just above the foot of her bed, was the statue of St Thérèse: dressed as a Carmelite, she looked down on Tessie early in the summer mornings; her shoes, shinily painted, were like the blackcurrant lozenges Tessie had for her cough.

There were many holy things in the house, and holy practices. Her mother often said laughingly, and always as a joke: 'I nearly became a nun.' Instead at seventeen she'd married a doctor ten years her senior, and at eighteen had Tessie; then two years later another daughter. From the beginning of conscious time there'd been just the four of them: mother, doctor-father, Teresa, and Patsy. Dear little girls, everyone said, dressed alike. Sadly, God had sent no more; but hugging them close, tears in her eyes, her mother said: 'Of course, if I'd become a nun I wouldn't have had *any*.' ('I should hope not, Peggy,' said her father.)

They lived in a small town on the Lancashire-Yorkshire border. 'The good he does,' the parish priest said of her father, 'he's a saint. No doubt of it at all.' The priest was often there for supper. Patsy would sit on his knee and read to him; she could read fluently at five while Tessie at over seven could manage only the largest print. Words needed hyphenating before they made sense. Her father brought out a book from his childhood, *Reading Without Tears*, but he had no time to do it with her. Some days the print danced, others it grew misty; one afternoon she sat with him and read a whole page through without a single mistake. But the next day she was stumbling again. 'How can it be "doil"?' said her mother. 'It's Big D goes that way round. The Saints grant me patience.' Then (surprise, surprise) Patsy laughed at her. It was incomprehensible, unbelievable, that anyone couldn't read.

They moved house: to a village in the Yorkshire Dales. It

was very beautiful with the moors up behind, and the sea not far away; but at school she and Patsy were put in the same class. This wouldn't do, so she was sent away to boarding school. From there she could have come home for weekends, if she'd wanted. But she didn't.

Near the end of her second happy term the nuns sent for her to tell her that she had a little brother. For Tessie, it was a complete surprise. Although family prayers had always included special pleas – the storming of heaven for another child – she'd noticed nothing. But God had heard their prayers after all; He was not deaf. She saw her mother, the baby lying beside her, smiling through tears of triumph: 'If only you pray hard enough, Tessie . . .'

The War came. Two terms later and every four or five terms after, Mother Aloysius announced in assembly: 'Such lovely news from Teresa Fletcher! Teresa has another little brother; another little sister; another little brother; another . . .' Fertility triumphing over sterility had run riot. One two three four – nothing could stop them. As Tessie grew older her mother explained, 'Catholics aren't – yes of course there are ways, but most of them are a bit disgusting, Daddy and I wouldn't. Anyway it's wrong, you see.'

Tessie wasn't the Little Flower any more: she was little mother. Her father, his young assistant gone to the War, ran the practice singlehanded. If people had paid their bills (if he'd asked for the money), they might she supposed have been rich; but it had not been so. Her mother, in a smock before each happy event (and after it too: she hadn't the coupons – and it wasn't worth it), looked distracted, her hair prematurely grey.

Patsy, clever, and growing cleverer, would probably get a scholarship. But her back was weak, and she couldn't play games. Nor could she lift babies in and out of baths and prams, or pick up whining, grazed sticky toddlers. Couldn't manage the endless journeys to collect orange juice and cod liver oil and National Dried Milk.

Teresa Cinderella Fletcher. Yet it hadn't felt like that at the time. Just later, as an adult, she would think suddenly: I was shockingly used; my good will abused, exploited. It wasn't the work, rather the lack of attention. No one else got it instead;

15

it was just spread thinly, amongst too many.

But school was still a happy place. It had always been so from the first day: she had never been homesick; she hadn't answered the nuns back; hadn't been too clever and yet not irritatingly stupid; she was pious at the right times, and yet not worried by her religion. They all liked her: dear little Teresa.

Although she made friends there she rarely stayed with them in the holidays. At home, she had no one. Until the summer of 1941.

A warm September evening; she'd been to confession and as she came out of the church she saw a boy standing in the porch. Dressed in long baggy shorts and a grey Aertex shirt, he had black hair and a small bony face; his arms and legs looked stick-like almost, as if he didn't get enough to eat.

'Hey – are there confessions on now?'

She pointed to the board. 'Till six it says.' She was already nearly halfway home when she heard someone running behind. 'Mind if I tag on?' the boy said.

'I feel better after that,' he said breathlessly. 'Going to confession, I mean. I hadn't actually done anything though, had you?'

'No, not that way,' Tessie said, 'just I've been lazy and I've been rude and, you know – '

'Yes, I know,' he said companionably. As they walked along together, he whistled: ' "I've got sixpence, jolly jolly sixpence." ' Then, 'I'm Mike Kelly,' he said, 'we only came yesterday. We got bombed out – ' A rabbit scuttled across their path: 'Hey,' he said, 'that's what I call the country.' Toes turned in he did a few quick dance steps: ' "Run rabbit run rabbit run run run." We've come here for the Duration, Ma says. We'd a terrible journey, standing all the time and I lost my new gas mask and nearly missed the train. "Don't let the farmer have his fun fun fun, he'll get by – " ' Do you like Flanagan and Allen?'

They were nearing the village. He wanted to know all about her. 'You look nice,' he said.

She told him quite a lot then, as they came up to the main street: 'I'm this end,' she said, pointing left. But he wanted her to come and see his house. It was small, part of a stone building: the vet and his family lived in the remainder. In the hall they clambered over two bulging suitcases, paper carriers dangling tipsily from their handles. 'Ma,' Mike said, rushing in, 'look what I found – '

Through the doorway of the sitting-room Tessie saw a large red-faced woman with braided hair, sitting in a low chair by the empty fireplace; she was reading a magazine and eating a plum. 'This is *Tessie*,' he said proudly.

'I'm called after the Little Flower,' Tessie said, standing awkwardly in the doorway.

'Isn't that lovely now? Did you hear that Mike? How old are you Tessie?' She reached for the bag of fruit, 'Go on, eat the two of you. Go on, Mike – look at the size of him, Tessie! Would you believe now he'll be thirteen on All Souls' Day? He's to go to Ampleforth, did he tell you that? His Da put him down for it. He said he was with the Jesuits in Dublin and he wasn't having – '

'That'll do, Ma,' said Mike.

'Och now, you,' she said, cuffing him as he passed. 'Call me Philomena, Tessie – Will they worry about you now, Tessie, where you've got to? Mike can play his banjo – wait now though while I put the supper on. Mike, wherever did you put the banjo?'

'I'll do Lupino Lane,' Mike said. All the time he sang and danced his mother shook her head to the rhythm. 'That's great, isn't he the greatest, isn't he the one, Tessie?' Then, when miming a piano he'd sung like Mickey Rooney, she called out: 'Now it's Tessie!'

'But I can't,' said Tessie, 'my voice is horrible.'

'Did you ever hear such a thing? Listen now and I'll do it – Mike what will I sing, will I sing "Nora Beag"?'

She had a little voice, slightly off-key; coming from so large a body it had a strange, haunting sound. Mike had brought in one of the suitcases and throwing jerseys, shorts, rolled up socks onto the floor, he lifted out his banjo.

'Give us an old one, Mike, give us "I Know My Love".' She sang the verse, her hands clapping the rhythm as he strummed: ' "I know my love by his way of walking, And I know my love by his way of talking, And I know my love in his suit of blue" ' . . . They sang the chorus together. 'Come on, Tessie, will we hear you sing? "And still she cried, I love him the best, And a troubled mind sure it knows no rest, And still she cried, bonny boys are few! And if my love leaves me what will I do?" '

At the end she wagged her finger, 'That's a wild song,' she said, 'a wild song.' Then passing round the plums again: 'Did you know a Mrs Willingham? Was it *Willingham* now, Mike? She was here this afternoon to see was everything all right. WVS she said ...' But Mike was dancing again. He made it look very easy: whistling while his skinny legs moved effortlessly to the beat. ' "Round the back of the arches, down Sunnyside Lane ..." '

'I'm sure I could make you sing,' he said to Tessie suddenly.

'Look at that now,' said his mother, 'he'll still be singing when the supper's burnt.' She leaped up heavily, 'Mother of God, the supper – '

They wanted her to stay. Mike would go up to the telephone box. But she couldn't hear of it; in the end Mike ran up the village with her, as far as her front door. 'I'll be back,' he said, his eyes darting.

With double summer time it was daylight till quite late. In her room, her body moving awkwardly, she tried tentatively to sing and dance: Judy Garland to his Mickey Rooney; her shoulders going up and down: ' "And when the band began to play, the moon it shone as bright as day. Good morning, good morning, to you ..." ' As it came out better she raised her voice, her mind and body full of the rhythm.

Suddenly, Patsy put her head round the door. Indignant, stooping, almost hunchback in her shrunk cotton nightdress. 'Do you *have* to? I'm trying to read, and it's like tanks, or elephants or something.'

Next day, Sunday, he was at church. Philomena Kelly, looking unfamiliar in a flowered hat tilted forward, waved over to her, and after Mass Tessie introduced them to her father and Patsy. On the Monday, early, he appeared at the house. He played with Joseph, two-and-a-half now, and together with Tessie held up Dominic who was just beginning to walk. Tomorrow he said, they'd go off on a picnic, all day. Then as soon as they were back they'd help with the little ones. 'We'll do everything,' he said with an air of great authority. Her mother looked surprised and pleased and flushed. She was expecting another baby at Christmas and was often tired now.

They took their picnic up on the moors. He told her very politely that he didn't like Patsy. 'It's just the way of it – I hope you don't mind. So I didn't want her tagging on.' As they puffed their way up, carrying thick doorstep sandwiches and bags of plums: 'We might meet a German parachutist,' he said, 'could you manage? I *might*. I thought I'd be in a funk with the raids, but I wasn't. Just the once. But with a German, it'd be adventure. Know what I'd say to him, Tessie? I'd say "Excuse me, are you *Funf* by any chance?" Then he'd say, "No, but after you Claude." "No," I'd say, "after you, Cecil." '

Tessie said: 'They usually dress up as nuns actually. They think that's a good disguise. But you can tell by looking at their feet.'

'I expect they carry the habit in their kit when they're parachuted. We'll have to catch him before he changes. I've seen nuns who jolly well might be spies, you know. Nun, Hun. Tessie,' he said delightedly, 'let's make a rude song...'

By that winter it seemed to her that there'd never been a time without Mike. She was at his house whenever she could. They had a piano there now. Philomena Kelly could play a little by ear and she would strum and sing for them her current favourite, 'Rose O'Day'. ('You're my philobegoosher shila-maroosher folderoldeboomdediay...') Mike could pick out almost any tune. 'My little song and dance man,' said Philo-mena Kelly, as she sat and knitted, very badly, grey socks for sailors. She was in the WVS now and went round helping to collect salvage.

Mike tried to teach her to sing, and to dance too. They did duets: Mickey Rooney and Judy Garland. But her voice wasn't good: it was very weak. 'Don't bother,' he would say, 'don't bother if you get it wrong.' Once he said, 'You breathe too tightly, that might be it.' He taught her to blend her voice with his; even to keep in step with him. And with him, she could do it.

'Tessie, this is *fun*,' he'd say, 'let's go on the halls. I'll run away from Ampleforth and you run away, and we'll join ENSA...'

All that next summer they played the gramophone in the garden; it drove Patsy wild. She wanted to hear Nelson Eddy and Jeanette Macdonald, but when she took the gramophone

19

off them, she overwound the spring and broke it. Up on the moors they found relics of a crashed Messerschmitt, and divided them proudly between Ampleforth and Tessie's convent; then relenting, they included Patsy's too.

'Aren't people awful?' her mother said, that September. '*Really* awful when you think of it. Barney Willingham was at a concert yesterday and when he came back after the interval there was a white feather lying on his chair – Margaret Willingham was terribly upset. He's still at Eton. Another year to go – '

'Mind you,' her father said, 'he looks all of eighteen. Bloody stupid though. It's elderly women, usually – they were much freer with them in fourteen-eighteen. I got one myself – '

'Oh dear,' said her mother, 'these things happen I suppose. I hope though he isn't killed – he always seems to me rather a *nice* boy . . .'

∞

Polly is late. Ten minutes too long trying to decide about a skinny knit (honey-coloured or pink?); rushing now up the underground steps, bumping bodies, seeing figures in the distance already going into the hall. Her mother would be even later. That was for certain; she, Polly, was going to be left standing, frantic, on the steps, watching out for the familiar, lumbering figure. And when she does come, she thought, she won't even try to excuse herself: condemned even before the trial – that's her, always.

A cab drew up just as she reached the steps. Muff, in a long purple velvet coat, was helped out by the driver.

'I am a little late, Polly. Teresa preferred to go to Mass – Barney's music, as always, comes a poor second to her religion.'

Inside the hall most of the better seats were taken but a few gaps could be seen here and there: with her stick Muff pointed at two centre aisle seats, halfway down. They had coats draped over them.

'Put those somewhere, Polly, would you?'

'I think – ' began a man beside them. But Muff, settling in, ignored him.

20

She turned to Polly, adjusting her lorgnette: 'Can you see him?'

'Yes,' (it's rude to point, Polly) 'there, third from the left second row.' His great spindly height, even when seated, showing above all the others. He was speaking to his neighbour, his head slightly inclined. That was how she imagined him looking all day in the City, politely listening, occasionally uttering, the air all around full of magic phrases: growth stock searching for a bullish market, speculative funds, net tangible assets enmeshed with parent and consolidated figures . . . Her mind embroidered.

Two women, talking loudly, came hurrying down the aisle. 'We should have left them in Cloaks, Margery,' then, head poked forward: 'hereabouts, I think, dear . . .'

Muff, her hand clasped round the silver knob of her stick, turned slowly. 'Ah! Latecomers. The choir are already assembled,' she remarked, reprovingly. 'If you would be so kind?' The stick shook a little.

The bloody nerve, Polly thought. The women had moved off now, muttering, to where their coats had been draped. *And she'll get away with it.*

Her eyes ranged over the orchestra. A girl flute; some very very young violins; an elderly cello; one small fair precise-looking trumpet and a second – by contrast perhaps – enormous one. Not fat, but large, shaggy: so much hair, such a lot of features; and looking from the way he was sitting as if he'd only remembered at the last minute to come along. Another player, leaning back, made a remark to him and he laughed, heavily, his shoulders shaking.

She turned back to her programme. Polite applause for the conductor now; beside her Muff sat very upright, gazing ahead.

Bach's *Magnificat* burst upon the hall. The trumpets (a hundred of them surely?) soared and in seconds she was back in the old, wild excitement. It will never get any better, she thought; it will always be like this.

Ten, eleven years now. A lifetime already. Her seven-year-old self playing the radio, flicking it from station to station. Then: 'Mummy, mummy, come *quick*!' Her body already moving, head nodding, the room not big enough for the sound. She must share this – at once. Her mother's figure filled the doorway. 'Listen, listen!' Swaying, bending; the texture of the music growing denser, her excitement growing wilder: her arms, legs going everywhere, exasperating in their failure to co-ordinate, to express what was happening to her. It was unbearable. Her mother, politely puzzled, eyebrows lifted: 'What a lovely dance, Polly.'

Later, they had gone to look up the music in the *Radio Times*. It had been Bach's 'Italian' Concerto for harpsichord; and it had been the last movement she'd heard. Music like that, her mother told her, was called 'classical'; they played it at concerts, and everyone had to sit very still.

Gradually now, of course, she calmed down: years of practice. And to help herself, she commended, and censured. The first soprano: too shrill, too tight. With the second, she was much more impressed. She checked on her name. Morwen Davies. Her singing was velvety, easeful, almost privately happy. She sang accompanied by the oboe, whose face Polly thought she'd seen somewhere, and the continuo, whom she couldn't see at all.

'*Omnes generationes*'. Next to her father was an old man. He sang not with the restrained passion she'd noticed in her father, but with joy. Lustily. He must be over seventy, eighty even. Wrinkled – the whole of him, she thought. Such joy: '*fecit potentiam*'. Scattering the proud. How I'd like him for a grandfather; because it's terrible never to have had one really, although when I see that photo of the famous Cecil by Muff's bed, I keep thinking that perhaps I remember seeing him. I imagine him terribly hearty: great guffaws, and not worrying enough about his golf handicap. Odd, that I think I've seen him when I couldn't have – while the other one I can't remember at all. Yet I must have seen him lots of times when I was tiny.

If that man were my grandfather we could sit and talk and he could tell me all about himself – like Muff does. And although he wouldn't say why he sings the way he does, I'd be able to guess. The odd thought – and I often have it – is that if Great Uncle Con had lived he'd be that sort of age. He must have been marked out though. I imagine them all marked out (what sign was he born under, I wonder?).

The trumpets hit high E, with joy, triumphantly. The

purity of the sound brought her out of her dream. A little later came the waves of applause: she turned to Muff, to see that she was all right. The second item, *Ich habe genug*, was short, a vehicle mainly for the tenor who, the programme said, had broadcast several times for the BBC.

Her father didn't come to see them in the interval: she watched the orchestra, the choir, file out. 'Shall I get you anything?' she asked. Muff didn't answer; appeared not to have heard; a moment later, she said:

'I wonder, Polly, if you could perhaps persuade Christopher not to call me *Gran* – it is most irritating.' She looked about her. 'I have already spoken to Teresa of course. But naturally – nothing has been done.'

The two women who'd been ousted from their seats passed by and Polly felt herself go red. Muff didn't notice them; then, as the orchestra and choir came back in, consulting her programme she said: 'As I feared, it is all Bach.'

Throughout the second half, sensing Muff's impatience, Polly kept glancing at her even when it meant tearing herself from the music: haunted always by the possibility that something might happen to her. And then, realizing suddenly how glad she was it was Muff sitting there, and not her mother, she bit her tongue. Yet the truth is, she thought, Muff and I sit together, and we are *right*. My mother – Tessie, Teresa – I'm ashamed of her in a way: she sits there, and she seems to be everywhere, sprawling, overflowing: not altogether, somehow. And I can't remember when it wasn't that way. I love her so, she thought. I wish I could like her.

Later, when it was all over, they waited for the first rush. Then as Polly was about to help Muff up, she saw her father walking towards them. He had a man with him.

'Mother,' he said, raising his voice a little, 'may I introduce Peter Kyrtle-Murray?'

'Harpsichord continuo,' Peter told them both, with a tight smile. He moved rather fussily; his glasses had slipped forward on his red face.

'Peter and I met in Zurich, Mother, ten or eleven years ago – '

'Quite a coincidence this. The purest chance. Their player fell ill yesterday evening. I stepped into the gap – through a friend of a friend . . .' His hair, in pageboy style, looked so neat, so fixed, that Polly wanted suddenly to lean over and lift it off.

Up to a year ago he'd been in Malta, it appeared. 'Indeed?' Muff remarked. Did he perhaps know the Fordyces? Angela and Clive?

He did not. They walked towards the entrance. Her father said: 'I can't, I'm afraid, come home with you. I've various things to arrange – to clear up. But – ' Peter rushed forward: 'Allow *me*. My task – my *pleasure*. Let me find you a cab.'

On the journey back, alone with Polly, Muff said as if to herself: 'Kyrtle-Murray? I recall a Kyrtle-*Mount*.' She rubbed gloved hands over her stick. 'There is something not quite about him, Polly. But then Barney was ever unable to tell dross from gold.'

She turned slowly. 'Did I ever tell you about Anthea?'

The creaking of the top stair but one woke her: Barney didn't turn on the light but walked unerringly, cat-like, through to the dressing-room. The luminous clock his side of the bed said three; she had no memory of falling asleep.

He climbed into bed: cold flesh against hers, hot with sleep, apprehensive, indented. Almost at once he turned away: 'I'm sorry,' his hand, ice-cold, accidentally brushing her thigh.

She lay very still sunk into the bed. Outside, the world seemed asleep; no traffic, no sound except a sudden gust of wind amongst the bare branches below the window. 'You're terribly late,' she said.

Search for the worst phrase: and when you find it, utter it. The words ballooned forth.

His voice, as cold as his flesh, came to her out of the darkness.

'Exceedingly. And so *deeply* sorry to disturb you.' Then changing from a sarcastic to a quite ordinary tone he went on: 'There was general clearing up of course. Then one was required to attend some sort of party afterwards. It went on rather.'

'Fun.' She added: 'The drink hasn't warmed you up much – '

24

'One was sorry not to see you at the concert,' he said. 'Polly seems to have enjoyed it. Muff – I rather doubt.'

'Who was this harpsichord something? Polly thought he was ghastly – did he come to the party afterwards?'

'Yes.'

She said in a rush: 'There's a piece of paper – something of yours. It was in your pocket, in the sports jacket, when I did it for the cleaning – '

'What do you mean "a piece of paper"?'

'A note. From – someone.'

'I can scarcely have received a note from no one. Mr Nobody as Nanny used to say. Was it perhaps from Mr Nobody?'

She said in a thick voice, 'I didn't understand the note, that's all.'

Cold limbs, cold voice. 'If a note is not addressed to one, why should one understand it?' She waited, breath held, for an excuse such as, 'Enough – I'm tired now.' But as if walking willingly into a trap, he said: 'Well?'

There was no answer to that, no answer at all. What had she meant to say, anyway? What had she expected him to say? Some flip answer, some throwaway line? The coy: 'I do believe you think I'm being unfaithful!'

'Well?'

'Cold hands, warm heart,' her mother had said, rubbing her potato-stained, red hands together in the wartime winters.

'What do you mean,' she said, ' "*Well*?" '

Perhaps he will touch me. Perhaps his still cold hands will reach down, till frozen-hearted, fearful as I am now, all of me will contract, shrivel, shrink, curl up, withdraw.

But he didn't move. His answer was merely, lying flat, a knight on his tomb, to fall asleep, silently, gracefully (it is I who snore, she thought). Slipping beyond her reach, he had not even wanted an answer to his question.

Chapter 3

Monday, just before nine. Guy Fawkes' day. Christopher, home again, and on his last day of half-term sits at the table eating cereal, slowly, methodically. 'I've got to get a fireworks party ready, I've got to help with the bonfire. First I've got to go swimming – '

Polly has a letter. 'Yes, lovey,' she says to Christopher. She opens her letter.

'Dear Polly,

I wonder if you will remember me? We met at the concert on Thursday night.

This Thursday I happen to have two tickets for another concert. More Bach! ! But some of the same singers will be there. As you will have guessed I'm not performing on this occasion. Perhaps we could go out for a bite afterwards?

Yours sincerely,
Peter (Kyrtle-Murray)
alias harpsichord continuo.'

'Oh God,' she said, sitting down. Her mother, sipping coffee, looked up, her hand still on the cup. Polly pushed the letter over. 'If you'd *seen* him. Shan't go . . .'

Her mother read it, frowning. She shrugged her shoulders: 'Well, it's music. For nothing. And a meal thrown in.'

'That's true.' Christopher, still eating, hadn't even looked up. She said, 'Do you really believe that'll make you grow?' She pulled his hair affectionately.

'Oh, stuff it,' he said, looking pleased. She poured out some coffee, then tried to drink it too quickly. 'Going anywhere, doing anything?' she asked her mother; a sort of ritual enquiry, not every day, but at decent intervals.

'Camilla. It's the day for Camilla.'

'Tell you what. One time I'll just turn up – a sort of ghostly third at the lunch table.'

26

'I wish you *would*.'

'I need black laces,' Christopher said. 'And laces for my football boots. I need them today.'

Her mother said, lighting a cigarette, 'I should have seen about everything. We can pack after your party – '

'I'll get them for you – I can do it in the lunch hour.' She kissed her mother quickly, high on the cheek. 'Don't worry about anything. Look nice, have a lovely lunch. If you run out of chat – just tell Camilla I've caught VD . . .'

∞

She reached out to the bedside table, to the covered jar where her teeth lay, and fitted them in, click. She preferred Teresa not to find her without them. Several times lately she had, and she, Muff, had felt no longer in charge: vulnerable, a victim rather than an oppressor. To make it worse, Teresa had appeared not to notice.

But the clock said only eight-thirty – she'd mistaken, perhaps, Polly's step? She fastened the lid back on the jar. Sans teeth, sans eyes . . . But her hair – that was still something to be proud of: she would put it up while waiting. The heavy silver-backed brush lay always to the right of Cecil's photograph. Her hand was halfway there when she stopped, and on impulse climbed carefully, slowly, out of bed. The dark maroon beauty case lay on the top shelf of the wardrobe. She lifted it down with difficulty; gently.

Even after all these years it smelled still of her mother. Every summer, from 1889 to 1908, carried always by the faithful Millie, it had travelled from Belgravia to Lough Corrib; from Lough Corrib to Belgravia. She had altered nothing in it: the brushes were the same, the folded curling tongs, the spirit lamp, the vinegar bottle – only the combs had fresh tortoise-shell. The gloves were there still, always at the ready: one pair grey kid, one pair white. Something spilling once in their sachet, (patchouli, sandalwood?) had scented the leather and the lining for ever.

But it was the tongs which most brought back her mother. Day in, day out, they had frizzed the light faded brown, later the pepper and salt, of her mother's fringe. Emily Delancey

27

had not been a beauty. Indeed as a girl there'd been nothing obvious about her at all, not even a complexion made soft, downy, by the gentle wet windless summers, the mild winters of her Connemara childhood. She was sallow, plump in the wrong places, and awkward in her gestures. And yet ... In the season of 1873 she'd come out very unsuccessfully. Her mother was already dead; three years later her father died too, and as unmarried daughter she went to live with her brother and his wife. She had a very kind heart, she could be counted on for good works of an unobtrusive sort, and she was wonderful with her nephews and nieces. By the season of 1888 she was thirty-three and in London for a holiday, as company for her brother's eldest daughter.

Surely though one must believe in the hand of God? 'Someone,' she would say to Muff, 'someone was watching over me. Over us *both*.' The other was Francis Gore-Lewis. Aged thirty-six and as yet unmarried, extravagantly handsome, he was heir to several thousands and a big estate in Breconshire. Quite a snap in fact. The fond mamas of 1888 watched him anxiously. Perhaps, this year?

And indeed he did marry – that September. But what a shock for them all! What a reversal of the natural order. For it was the aunt he fell for: meeting her at an exhibition at the Doré Gallery. Never looking back, or forward, or at any one else. A seemingly never ending conversation. Taking her down from her place on the shelf, giving her his undivided attention.

All those soirées, balls, supper parties, dinners to which he'd been invited! All the *trouble* taken. Why could he not have noticed her when she was on show, fifteen years ago? 'I think people generally were a little vexed,' she had said mildly, telling Muff of it.

But afterwards: such happiness. It shone out in all the memories, all the allusions. The only shadow was worry about children. Time was short: she was thirty-five now and still no sign. Francis was an only son (yet another reason why he should have chosen a young filly); even were she to conceive, it might be a girl.

Then at the end of 1890, she became pregnant; but Theo, born while they were at Lough Corrib, was puny, a sickly baby: changed to bottle feeding after his wet nurse caught diphtheria, he seemed unable to keep food down. Would he live? In the spring of 1893 she conceived again and at Christmas in London, a daughter, Margaret Ursula, was born: seven-and-a-half pounds, and the picture of health. Theo, growing stronger, was interested enough to twist her little finger as she lay cradled in the house at Hill Street. It was Emily who wasn't so well: in May 1894, she and Francis went to Italy for a month, staying in a villa at Gardone. And there, disobeying doctor's orders (but with what delightful results!), she conceived again. 'Italy has a rather odd effect on people,' Cousin Livia told Muff years later, 'or so Emily hinted. The hot climate, you know.'

But she felt well, superbly well, all the nine months. It was another son, she told everyone, and on St Valentine's Day she was proved right. Francis Conran Gore-Lewis – never was there such a baby: crying lustily, kicking from the start, with a head of thick dark hair, and weighing almost nine pounds. Triumph for Emily. For although Theo (smelling faintly always of Scott's Emulsion) is much better now – and God forbid anything should happen to him – even if it were to, the line is assured. (How well Francis chose after all, people say. And those dark vivid looks – they must surely come from the Delancey family?)

Now it is Margaret's turn though to have her nose put out of joint. Who *is* this nuisance? Only a few months ago every visitor, every relative, was admiring the flaxen ringlets, the velvet slippers, the lisping recital of: 'Once I saw a little bird come hop hop hop. And I cried Little Bird will you stop stop stop?' Now, they only have time for the newcomer: he too is brought down to the drawing-room, takes his first uncertain steps, and captures all the attention. The photographer calls – too often. The years pass: she is photographed too; painted; drawn by an artist house guest during those long Corrib summers. The relatives gather: 'How big the catalpa tree has grown!' and then, 'how *pretty* Con is!' At five, he is painted in historical costume, with the Joyce mountains as background.

He isn't very good at reading though or writing. Struggling with his Darnell's copybooks, he blots frequently. Their governess, exasperated, praises Margaret in front of him. But he doesn't mind at all.

Theo, they see little of; he has gone away to prep school and in the holidays he really doesn't share their interests – condescending only now and then to show them his butterfly collection or to join in a ball game.

Summer 1904. They are on Lough Corrib. All the cousins are there. Theo, thirteen now, will begin at Winchester in the autumn. They all play on the lawn behind the house: Con, his tongue between his teeth, catches the ball – then throws it on – to his sister. She, the graceful one, aims – and misses it. She misses the next one too. And the one after.

'You *can't* muff it again!' declares Theo. She does though.

Last week she was kept in her room with a sore throat; for two or three days since she has felt clumsy. Twice, she's missed a step on the stairs. Growing pains: some of the relatives are impatient. (Although Nanny O'Hara is understanding.) She doesn't know what to do with her limbs. If *this* is growing up!

But they go on playing ball, in the long summer afternoons. (Cousin Denis says, teasingly, 'Not again! I say you know – I think we'd better call you Muff . . .')

On the boat going home she fell, badly. Clinging to the railings and missing them. Dropping the hot drink which they had brought her, sitting wrapped up on the deck. Back in London they sent for a specialist at once.

Sydenham's Chorea; St Vitus' Dance to you and me. Instant bed rest is prescribed. Great care must be taken not to damage her heart.

How then to pass the time? It's autumn now. Theo has gone. Con irritates her by looking so fit. She spends her days, a rug wrapped about her, lying on the sofa in the library. There is a piano in there and Con comes in and practises Mozart; when she tells him she doesn't like it, he looks crestfallen. 'What *would* you like, Muff?' (the name has stuck now – it will never be shaken off). Peevishly, she fancies she'd like to be read to, or puzzles made. So in the darkening afternoons he makes hand shadows for her, cuts cardboard shapes – the Japan Square, the Army Square; colouring newspaper, he cuts them both comic masks. While she sips Brand's Essence, he reads about Kit Bam, the British Sinbad; and when she doesn't like that, there is the Memoir of Bob, the Spotted

Terrier. Together, on paper, they fight their way out of Hampton Court Maze.

The surprising thing is – she likes his being there. She sees suddenly that he's not a rival, but an ally (against many of the adults, against the superior sarcastic Theo). More than an ally – a friend. He worries for her constantly. It is incredible, unbelievable, how much Con cares.

She gets better slowly; her heart fortunately quite undamaged. It has taken several months: but all's well that ends well, and it has ended very well indeed. Life has taken on a quite different meaning. Henceforth it will be Muff and Con against the world (yes, even against the Kaiser and all his men).

Three years later and it's his turn to need her. His lessons aren't going well. Prep school is not recommended and a stern no-nonsense tutor comes to do his best. Con is intelligent they say, but not clever (there is a distinction it seems), and although he has considerable, almost remarkable musical aptitude, *cui bono?* since he cannot construe. He can make nothing of *De Bello Gallico*; an ablative confounds him; and why the gerund? he asks. 'It doesn't matter,' Muff says. 'Oh yes it does!' he cries. The relatives nod their heads; his tutor queries whether Winchester will in fact take him. Founder's Kin has been abolished for twenty-five years now; the Gore-Lewis ancestors can no longer reach out a helping hand.

But she is there to defend him: all the time now. Theo teases her about it even. 'All right, all right, I only *said*. No need to get into a bate ...' And Uncle Algy: 'Con can look after himself – can't you, old chap? You don't have to fly at me, little martinet ...'

And yet in the end, she thought, he wasn't able to look after himself. Which of them, at Armageddon, could?

The little French clock struck nine. Picking up one of the brushes she pulled it gently through her hair. The bristles were slightly flattened, too soft even for her fine hair. She put it down and a moment later heard a knock at the door.

'Come in!' Really, it was almost as if Teresa had been waiting outside. Perhaps she has been listening? she thought. Then a second later: but that is ridiculous.

'Absurd, how absurd!' she exclaimed out loud.

31

'What was that?' asked Teresa, putting the tray down, crossing over to the window.

'I did not speak, Teresa – my pillows, please.' She arranged herself: 'I was not aware that I spoke?'

She would say nothing today about the grapefruit: it appeared to be perfectly cut, the skin just possibly a little thinner. But the condition of *The Times*!

'Teresa. Barney was surely not the last to read this? It has the appearance already of yesterday's newspaper – my father always received his ironed. Admittedly, he scarcely noticed. He was not an observant man. I shall have to consider ordering my own copy – indeed, I can't imagine why I haven't done so before.' She saw that Teresa had walked over to one of the potted plants and was tapping its side. 'Leave that!' she said sharply.

There was a moment's silence, then exasperation welling up again she heard herself say: 'My plans. You have not asked me what my plans are for today.' Her anger grew even as she spoke: 'It seems to me sometimes that no interest at all is shown in what I do, where I go –' She pressed her back against the pillows. 'But why should you bother? My life is over.' She felt her lips begin to tremble: 'And no doubt that is exactly what you are thinking? Well, you may spare me your thoughts, Teresa – I have no wish to hear them.'

It is her generation, she thought, Barney's generation. They are so selfish. Warmth came to her with the memory: '*Polly* cares,' she said.

'I'm sorry,' Teresa began. 'It was just that last – '

'That is enough.' She could feel inside her anger becoming diffuse: when she was alone again it would spread and grow. She brought it, quickly, to a point.

'And what shall *you* do today?'

'I'm lunching with Camilla.'

'Ah yes, Camilla. A tedious gel. Her teeth are too large. And she has far too much to say for herself always. A time-waster, Teresa.'

∞

'Tessie!' called Camilla from a table right up near where

the head waiter ordered his minions about. Shouting as if the half-filled restaurant were the length of a street. 'Gorgeous,' she said as Tessie came up, 'you look gorgeous. That hat, sweetie. What I wouldn't give to be able to wear hats. They always make me look like something out of Enid Blyton – Noddy or Plod or somebody.'

When Tessie had sat down: 'Now,' she said, 'tell me everything. *All* your news.' She looked about her. 'We need a drink. A Cinzano – or a Campari, let's have a Campari. Mario! *due* Camparis – please.' Then as the waiter moved away, 'He's an absolute sweetie. Gives the most *marvellous* service. I'm not completely sure his name is Mario but I thought I heard Luigi call him that the first time. And he's never corrected me . . .'

Tessie looked at her. She was dressed as usual in a suit: pink wool, very furry, with a spotlessly white frilly blouse. She'd put on her spectacles. 'Now,' she was saying, flapping the big menu card, 'what shall we have, sweetie? Soup. *Stracciatella alla romana* – gorgeous. It never comes out quite the same when I try it though, it's the bouillon cubes I think. *Gnocchi*, mm, yes, mouth watering – but murder for the figure. Let's go onto meat. Veal, sweetie, you must have veal. Though Luigi does do this gorgeous chicken thing, with fennel – no, it's not on today. *Finocchio*. It's got ham and garlic and brandy – Rodney always has it and then wishes he hadn't.'

Her white, even teeth stuck out. It was impossible for her to close her mouth. ('I suppose the silly old parents should have done something about it,' she said once. 'Only, what with the War and everything.')

'I think *this* one,' she said now. '*Bracioula di vitello*. With marjoram and raisins and eggs and things. Fiddly, awfully fiddly, sweetie, don't try and do it for a party – ' She frowned, running her finger down the page; her hands were a little gnarled and she wore, as always, a lot of rings. Pushing the menu aside she looked up suddenly. 'Sweetie, you haven't told me a *thing*,' she said reproachfully, 'I can't believe a whole month has gone by without any news – married to that divine Barney, you can't ever have a dull moment. Rodney, poor lamb, is an absolute yawn these days. Liver really is the most revolting complaint – only a Frenchman could get away with it. And even then . . .'

33

The waiter stood before them. Camilla ordered with a great flourish. Then turning back to Tessie: 'Now tell me,' she said, leaning forward, her protuberant eyes seeming about to pop out with friendly curiosity.

It was the same face in which, on and off, for over twenty-five years now, Tessie had confided, however unwillingly. I am in her debt, she'd said to herself once, feeling that that described it all. As in a sense it did. For when in 1947 she'd begun her seven-year stint as mother's help in the Marchant house (Julian, two, Amanda, one), it had been Camilla, home for the weekend from her Oxford secretarial course, who'd found her weeping in the bedroom. Child of an earlier marriage, Camilla was her own age: but with her string of beaux, her string of pearls, and her expensive Braemar twin-set, she'd seemed much older than raw Teresa. She'd seemed self-sufficient; all right. Tessie had not been all right. But Camilla had said: 'Sweetie, I used to feel like that, last year. It was too ghastly. And the parents were *no* help. Are they overwork-ing you?'

They weren't of course. The work was light really compared with what she did, unpaid, at home. Here at least there were fixed hours – and only two children. The family were related to one of her father's patients and the job had been found for her when, standing sullenly, head down, she'd been asked yet again, 'But don't you want to do *anything*?' and had been unable to answer, because all she could think of was: 'Yes, I want to marry Mike.' So she'd taken the job which was at least doing something, although a dead end in itself. It had really been essential she got away. Over eighteen months now since the convent had expelled her and she'd done nothing except help at home. She'd intended to work for School Certificate, arrangements had been made tentatively, but some-how it had never got done. Patsy, who'd been held back out of consideration for Tessie, was furious ('I could have got it all over and done with. Maybe not distinctions – but lots and lots of credits . . .').

'Are you sure you don't want to go out more?' Camilla had said, comforting her. 'I mean I expect the parents just haven't *thought* –' But in fact the little social life she'd had at home earlier that summer had terrified her. Theirs was the

34

sort of village where, because of her father's position, she could have gone out a great deal. Her mother had encouraged her. 'I can cope,' she'd said bravely, pressing on the old iron mangle, piles of steaming washing beside her. Tennis parties, dances, cocktail parties, picnics: she could have been a great success. 'Expelled from a convent? But – that's awfully exciting! What exactly did you do?'

All that summer it was jolly good bathing weather. Once, at a dance: 'Isn't that Barney Willingham over there?' said her partner, the vet's son from the next village but one. Barney was standing, drink in hand, by some french windows. The evening sun was behind him. He looked around: his eyes, resting on her for a moment, didn't recognize her.

'Know him?'

She shook her head. He seemed little changed. How odd she'd thought then, to go half across the world to save your country, your empire perhaps, and to look the same as when fresh from Eton.

Floreat Etona. 'Sweetie!' Camilla shrieked, 'we haven't ordered the *drink.* No, but really, it's all on me. *All* of it. What about this Falerno? Would that do us? I don't know a thing about wines, I'm positively cretinous when it comes to which what – Rodney nearly had a seizure last time I tried to handle that side of things. Which reminds me, he's bringing some people back this evening so I absolutely *must* be home and compos mentis by five-thirty – he froths at the mouth these days if things aren't just so. Honestly, sometimes – I mean I'm sure it'd be utterly different if I had someone like Barney to come back to. Really you are fantastically lucky, sweetie. I said – don't you remember me saying, that time when you first came to our house and you were so absolutely ghastly miz and I said, "You won't believe me," I kept saying, "but some absolutely gorgeous man will come along and sweep you off your feet – " and look what happened. I know it was *years* after, but still ... I'd have waited I must say, if I'd thought something like that was coming my way.'

Their order had arrived. Tessie, wondering already if she would, could, manage to get out of the restaurant without telling Camilla anything, felt her appetite slip away. An omelette would have been sufficient

She watched the white wine sauce being spooned over her meat. 'Oh, but look at all these calories!' exclaimed Camilla, 'absolute murder. Mario, tell me – do you like fat women? *"Donna grassa, come me?"* Really, sweetie,' she said, as he moved away, 'I do rather tease him, don't I? What Mummy always called being familiar. Poor Mummy – hardly anything I can remember about her now. *Polly*,' she said suddenly, 'you haven't told me anything about Polly. I keep thinking if only she and Mark really got on, you and I could be lavender and lace grannies together. Fabulous.' She took a mouthful. 'No, but they do do this veal superbly. Sweetie, you're not eating! Where's the wine? *Mario!*'

But it was delicious, Tessie told her, really. 'It was just that I was listening – '

'And Muff – how's *she*? Still absolutely wonderful? A teeny bit of a martinet of course but then she's entitled to it – Where *is* that wine? You know the trouble is, sweetie, you just haven't given me *any* of your news at all . . .'

And so it was that between the *insalata di cavolfiore* and the *zabaglione* (special order, fifteen minutes' wait), she found herself confiding yet again, as if discharging the debt, in Camilla.

'The thing is,' she heard herself say, haltingly, 'the thing is, I rather think, I don't know exactly, I rather think there's Someone Else – '

The pain of saying it, thus poorly, was if nothing else proof that the time had come to excise the festering sore. And very silly it sounded too – in this day and age, she thought, in the year of Our Lord 1973. But she had reckoned without Camilla.

'What?' Fork arrested on its journey, salad speared, a little juice dripping: 'Oh Tessie, but sweetie, *no*! Not *Barney*.'

Anyone sitting around, anyone within a mile, must surely think it was he who stood responsible for the collapse of Consols, embezzlement of Government funds or at the very least fraud on some marathon scale. 'Sweetie, he *can't* have – '

When she'd given an account, 'Have you got it with you – the note?' Camilla asked, wiping oil from her lips. 'What did it say, anyway?'

What had it said? She couldn't remember a word.

'No, but really – I'd better lower my voice – have you asked him about it?'

'No, yes, I did, but – '

'Well, honestly sweetie, I think the whole thing's imagination anyway – I mean I k*now* human nature, and I mean it's just so absolutely out of character ...' All through the *zabaglione*, for every yellow spoonful: 'Anyone *else*, sweetie – God knows Rodney's up every skirt and I'm used to it, at least it makes him too tired – it's just that I have such an *image* of Barney. I used to think – I know I do get silly ideas about people, but I used to think, you remember I've often said, I'm sure he's always seen you as a sort of *refuge*. I mean after all that Anthea business – years ago when you first told me, I thought, Tessie will make it up to him. And it made him so interesting. You know, people who've suffered. I mean Rodney's a bit of a slug, really, in a way. Such an easy War and – '

Tessie said: 'And I haven't mentioned it since.'

'Oh, but you *must*. *Due espressos – espress*i, Mario, please. You'll just have to ask him straight, sweetie. I mean what else can you do.' Then a little later, spooning brown sugar in: 'I think you're going to have to tackle it head on – if I can use that expression. Let's have some more coffee, otherwise I shall just drop off to sleep when I get home. Mario! The thing is, sweetie, I can quite understand anyone falling for him, after all he's madly attractive if you think about it. He's caught in somebody's web, I'm absolutely convinced. Another hard-faced bitch, another Anthea. He always looks so terrifyingly cool, sweetie, which is a certain sign that he's all soft inside so that any clever woman who's made up her mind could get him – '

'In the note though, she sounded rather nice – '

'Sweetie you're incredible. *Incredible.* You'll have to get a little more malicious. No, but what we want is a plan of action, and what I think, my advice is – just ask him outright, as soon as you possibly can, I don't mean the stupid sort of "I have a right to know", just a straight question – but casual, for God's sake, keep it casual, sweetie.'

It seemed to Tessie that she would never stop. The restaurant was nearly empty now: only three businessmen still talking at a far table.

'God, the *time*,' cried Camilla, 'let's get the check. *Il conto, per favore*, Mario – really my Italian gets worse every day, the only practice I get is in here – the one place you never need it now is Italy. On Elba last year – I don't know why Rodney chooses these places, all that wine and the oil and the cheap brandy – he's positively ghastly bilious practically the whole time. On Elba – '

She talked on, even while paying the bill; first accepting then rejecting Tessie's money. On their way out:

'Oh, but it's awfully sad, sweetie,' she said. 'Thinking about it, I mean, couldn't he have done something just a little more, you know, trendy? I mean it's so frightfully – so *ordinary* somehow. It's like getting *vino da pasto* when you thought you'd ordered Est! Est! Est!' Standing on the kerb, she clutched at Tessie. 'Sweetie, I'm *so* disappointed . . .'

Chapter 4

The taxi braked suddenly, pitching Muff forward. She rapped
sharply on the partition; the driver, pushing the glass back,
scarcely turned his head: 'Sorry, Your Majesty.'

They were stuck in the traffic now. Sitting very upright she
watched the passers-by. Last week, held up just here, she had
seen Polly rounding the corner of Beauchamp Place together
with a charming boy: they had both come over to speak with
her. 'My grandmama,' Polly had said with pride.

How I dread, Muff thought, the moment when there is no
more Polly. Marriage, a career, even this modern aimless
wandering – all of them will take her away from me.

And yet when it was Barney: it seemed to me sometimes
that I would never be rid of him (I shock even myself by that
thought). The years passed and still he was there, a responsibility I never asked for. Anthea. How *typical* all that was in
retrospect. Almost as if he had wished the mishap upon himself. She would have led him a dance. He gives in of course,
at the first obstacle. How I dislike that trait.

She stared out of the stationary taxi, hoping still for Polly,
but seeing only a blur of harassed faces, hurrying bodies,
indistinguishable, undistinguished.

June's, her hairdresser's, had a big plate-glass window. The
taxi driver didn't help her out but waited impatiently, engine
ticking over, while she arranged her money.

The receptionist had seen her though. 'Thank you, most
kind,' she murmured, as arm held she was helped through the
swinging glass doors. Going through them by herself was to
be dreaded; second in difficulty only to the once convenient,
now terrifying revolving doors (and as for moving staircases – I
shall never use them again, she thought, they are no longer
possible).

June herself had come out to greet her at once: creating,
as always, the illusion that the whole salon was founded and
maintained solely for the care and planning of Mrs Margaret

Willingham. But what better way to be successful with the customers? Muff thought (except that today they are all called clients. Astonishing; as if a change of name could suddenly elevate a trade into a profession. Rodent officers, refuse disposal men. What next?). And yet June had done well: she had come a long way from the day when, a mere twenty-year-old, she had attended her at Harrods. ('Too young,' I said then; and grew to depend on her.)

A little girl was hanging up her coat; helping her into an overall: 'It's an awfully cold day for you to be out, Mrs Willingham.'

'It is the same for everyone,' she said. She felt her stick sink into the thick pile of the carpet. 'If I were to take notice of the weather – '

There were two cubicles for older customers (advice that she had given June). She could not imagine what she would do if she were forced to sit in the open as was the custom nowadays. A flock of sheep in the market-place.

Her hair was being taken down. 'It's lovely, so fine, Mrs Willingham. Just a mo now and I'll fix the basin.' The little girl's name was Lesley. Her fingers when she shampooed were very gentle and thorough. 'I'll have the chair right in a jiffy. Now, carefully with your head – there, how does that feel?'

All the girls kept up this sort of patter. She fancied they thought they were reassuring her – elderly, shaky, easily alarmed. *She* knew they were reassuring themselves.

'You tell me now, if it gets too hot ...' How could they feel at ease with her? I have always been waited upon, she thought; and they know it. Yet today, when the newspapers, the wireless, the television shriek at them that we are all equal, how can they know their place? They have every chance – no, every right now to equal parts of leisure, to motorcars, to holidays abroad, to chicken in baskets (whatever *that* may be) ...

'Just a teeny bit nearer, if you don't mind, and we'll have you finished – not getting splashed, are you?' But even as they try to ape our ways, they are sold up the river. Their food is inferior, overseasoned, underflavoured, underhung – just as they are underbred. They buy what they see advertised. But goods of real quality are not advertised, they are not to be seen on the sides of moving staircases or made into simple stories on the small screen . . .

'I didn't ask about a rinse, Mrs Willingham.' June came into the cubicle: Lesley said, 'Does Mrs Willingham have a blue rinse, June?'

No, Mrs Willingham didn't: June could be seen in the looking-glass, shaking her head, trying to pretend the remark hadn't happened. 'Just a nice conditioner then,' Lesley said, 'we'll rub it on the ends and not rinse it off. I hope when I go all white it's that lovely colour, is it in the family?'

My mother never lived to go white – but why should I tell her that? Why should I behave as if familiarity came naturally to me? 'The towel's nice and warm, isn't it? How's your grand-daughter, Mrs Willingham? How's your little grandson?' She felt irrational anger well up. We are not equal, I do not admit their equality. With their polluted blood – a century ago only and they were living, many of them, in alleyways and under arches, gin-soaked, phossy-jawed, bow-legged, half of them unfit to fight the Boers. Sweetened tinned milk, margarine, strong tea – what sort of blood can that have made? The Willinghams – upstarts of course – were at least yeomen stock before coal made their fortune . . .

June said, 'Well, it's no better in Ireland, is it? My sister's second boy is out there – she hasn't been sleeping with the worry. It's all right till it's someone you know, isn't it?'

Cromwell, bestowing land on those anti-King's men, her mother's ancestors: origin of her Corrib summers. And further back still, the Gore-Lewises in Breconshire. What else but fresh spring water, good red meat, and claret went to make up their blood? Con's and my blood (and Theo's I suppose). But Gore *means* 'blood' – I have never thought of that before.

'I'll put the switch right beside you – so that if it's too hot . . .'

The blood of us all; I wish I believed in a God still. The dryer was making her head throb. She felt imprisoned. Years ago there had been the processions. Feast days, and the Irish – their religion was everywhere – processing along the road from the church, below the lake: she could see them as she peeped through the hedge. A litany. Solo and chorus: Queen of the most holy Rosary, pray for us, Queen of Peace, pray for us, Lamb of God who takest away the sins of the

41

world – spare us O Lord . . . Why should I remember so much, from so long ago? That meaningless chanting. I didn't even know that I was listening.

Spare us, O Lord. And most especially thy servant, Con. She fumbled, turning the dial to 'Low'. But too heavy for her, it slipped back each time. Angrily, she banged it against the edge of her chair.

∞

'I was rather wondering if you would recognize me,' said Peter Kyrtle-Murray. He was standing on the steps of the hall; Polly had had difficulty in finding it. She was regretting her Zapata shoes – their stacked heels made running dangerous. 'We shall have to hurry, I fear.'

Oh God – he was looking impatient. And in a particular way too which placed him at once as her father's generation. An avuncular impatience. Reproach, reprimand almost. Her own friends would have looked just fed up –

'I was rather wondering if you would recognize me?' Last week he had seemed harmless, colourless almost. But today, fur-coated (racoon surely?) over a green tweed jacket, knee boots gleaming ostentatiously, he could scarcely pass unnoticed. His face was redder than she'd remembered: but perhaps that was his annoyance at her being late. 'I expect you had trouble,' he said suddenly, heavily, as they were walking in, 'tearing yourself away from your mod friends.'

'My what friends?' She hoped she hadn't heard him right. 'I'm terribly sorry,' she said again, feeling anything but. 'Always late everywhere.' He'd bought only one programme and was obviously slightly myopic since he bent very close to her to read it. His face was almost into hers, his breathing so heavy it sounded passionate.

'*Wachet auf*. This first item. "Sleepers Awake". Very overdone.' He underlined it with a stab of his finger. 'I rather *dig* it though.' He said the word with distaste as if it left a bad flavour in his mouth.

A burst of polite clapping greeted the conductor; Peter whispered, his mouth unpleasantly close to her ear: 'Risen

42

from the ranks. He was originally with some South London choir, just in the choir. But he had ambitions.'

'So what and how else?' she said tartly. 'We can't all have Beecham's Pills behind us.'

He raised his eyebrows. 'Oh – so it has a temper, has it?' But then a few seconds later, just as the conductor was about to raise his baton, he patted her hand reassuringly, patronizingly. 'Touché,' he said.

During the opening chorus he seemed a little more relaxed; she almost forgot him. But then as the tenor stood up, singing in German that the Bridegroom cometh, 'cometh in haste from on high to your dwelling', he began, horribly, to fidget. His cream polo neck sweater didn't fit round the throat, tickled him perhaps? He was making violent efforts, contortions almost, to get comfortable; without actually looking she could see him. She hoped at first that the explanation was something simple, such as that he was in love with the tenor. But it continued rather worse right through the bass-soprano duet. This time it was his bottom. He shifted his weight from one buttock to the other as if neither could bear the pressure. Perhaps it was piles? Trying to keep it all out of focus, not to feel (because now his foot, shuffling, had pushed against hers), she concentrated on the soprano. It was a part she knew, and easy to follow. The soprano – only one today – was the same as last week, ditto the bass; only the tenor was different. Amongst the musicians she recognized the trumpeter, looking if anything even more crumpled, tousled, than last week.

'*Die Liebe soll nichts scheiden* – our love nothing can sever!' sang the soprano and bass. Feeling it within her, she wished she could sing it; even more, she wished, suddenly, that she could be in love. It seemed to her, sitting there, all at once that she was empty: there was nothing there and never had been. I feel it only about music, and even then it's an aching void. It's become that. To sing with such passion, though it's about God, they must be each of them able to *feel* it: she sings with such joy. Mine lasts the music through and then I'm left. I suppose I'm meant to find religion – what was that bit they kept reading to us, at us: 'Our hearts are restless' – If I could feel it for Patrick, I would. Oh, I would. If it were a good thing I could *do* – only it's *be*, not do – Oh God,

43

I would do it. It's like a black tunnel – no, not a tunnel, a great wide open plain, dry, with no idea where to go. No direction. Why should one direction matter more than another? Most of all, I suppose though, I dread being like her, Tessie. A nothing. Not a nobody, but a nothing – I can't imagine her ever feeling anything overwhelming, ever going overboard about anything, anybody. Disorganized – well, I'm messy – but it's her not wanting anything, not pointing in any particular direction. I mean, what's she *for*? Not for marriage anyway. And who wants marriage if that's what it's like. And it *is* like that ... But then the truth is, they both drive me nuts. We're back to music, aren't we? It's – he's so ... His voice, it's like hearing another person; but if he cared, really cared, he'd have given up all this stuff in the City and gone in for singing. Money's all right – he's always saying so. 'If it's money, forget it.' For all the heart he has in that work he does. Or his life at home – oh God, *marriage* ...

Music brought her back, kicking, to the present. Time lost: unlike her, not keen on using music as background for her thoughts. She felt drained. And once again aware of Peter: all the last chorus he was the buzzing of a bee, the tickling of a crawling fly. Then all through the *Missa Brevis* his legs – in well cut dark grey wool (they'd look wonderful on anyone else she thought) – rubbed against hers; tainting the music. The interval when it came was a relief. Peter got up lightly, glad, it seemed, to have something definite to do: 'No booze, alas – the nearest ale house is two streets down. Coffee in the basement however.'

When they got down, it was Nescafé in plastic containers. Handing her the squashy mug, he managed to splash some down her white smock. But instead of apologizing: 'It rather amazes me,' he said, 'what you dollies wear. Time was when a smock meant only one thing – '

Her eyes on the creeping brown stain, she said rudely, 'What was that, a cowgirl?'

'Harry preggers, my dear. Harry preggers.' On the far side of the room, hemmed in by the crowd, were some of the musicians and singers. Looking over, changing the subject: 'I'd have liked,' he said, 'to have got you over to meet Morwen – the slightly voluptuous soprano.' He looked with distaste

44

up and down Polly's spindly frame: 'Personally, I like an armful. I used to *fancy* – correct me if I don't use the in word – I used to rather fancy Birgit Nilsson. How horribly dating. Now I've surrendered quite painlessly to the charms of Rita Hunter.'

A moment later, holding her arm tightly, he tried to take her across, but it proved too difficult. Instead, halfway there, he introduced her to a leathery-faced woman who smelled strongly of mothballs. 'I'm just off for a quick pee,' he said, with an air of bravado.

She and the leathery-faced woman, whose name she hadn't caught, began a semi-shouting conversation. A friend's son had been to Hatter's. A great aunt of hers, oddly enough, had once lived in the house next door.

'Ghastly place,' Polly shouted; finding herself thinking about Muff suddenly, and worrying because tonight she was left alone in the house. She broods, she thought, and she hasn't seen me all day. 'Just a matter of getting "A"s there,' she shouted, 'and getting the hell out – '

'Don't wish your life away,' the woman was shouting back when Peter reappeared. Polly realized that she should have gone to the lavatory too. 'The bog,' she said, 'have I time?'

'Go ahead,' he said, waving his hand airily. 'Permission to leave the room. Piss off – as they say.'

She came to the top of the stone steps and a bell rang. Rushing, following the arrow 'Toilets' down the corridor, she saw that it had all been done up recently – a notice still read 'Wet Paint'. She came to the doors; they gleamed; frantic with hurry she wondered absentmindedly – she seemed to be all bladder now – why they'd put the pin-figure woman in Oxford bags. She flung the door open, and rounding it hurtled into a man fastening his zip. Putting out a hand to save her balance she hit him in the chest.

'Oh golly, I read it wrong – ' She saw then that it was the trumpeter.

'All right,' he said. 'Steady,' gripping her arm.

'I'm so sorry – ' she began. The door opened; an elderly man hurried in. In evening-dress – so one of the orchestra. Head averted he rushed past them. 'Look here,' he called – the place seemed to her suddenly to be all white porcelain and

45

rushing water – 'there *are* other places for – that sort of thing.'

'I say I say I say this isn't Unisex Hall you know,' the trumpeter said, laughing. They were standing outside now. 'I'll explain,' he said, 'not to worry. I know him of old – ' He turned to go, hurrying.

'Sorry, sorry,' she said stupidly.

'Oh any time,' he said, lifting a hand in farewell. 'Any time.'

When she got back Peter was already in his seat. He had on the same slightly reproving expression as earlier. 'I thought perhaps you had stood me up,' he said, 'gone home in disgust – *freaked* out.' She slipped into the seat beside him and realized she was shaking all over. She tried to calm herself. How could I have been so silly? Fortunately Peter was a little less restless in the second half and at one point she even thought he'd gone to sleep. Then, while the trumpeter was playing a long and difficult solo passage, he woke up suddenly and began fidgeting again. She'd gone fiery red; she couldn't look at the trumpeter. Picking up the programme, she searched for his name. Sam Zossenheim. You are a nit, really, she said to herself, how could I have been so thick, how could I have done it? Then she thought suddenly: I'll tell Patrick tomorrow; it'll cheer us up, *he'll* like it.

It was all over. As they went out, taking her arm, 'Well, I could do with some grape or grain, or whatever,' Peter said. 'Supper of course? Yes please, Uncle Peter?'

He took her to Drone's in Pont Street. 'Is this near enough to Hatter's?' he asked in a disdainful voice, head turned in the direction of the crammer's, as if miasmic air rose from the place. She ignored him; but a moment or two later when they had been handed menus: 'I wonder how many of your young men, your *beaux*, can afford to bring you in here?' he said.

He ordered flamboyantly, loudly; looking around him a lot of the time. Once or twice he raised his hand, gave a smile of recognition and looked knowing. But when she said, 'Well, and who's that?' he said hastily, 'Wouldn't you like to know?' colouring, so that she felt certain there was no one there at all.

The meal was going to be a drag: even before the avocados arrived she had had enough. He tried to draw her out about music, but it turned out to be only a guise for his need to slate the conductor. 'He made an absolute mess of the Carissimi. Behaving as if he had a train to catch – and then *no* idea what to do with his left hand. Frankly, I slept after the first ten minutes. But then as Winston Churchill said on another occasion, sleep is an opinion. *I* wouldn't perform under him, I must say.'

She thought this was probably her cue to ask him about his playing. It was. 'I should of course have persevered. It was hardly lack of *talent* I suffered from but – I play the organ of course – the general lack of opportunity. So discouraging. I have played on several *very* famous organs, but I was of course in the end driven into the world of business.'

She looked down at her salad, and wished that she was eating it with Patrick – or if not him, anyone of at least a dozen other people. (Anyone, in fact, but this person.)

'You can't imagine how delighted I was to run into your father again last week – I can almost say that I *flipped*, is it? when we coincided at the concert. I haven't seen him since a Concertgebouw Beethoven Nine we sat through together – I've been out of the country many years of course. Making my small fortune.' He sipped at his hock. Then:

'Do you have a *fella*?' he asked, fork poised over his salad.

'Hundreds,' she said. 'Hundreds and thousands actually.'

He stared at her for a few seconds as if trying to discomfit her, then he said after a little reflection: 'You *could* have dressed up for Uncle Peter, you know – it's a dear little outfit, but – ' He sighed. '*Autres temps, autres moeurs*. Is your hair natural? I've been dying to ask.'

'Yes,' she said savagely, feeling as if his fingers were rumpling through it. Was the evening never going to finish? He sat on through pudding, cheese, two servings of coffee. And then, miraculously it seemed, it was all over. He got a taxi – which was to drop him first, thank God. It appeared he lived near Victoria. But just when she thought she was almost safe, he said, looking out of the window: 'There's a party later this month. Amusing I should think – some of the same crowd, musicians and so on. I think I'm invited – if that doesn't sound too modest.'

'It doesn't.'

'Nasty, nasty. Temper. Look, Uncle Peter's trying to ask

you – would you like to come?'

Oh God, she thought wearily, oh God. What have I landed myself in for? Guiltily, she gave some off-putting reply. The towers, the office blocks of Victoria had come into view. It couldn't be long now. She ran through Cleopatra's dying speech, learnt ready for the morning. But she'd reached only 'the stroke of death is as a lover's pinch' when – oh joy – the taxi stopped.

∽

She had caught 'flu off Sandy. She was seldom ill – tough Tessie – and almost never ran a temperature; now she just gave in, collapsing into bed as if her spirit had been waiting for the rest.

They were due to give a dinner party in six days' time. Looking down at her from what seemed a terrifying height, Barney said: 'It's to be hoped that you will have surfaced by then . . .'

She feared indeed that she would. It would have to be gone through with. As usual a girl from an agency would be coming to do the cooking: she'd help with the menu-making too. Once only, Tessie had made a stand and insisted on doing everything herself. A masterpiece of ill-timing, Barney had said. A saga of disasters. Mouth watering in her pre-dreams, in actuality nothing – sometimes quite literally – jelled. Barney explained that she hadn't decided on her style beforehand. She had mixed, he said, traditional English, French cuisine, Greek peasant and nursery food. Now one of these girls came always. And always, without exception, Tessie liked them. They were charming and efficient, and tactful. Nothing was left for her but to be the perfect hostess. So easy, Barney said impatiently: when one thinks what most women have to manage. Muff was at a loss to understand, she said, what problem there was. 'What is the problem, Teresa?'

She turned in the bed, trying to get more comfortable. The transistor radio lay on the pillow beside her. Between dozing and waking she twiddled the knobs: half a tune here, half a tune there. 'Won't somebody dance with me?' She didn't want to listen really. 'You'll never find another fool like me . . .' Any tune heard more than once would belong forever to these

48

few days of fever: would join the vast library of tunes associated with people, with incidents, with states of mind and body.

'Put another nickel in, in the nickelodeon,' sang her name-sake, Teresa Brewer, in 1950, over and over again on Camilla's borrowed gramophone, 'All I want is loving you and music, music, music.' She had battened down the thought then, that Mike would love this honky-tonk beat. 'Closer, my dear, come *closer* . . .'

It was the New Year. After only five days at home she'd been SOS'd by the Marchants: they had a round of parties and entertaining, of days out hunting: both the children had 'flu.

Camilla, noisily healthy, crashed in and out of the house. She had a love affair on: the telephone rang at all hours. Soon, she hinted, she might be leaving for far-away places with strange-sounding names. Tessie, feeling the symptoms of 'flu, was reminded of her father at epidemic time. 'Good God,' he'd say, mildly irritable, '*I* haven't time to catch it – ' And so it was with her. When finally she crawled into bed, it seemed to take not days but weeks to recover.

While she was ill her mother wrote three times, as if guilty that during her short visit home Tessie had worked almost non-stop. Her letters, scribbled at a corner of the kitchen table, were a catalogue usually of who'd been ill with what, how busy Daddy was, and an explanation of how she'd really meant to write earlier but . . . This time though, in letter the third, her pen could hardly keep pace with her thought:

'*Terrific* excitement in the village! ! ! You'll remember that I was rather dreading dolling myself up for the Barney Willingham wedding, well there's been the most awful scandal and it's all *off*! ! Margaret Willingham is *very* put out I hear, it was going to be a terrific do, very non-austerity. Lots of *his* relations had come over from Ireland and two from Canada. It was going to be here because Anthea the girl had no parents, evidently she's a war orphan. The Hadley-Taylors had her staying with them for the last few days then you'll never believe it – on Saturday the actual *day* of the wedding her room was found quite empty! ! just a note on the pillow, Mrs Hadley-Taylor was terribly upset, she felt she should have guessed. They say she panicked and it was her war experiences upset

49

her, I don't know – I got the story from half a dozen people and patients, Cecil Willingham was furious and said she'd made a fool of the whole family. I keep thinking about him, poor boy, still I expect God has another plan is all I can say, surprised really, I've never run into him . . .'

'Gosh,' said Camilla, 'how absolutely dreadful – how simply terrible. What's he like, what did he do in the War? Is he terrifically good looking? He sounds it somehow – I'm awfully surprised really. I've never run into him . . .'

∞

Muff held the paper well away from her, her glasses sitting uneasily. The lamp above her desk made a little pool of light around the box of Con's letters. Their ink was discoloured, the paper crackled with brittleness – victims of the gas fire, the central heating, the years.

'Dearest Muff,

Terra firma – I was never so glad to see it. The Mothersill was useless, but since it never used to work for that Irish crossing, I don't see why it should have worked for this, and we were a long time outside Boulogne tossing about like a cork. I just held my head; some of the others were pretty greenish too.

So far it hasn't been at all like I imagined. In the silly way I did over school when I tried to picture and 'feel' it all beforehand – what would Little's house be like, the other boys and so on – I've been caught out again, because it's quite different. The town for a start is still pretty civilized, shops and restaurants and so on, and I can think of what it would be like taking you about, and being proud of you because your French is so awfully pretty (and of course, so are you!). And the other thing is – the billets. We've found ourselves in what is really a château, smart as paint and awfully roomy and warm (they've got hot water pipes). Any sort of clean straw, as we used to say at school, would have been welcome, but of course it's all fine linen. And nothing's too good for us. They're tremendously nice. You'd like them I think, Muff. *She* reminds me awfully of Aunt Victoria: she has the same sort of cheeks, very pink and white, and funny little hands which she flutters.

50

And she fusses about us in the very nicest way.

... So you see, don't you, how in many ways it isn't real yet: although you can hear the guns rumbling all the time; it would only take about twenty minutes to walk over to the trenches – and we'll be there soon enough.

... I miss you all the time. Is it because we're orphans that we're so close? But it began long before that, I think. In fact, I *know*. Although I can't really remember a time when you weren't the most wonderful sister a chap could have. It's much easier to write something like that than it is to try and say it to you. I'm afraid for us both. '*Usque adeo ne mori miserum est?*' Yes, I think it is.

I shall look forward to Fortnum's offering. (Have Harrods offended? Please explain!) ...'

Pages and pages. He had known that was what she wanted. His first letter: and she could remember now where, how, she'd been sitting when it came. It had been a Sunday and it had snowed all day. Two days later she saw her husband for the first time; although he didn't see her.

It had been at a charity matinee for Serbian Relief. Coming down the stairs of the Drury Lane, she'd seen him standing in the foyer: he was with a group of friends, and was laughing loudly, head tilted back – as he laughed he struck his thigh with his swagger stick. Immensely tall, immensely thin; his head forward now as he listened to one of the women.

She stopped for a second, her hand on the stair rail; then turned to query. 'That's Cecil Willingham,' said her companion. 'The Yorkshire Willinghams. You know – the coal people. He's just back from India . . .'

Something about the nature of his laughter impressed her: an assurance she didn't confuse with languor or arrogance. And there was something else too – an intangible which she was beginning to recognize but couldn't name. So that, although he hadn't seen her, it was as if he had.

∞

Teresa and Barney coming up the stairs, slowly. The grandfather clock on the landing striking twelve. Muff's light, as they pass her door very quietly, is still on.

'Are you going in to her?'

'No.' His voice, because of the drink (and there'd been a lot of it), came out louder than she thought he'd intended.

She herself was shaking: a fine preparation for the casual remark advised by Camilla. 'Oh, ask in *bed*,' Camilla had said in the end – as if smelling her fright and reluctance.

The bedroom looked beautiful, it looked inviting too. She thought, I'll get straight in and not bother with any of it. But almost at once, standing in the doorway just a little behind her, one hand fingering his cuff, he said:

'Had you asked me in good enough time – I should have strongly advised against that outfit.' He paused. 'Is it the top, or the skirt?' He put his head to one side: 'Something is wrong.'

'It's the bit in the middle,' she said sharply, caught off-guard; the only time really when she could manage a tart rejoinder. 'It's me.'

'Probably,' he said, smiling; the smile, although cool, was gentle. This is the moment, she thought, when I should smile too – however reluctantly, however feebly. But the moment passed.

'I also thought,' he said, coming right into the room, 'at various points during the evening, that either you hadn't done your homework or else you were being deliberately obtuse. Woundingly so, on two occasions. Piers lost a *great* deal of money – a small fortune in fact – not fifteen or even five years ago but last Friday.' He went on in a mock patient voice, 'So we don't say "and how are all the little bags of gold?" or whatever the inanity was you let slip with the Chambéry . . .'

She pulled at the buttons of her blouse, straining the fabric. I shall ask in a moment, she said to herself, because I've grown angry and that in a way will make it easier.

'Sin Two?' she said.

'I like the cardinal,' he said. 'A nice touch. Actually I picked them at random from too many to count. But for example, Deb Fortescue lost a baby last spring I think it was – anyway Clive not only told us all about it, he also said that she'd nearly cracked up over it, so that a feeble joke about – misconception was it? I forget – is *hardly*. One wonders continually what you're doing, thinking, when I – when people, tell you things.'

She wiggled her hips and the skirt, unfastened, fell to her feet. She stepped out of it, at the same time saying: 'By the way, who *is* this woman you're going about with?'

'And there's another thing,' he said. 'I thought also that in view of . . .'

Oh no, it could not be. Trying to be offhand she had not so much flung the remark as muttered it, into her skirt, into the carpet. Lost for ever; how could she repeat it now?

'I thought too that – You're shaking. What is it? Look, one knows nothing about dress. Doesn't presume to criticize.' He pulled at the knot of his tie. 'This goes deeper. I suppose once one found it entrancing, or shall we say entertaining? But at forty-three – to be so completely unsophisticated. It's unbelievable. Your gaffes – floaters as Father would have called them – they're bad enough. But it's as if, somehow, the nuns had *just* let you out.'

'I'm tired,' she said rudely, shouting a little; but he had closed the connecting door.

She got into bed with her make-up still on and thought she was going to cry; she could feel an obstinate lump, undissolved emotion. After a few moments she lit a cigarette. Lying back very still, she watched the smoke making rings of calmness.

He came back into the room. She asked him: 'Did you ever know a Tom Babington at school?'

'I wish you wouldn't,' he said coldly, 'I could smell it from next door. I don't know – the name has a faint ring.'

'He was a Catholic.'

'Vaguely, I suppose. Not the same house, or year.' He reached for her bedside light, flicking it off. 'Why Tom Babington, suddenly?'

∞

'A very old Catholic family,' Mother Aloysius said, two weeks after D-Day: taking Class Four into her confidence. 'The Honourable Teresa is the youngest and Lady Babington was *most* anxious to find a suitable convent. It appears that at St – ' she blushed, began fumbling hurriedly through a pile of papers. She had surely been about to name another school, tried and found wanting by Lady Babington? 'I should like you to be very welcoming. The Honourable Teresa will come to us in the autumn term. May I tell Reverend Mother that I can count on you all?'

Later that week Tessie was sent for to the convent parlour. She hadn't time to tidy herself, and after running the length of the corridor ('*Hurry*, Mother Alouie wants you *at once!*') she had to stand for a few moments outside the door getting her breath back; and hearing the voices inside.

'I quite understand,' Mother Aloysius was saying, in her oiliest voice; the one she used for asking whether so-and-so had begun her periods, 'yes, yes, I understand. Of *course*, Lady Babington . . .' Then, raised, the definite voice of Lady Babington herself, snapping out the words: '. . . her companions, dear Mother – I should like a *great* deal of care taken over this.' Tessie eavesdropping, fascinated, was frightened now to go in. 'You will understand of course, our concern over purity. Teresa, at *present*, is so pure. Quite untouched. But the world of today, Mother – the War. What we hesitated to speak of, knew nothing of, at seventeen, eighteen, is discussed freely, openly now. Teresa, you will understand, as the youngest, possibly she has been over-protected. But I have come to realize that one *cannot* be too careful. The arrangements at St Francis – the dormitories – I was not at all impressed . . .'

'Of course, of course,' murmured Mother Aloysius. Pause.

'So – I can trust you, dear Mother? This gel is suitable?' There was a flurry of movement, and hastily Tessie knocked on the door.

'Little Teresa has been with us since she was eight,' Mother Aloysius told Lady Babington. 'Such a delightful family. Five – no,' she corrected herself hurriedly, '*six* of them now. Her father is a very busy doctor.'

And so apt, Lady Babington remarked, that both should have the same Christian name: the happiest of coincidences. Her Teresa was named, she said, after St Teresa of Avila. Big St Teresa.

Yes, yes, Tessie told her – biting at the skin inside her mouth, her voice thick and awkward – yes, yes, of course she'd look after her Teresa, show her round, share a room with her, be her *friend*.

Their bedroom was the second on the right as you went up the main staircase. It was September now, and the Armies were making great advances in Europe. The Hon Teresa had bagged the bed nearest the window. She was already sitting on it when Tessie, lugging her suitcase, came puffing in.

'So you're you?' she announced, looking Tessie up and down. 'Come on in – Guardian Angel.' She leant back against the windowsill, pulling down the corners of her mouth. She had a small, ravaged face and long blonde hair which needed washing: her pageboy had separated into strands.

'Oh God, leave that,' she said when Tessie, humping her suitcase onto the bed, began to unpack. 'Let's have a drink.' She jumped down and crossing quickly to the big old-fashioned wardrobe came back with a large medicine bottle. A measuring glass stood on its top. The label read: 'Teresa Babington. One tablespoonful three times daily.'

She uncorked the bottle lovingly. 'What's the school chaplain like?' she asked, 'I mean, is he halfway reasonable?' She wrinkled up her nose and then downed the medicine at one gulp, 'I mean – is he even presentable?' She measured out a dose for Tessie, and passed the glass over. Tessie shook her head. 'Go on,' she said. 'If we've got to live together, we might as well be pickled together . . .'

'Oh God,' she said that first night, as they lay outside their beds unable to sleep in the September heat, 'this is *the* most incredible drag. I never thought Mummy'd actually do it you know – actually *send* me here. She got round Daddy when he was down for the weekend. He only comes because there's no wine left at his club. We've still some in the cellars, you see. Oh my God,' she said, 'I shall go mad here.'

She talked, on and off, most of that night it seemed: casually, about Giles who'd just gone out to India, about Elizabeth who was in the ATS, about Tom at Eton. Her voice, a little harsh, somehow matched her elegant, rangy body which looked not fourteen, but an easy seventeen. 'How ghastly,' she said when she heard all about Tessie's brothers and sisters, 'how absolutely too frightful.'

They settled into an easy relationship. Tessie, the safety valve, would listen to the Hon Teresa letting off steam: although she was never to talk as much again as that first night.

55

Later in the term Tessie tried the medicine – the Hon Teresa was recklessly generous with it: 'I don't give a damn if you split on me,' she said. But the fiery spirit choked Tessie and, setting her heart beating, frightened her. 'Giles got hold of it just before he went out. It was stinking expensive. Tom was livid, *green* – '

Airgraphs came from Giles. She would toss them over to Tessie: they were terribly dull, with occasional secret allusions. One day the Hon Elizabeth came to see her. Her hair was the same blonde as her sister's, but under her cap shorter and neater. She was prettier too, softer, with large brown eyes. She came and looked over the room: she seemed always about to cry. 'Taggy,' she said, 'it's awfully quaint – positively touching to see you like this.'

'She's frightfully nervy,' the Hon Teresa said in the evening. 'The chap she wanted to marry has just been killed, and she doesn't know but she rather thinks she's preggers. Christ, isn't the whole thing just too ghastly? *I'm* never going to fall in love.'

Early the next term Tessie asked after her: 'Oh God, *that*,' said the Hon Teresa wearily. 'She got rid of it, it cost the earth she said and was revoltingly messy. I mean, Christ, who'd be a woman?'

The last week of that term Tom came to see his sister. 'You're awfully well behaved,' he told her. Then to Tessie he said, 'Hasn't she corrupted you yet?'

She hadn't of course. But on the other hand she was, surely, an example of what it meant to be sophisticated, to be worldly? For years after Tessie would measure those words against the Hon Teresa's conduct; for it hadn't been, as with other girls, a veneer, a careful, overdone act: it had been the very air she breathed. Indeed, had she from the age of ten or eleven breathed any other air?

No one, nothing, was sacred; no one her idol. Her father the only person able to keep anything from her. Otherwise, she knew it all.

'. . . and at the time poor Mummy was absolutely loopy about Father Bede and she really thought Elizabeth didn't notice – and all the time *he* was lusting madly after Harry Turner on the estate, our altar boy . . .'

56

Surely sooner or later she would be expelled? It wasn't just the lingering smell of whisky (one day she'd spilt it in the bed), or the Turkish Pasha cigarettes which she hadn't liked and left lying about: it was the walks out to the town without permission and the careless excuses when discovered missing, the damns and bloodies within earshot of the nuns. Oh but *how* she must have wanted it! And yet they hadn't.

For a while, after her own expulsion, Tessie had vaguely expected a letter from her, some sign of life. But nothing, ever, had come. She'd been too proud to write herself even though she knew by heart the home address. For the Hon Teresa, she realized, Tessie Fletcher had existed only while she was there.

In the years that followed she had half hoped, half expected that sooner or later she would find herself (most likely of chances) next to the Hon Teresa on a bar stool, in a railway carriage, at a shop counter. Once, about three years after the War, she saw her in the *Tatler*: at Cambridge for a May Ball. Then a year or two later her engagement – or was it the actual marriage? He was Brazilian, and a diplomat. Nine or ten years after that she was photographed in one of the glossies, sitting on a regency sofa surrounded by children in frothy white, all ribbons and laces. He had been posted to London: they would be here for three years or more. She looked taut now: thin, hard: yet with a look about the eyes far more vulnerable and tender than the girl who had talked into the night all those years ago.

She would have been easy to locate, to run to earth, and for a while Tessie meant to do it. She would have liked after all to hear the end of the story. But it became just one of the many things not done; opportunities lost. Probably, possibly, life had gone all right for the Hon Teresa (how ever really would one have known if it hadn't?). The little she'd asked from it she'd probably got.

It was I, Tessie thought sadly, with sudden passion; it was I who asked for the impossible.

Chapter 5

By the time she got in from Hatter's, Polly was whacked. She said to herself, it's been one of those days. Badly begun; pushing the alarm off, then coming round with a fright too late; rushing into the kitchen all scatty, scarf flying, shaking her head to the offer of coffee. And then sitting on the bus, coming to suddenly: cold and hungry. And it was test day too – which was probably why she hadn't wanted to wake. She'd rummaged in her bag for her history notes. Her text books spilled out and she said to the boy in the next seat, 'Sorry. *Sorry.*' (He was very thin, if she jabbed him with her elbow she'd surely pierce his ribs.)

A moment later, a cheerful discovery: at the very bottom of the *tagari,* a double piece of Harrogate toffee, reminder and remainder of Patrick's half-term visit to his grandmother. She broke it with difficulty and offered half to the thin boy; he looked very frightened and said no at once, so she put both pieces in, one either side. Then coming up to Victoria – it happened. A yank with her bottom jaw, a sudden jab of pain: and out came a filling. Oh God, why me?

All during the test it was exquisite. Patrick, who'd been seated as far away as possible from her, seemed absorbed, head down. But she couldn't concentrate at all. As soon as she began any serious thinking, her tongue probed till it found the hole; then the nerve would throb alarmingly and up would shoot the pain. 'Christ,' she said, coming out with Patrick, 'I've mucked up just about every question.' In the street the icy cold set her whole jaw aching. Patrick was all sympathy: during lunch she opened her mouth for him: 'A souvenir of Harrogate,' she said. 'I should skive, beautiful,' he said, 'don't stay on for the Lit. You look ghastly – go straight to bed. Wish I could come too . . .'

She thought, I can't feel that bad just for a hole in the tooth, but when she got into the house that was all she wanted to do: just go to bed. There was nobody about. When she knocked on Muff's door, there was no answer. Out. She went straight on up. She wanted just to lie absolutely still, quite alone, in the dark. Then it would all fall into shape. She'd read somewhere that like a computer the brain, the human mind, needed time to sort impressions. Dreams were meant to do it – she'd been snatched from hers perhaps this morning. In the dark it would all, maybe, make sense.

Sometimes at school it had been like that; only then there'd been no real escape, nowhere to hide. She'd solved it in those days by giggling with her best friend, Alice. For years and years – from ten or eleven was it? – everything had been punctuated by giggles. Sitting hidden, they'd talked and talked and talked; and giggled. In those days, she thought now, it had been in some weird way possible to say everything. A kind of thinking out loud. It worked very well. At the same time, like an undercurrent, there'd been reality. Some of it horrid. The dried up beefburgers at lunch, the very long, very grey hair on Sister Scholastica's chin, the Instant Whip with big lumps in it. And then happenings: not thinking much of the Monkees, Alice's uncle in the hotel business who'd got them Engelbert Humperdinck's autograph, letters from home with no news in them at all. Lots and lots of interwoven strands and everything somehow coming out right. But those days were over: they couldn't anyway have continued so simply, even had Alice stayed. They'd gone before she left.

I suppose, she thought, lying in the dark, I need a friend like that again. Not a brother-cousin like Patrick but that better-than-sister relationship I had with her. There wasn't the jealousy I've seen between sisters (not that I've had the chance to find out).

So, when did Alice go? Not after that one fraught sixth form term – we were out of touch by then already – but that last summer surely? The summer I lost my virginity (lovely phrase), that commodity we'd both been carrying round sixteen, seventeen years, and noticeably so for four or five. Alice's had gone first. It had been turn and turn about for such years anyway. First to have a kiss (Polly), first to have a *real* one (Alice); first to have her tits looked at (Alice), first to have them felt (Polly); first to have a hand up her skirt – unwillingly (Polly), willingly (Alice). Then, first to get laid. Alice had been very

59

pleased with herself. It had been a great success. He was quite old, at least twenty-three, and she had promised not to tell anyone, anyone at all. 'Not even my best friend.' (Well perhaps – *just* her best friend.) The difficulty was that the success hadn't been repeated. She'd searched around – slept around – for just such an explosion. 'If you knew,' she kept saying. 'Polly, if you knew.'

That last summer they'd both of them been ratty, aimless. 'O' levels all finished and nothing known about results. What to do with themselves? They made all sorts of plans: jobs they were going to take, places they were going to hitch to. They'd been talking about it since Easter but no decisions had been made. The summer suddenly loomed before them, stretching out endlessly, unprovided for. Alice's family had a house on the Norfolk coast. An old couple who'd once worked for the family were caretakers and it was always warm and welcoming. They decided to go down there. Alice's brother, William, who was going up to Sussex in the autumn, would be coming some of the time, possibly bringing a friend: both of them were off to Greece in August. At the weekends Alice's parents would be there.

In the event they did absolutely nothing all day. They stayed in bed till twelve or one, then tired out with lying still and not eating they sat about all afternoon, coming to life in the evening just enough to play records, or talk, or watch telly until late late bedtime. 'I wish something would happen, or someone would turn up . . .'

William turned up, eventually, with his friend Rory. 'He's frightful,' Alice said as soon as she saw him. 'Honestly, he's so *young*.' He didn't seem so to Polly, or not particularly. Very very lanky so that he might have been her twin, he had a face that was all angles, with upturned eyes, puckish in a cold way. He was exaggeratedly polite to her when they first met, then ignored her. This irritated her; that it should, made her even more irritated. William whom she knew already she found very heavy going, but by an unwritten arrangement she had to go with him, solid as he was, so that Alice could have Rory – whom she didn't want. 'I'm afraid you're stuck with William,' Alice said. 'He is bloody boring, I know. But I'm not trying incest even for kicks.'

The weather, never very good, turned worse. The days dragged. The town was small and uninteresting and they'd soon exhausted it. Records, the cinema, table tennis in the dark basement; it was only five or six days, but it felt like a month. Polly felt that she couldn't endure another moment of William's devotion, his inability to disagree with her, his dead-pan expression, his heavy considered answers to anything that could be, however faintly, construed as a question. Alice was fed up too. At first she'd parried Rory, now she couldn't be bothered.

'He's awful. He's got verbal diarrhoea. How long are they staying? Let's *go* . . .'

They talked a lot about going and made lots of telephone calls about possible holiday jobs. For a whole afternoon they were set on farming in the Valais. Then running out to the shops just before they shut, Alice saw five unlikely looking people strolling through the centre of the town. They were all utterly and completely beautiful, but the most beautiful of all was one of the two men. He had long fair hair in a plait, and a moustache, and just to look at him, she said, just to think about him, and she felt faint. She went up to bed early without supper.

She stopped talking too about going off anywhere. 'We'll stay,' she announced, and as if by arrangement the weather altered. For two days in the hot sunshine they went on picnics, bathed, even played tennis. Then on the third day, 'I've got to walk my passion off,' Alice said. There was an elderly spaniel, Nelson, who went with the house but which no one bothered much to exercise. She persuaded Polly to walk him out with her and then the most marvellous thing happened: from the cliff top the beautiful people were spied in a cove. Nelson, encouraged that way, dashed down to them. At once he stole what looked like some pasty, moving aside to eat it in great greedy gulps. No one seemed bothered. One girl gave him a lazy half kick, half push. Alice rushed down after him; Polly waiting in the grass saw her talking to them. She couldn't be bothered to follow – couldn't that summer be bothered to do anything – and in a while, when Alice didn't come back, she got up and strolled on home.

Ecstasy. Alice came back. She'd been asked round, she said:

61

any time, just drop by. They were sharing a house – they were a commune really the other side of the town and all of them were quite wonderful, but of course especially the fair one. Halfway to the bus stop that evening, they were going to the cinema with Rory and William, she said: 'Well I think I'll just drop by now, while I think about it.' 'Hey, what about me?' Polly said angrily.

The evening went badly. She sat in the cinema between the two of them. William rubbed his knee against hers, up and down; in the darkness Rory was looking at her; then he entwined one long leg round hers, pulling at it. William had only to do the same, she thought, and she would split down the middle. It was very hot: William ate a choc ice and said he felt lousy. Home again, he went straight up to bed, giving her a soulful look as he went by: being ill accentuated his flabbiness, his hangdog expression. She was left alone with Rory.

He announced that they were going to swim. 'Get your things,' he said in his superior, slightly high pitched voice.

'I might,' she said, but then stopping to think could come up with no possible reason why not. She enjoyed it too: cool now in the evening, nearly a full moon, the waves crisp and gentle. Probably she stayed in too long. He chased her in the water, unfastening her bikini top, trying to swim away with it. Walking back up to the house, twined round her again, arms this time, tripping her legs as they crossed the wet sand, 'I don't think I shall collect panties,' he said. 'Girls don't seem to wear them any more.' He gave her a salty kiss, his thin body pressing against hers. He said, 'You must admit, I have style.' 'You haven't, you're unutterable, sickening,' she said with easy confidence. She shook her wet hair. 'That was fantastic – '

There was no sign of William, or Alice. She went through to the kitchen. They were both hungry; he could eat an elephant, he said. She fried some bacon: 'All right,' he said, 'could eat a pig then.' He followed her all the time she was cooking, standing just behind, moving when she did, jerking, sidestepping, teasing. Then he took her hand in his: she liked the fantastically long fingers. When they had eaten they crept up the stairs together, along to the room she shared with Alice.

'Lock it,' he said. 'Let her crave admittance.'

Thinking about it later, she remembered more about the ending than the beginning. The petting was never aimless. Then he had said, pushing back her shoulders with his thumbs, looking at her, eyebrows raised: 'Well, shall I?' She'd admitted that no, never, and so – 'Oh *I* shall take care of all that,' he said.

It was like the bathing. There seemed no particular reason why, no particular reason why not. Her mood changed from second to second – she felt suddenly wonderful, then frightened, then angry. So much time too to stand back – lie back rather – and think; and yet she couldn't think. She couldn't believe afterwards in such purposeless inevitability. Grown cold, half wanting to laugh as the long fingers unfolded the sealed envelope – 'has your Pope had a hand in puncturing this?' – watching fascinated as he rolled it on with loving care (love for whom, care for whom?). 'This is Big Claus,' he said. 'Little Claus you met earlier of course. You must admit,' he said again, 'I have style.'

She didn't speak; she thought perhaps she would never speak again. 'Are you ready, Big Claus? He does it like this, and like this, and like *this*.' His eyes were shut. It was a little painful and rather surprising. Then, very soon, rather as if she weren't there, it was over. She supposed it must be since he brought his thing out hurriedly, still a size. He had a high colour: 'Well ploughed, Big Claus,' he said, then after a moment, 'you may get dressed.' While she was pulling on her jeans, he said, 'It's his third virgin, he does rather well, don't you think? I'm aiming though at *seven* – that's symbolically more perfect. I must say though that I honestly prefer the initiated. I mean, who wouldn't?' He watched as she slipped on her shirt. 'And another thing,' he said, beginning to dress too, very slowly, 'another thing, I do prefer a bit more of everything, a bit more of a handful. I mean, fantasies of raping a Renoir wouldn't get anywhere if one landed you, would they? I should fill out a bit if I were you.'

She felt very cold, torn and empty. She thought she heard a door downstairs. 'I expect you're wondering what I thought of your actual performance?' he said. 'Quite moderate for a first time. I got in surprisingly easily but then I expect you've been working on it yourself. Beta minus, shall I say?' He

63

seemed compelled to go on talking. She got up suddenly and unlocked the door, shouting in a stage whisper down the stairs, 'Alice!'

The evening ended smudgily. They all three sat in the kitchen drinking beer till two or three. Alice seemed inclined to be tolerant of Rory, as someone in a good mood might tolerate a buzzing insect. She told Polly nothing of her evening, but wore all the time a secret, ecstatic smile. She seemed to have it still when she woke next morning. Polly in turn told her nothing. It was the beginning of the end. The next day, she was sick with a temperature; William seemed to have the same bug. Alice came in only to sleep and hardly that. As soon as she was well enough, Polly went quietly home.

The next term had begun normally enough, except that it was obvious Alice had some secret. She did no work, and obeyed none of the few rules applying to the sixth form. Sometimes she and Polly giggled together; but it was different, the conspiracy of strangers trapped in the same circumstances, not that of old friends. Polly felt herself to blame too.

After half-term Alice never came back. The nuns announced that she had left, and her elder sister wrote to Polly that Alice had cleared out completely. 'Mumps is absolutely devastated and we haven't got any kind of address or anything but William says he thinks he knows who it is and it's somebody absolutely *awful*. Anyway she says she's living with him and that's that and we can't find her; we don't know yet if we're going to do anything with the police . . .'

She had limped somehow through the rest of that school year, till they had asked her to leave. 'Polly has outgrown us,' was the polite phrase. But she would have wanted to leave anyway. Now one way and another, she was healed. All in one piece and going nowhere in particular. She scarcely thought of Rory, had never seen him again. Just sometimes he would come suddenly to mind, then she would say as she had said that evening, over and over again lying in bed: 'I'm still me.' He hadn't taken any real part of her. Just an outmoded piece of property – and better lost than stolen or strayed. But then she would think suddenly that he *had* taken something. 'You've taken it,' she would say angrily, waking in the small hours:

64

taken it and given me nothing in exchange. (But that was greedy.)

This evening, remembering it all, she wanted on an impulse to have it back. 'Give it me back,' she said suddenly, sadly. She could never now give it to anyone.

∞

A hired car ('however did you get one?' Polly asked) took Muff to the Home. The matron who was possibly slightly in awe of her, but more probably very busy, wasn't disposed to discuss at any length the patient she'd chosen for her.

'My time I'm afraid is very limited. We have – '

'I, too, have limited time,' said Muff, rising; ending the interview. 'If I could be shown up?'

Frank Robertson was seventy-five. He'd been wounded and gassed in the summer of 1917, at Messines. He'd never been able to work again or to marry, or indeed to live outside the Home. Nowadays he spent two-thirds of his time in bed: occasionally he was wheeled out. 'You will understand,' Muff had told the matron, 'that I am hardly fit for wheeling a chair . . .'

She sat very upright now, beside his bed: her stick propped up against his screen. The chair was not very comfortable. Her hip was beginning, already, to protest.

It was three weeks now since Con had spoken to her. In the dream she had tried to listen but – the old terrifying dream-nightmare – she could only keep thinking, half sobbing: it's all right, it's all right, he's here, he's safe, he's *alive*. He had spoken earnestly; he was lying back in a deckchair – Corrib again, it was always Corrib – then leaning forward suddenly, chin cupped in hands, he had said: 'You mustn't think you're not needed, Muff – we didn't all go you know.' Then he had looked at her in an odd way: puzzled perhaps, disappointed even? But when frantic, her heart bursting, she had tried to speak to him, to reach out to him, she saw that it was already evening; his chair, all the chairs around the lawn were empty.

She had had to puzzle out the answer for herself. Now, two

letters and a telephone call later she was here by a bedside. And visiting not an officer, but one of the men.

The introductions were over. There was a pause:

'Well, and how have you been? How are you today?'

There was another pause. But this is terrible, she thought. It was straight out of the times when she and Aunt Lettice had gone round to see the men's families. When they had had to say the right things to mothers of seven who had lost the breadwinner, to mothers of five who had no children left at all.

She tried now to ask the right questions. But it was not like the dream: that was the mischief; there was no reason, conceivably, why she should be needed. Frank was playing his part: he was the gardener's son, the stable boy, the blacksmith's son; he answered questions as he'd been taught to. 'Yes, Ma'am,' he said and 'No, Ma'am – that bit I can't remember, Ma'am. It's gone that. Jerry did for that – ' Then: 'I were sixteen when I went, I told a lie – they were sorry, the Family was very sorry. Me going off. That's very good of you, Ma'am, it's very good of you to take an interest. They haven't been since thirty-four you see, they went to Australia, that's what they said. There were only the young ones and they couldn't remember me because they'd been in perambulators you see when I left. So you couldn't expect them to keep calling. Dad, he came till forty-six – he used to take me out. But his chest were bad then. He's gone now. And Mother – she's gone. I had nephews, they'll be in Canada, Ma'am. But the Family, the young ones, they went to Australia . . .'

She thought suddenly, the place smells. It was not he who smelled but the place itself. Disinfectants warding off decay, masking in a horrible false refinement the smell of being human: Dettol, carbolic acid, TCP, mingled now with cabbage; and steamed into the very walls, a million cups of strong sweetened tea, filming orange round the cup.

The dream had been in a language hard to translate: she had thought that she had understood it. But now as she watched him, his shaky mouth with the ill-fitting teeth, the trembling hands which pulled at the sheets, the stained brown skin, it seemed that this was not after all a message from the past. It was a separate sadness that Frank (stable boy, head gardener's son? whatever) had been serf-like lover of some

66

family, and now was forgotten. She doubted, even with what she recognized as a great gift for self-deception, that she was giving pleasure. It was perhaps too late. Old habits died hard: already she could feel rising in her a remembered angry impatience at 'their' lack of appreciation. 'They' never showed – could not express – gratitude for the time spent on them, the money, the gifts, the thoughtful enquiries about their (usually too numerous) offspring. It was all their own fault: they stood mute victims ready for the slaughter – the sword, the block, anything that life could do to them. The tragedy was when the proud were struck down.

'... we'd been letting Jerry have it all night then come the morning we'd thought we was done – then it were only after I were hit, Jerry was using this stuff – I don't remember not rightly. It's my chest, you see, Ma'am ...'

Between the silence, his voice came and went: to hear him at all she had often to lean forward. She thought that probably he was tiring. She looked at her watch. She had acted on the dream, she thought. And because she had done so she had learnt that between her, Margaret Ursula Gore-Lewis and this terrible pass, this life amongst the smells and the slow inevitable decay, lay not so much birth and breeding (which all her life she had used to get her way, or to stop others getting theirs), but rather a bank balance, assets, and not least, Cecil's elegant provision for her. She had not to say, there but for the grace of God go I; but rather, there but for Hambros, Hill Samuel, Consols ...

'I have telly on Tuesdays,' Frank said, suddenly coming back to life. 'Tuesdays, and Thursdays.'

There was silence. She forced herself to speak. 'And what type of entertainment, what shows, do you enjoy?'

'*The Saint*, they have *The Saint* on. And *Beryl's Lot*. They have that. I only watch Tuesdays though. And Thursdays.'

His head touching the pillow, seemed scarcely to dent it. He began to cough, seriously.

The visit, the interview, drew to a close. As she rose to go: 'I shall call again,' she said.

'That's very kind of you, Ma'am, they'd have kept calling you see, except they went to Australia.' He turned his head

67

away. Then, his voice querulous almost: 'I have my tea now,' he said. 'Now's when I have my tea ...'

∞

Occasionally, she found herself thinking about Peter; thinking with irritation: he fancies me. But she hadn't heard from him, he hadn't bothered her about the party. A good thing. She wanted to forget that whole evening; wrong loo and all. Didn't want to think about it.

But these days, what *did* she want to think about, what remember? Patrick perhaps? 'Our beautiful friendship,' he'd say, pulling a face. Tonight they were going to the Rainbow. It was his idea. 'You're terrible,' he'd said that morning. 'Impossible. You're going to bits and pieces.' (Then mock-pathetic: 'Please – can I be around to pick them up?')

They were to meet at Finsbury Park at six-thirty. In a wandering, or was it a wondering mood – who cared about the difference? – she walked from Knightsbridge to Green Park and down Pall Mall to Trafalgar Square, taking her time. She tried to look at the familiar landscape as a stranger, a foreigner might; as someone in love might.

Nelson's column rose gauntly. The air was misty; Big Ben struck five, sounding as through fog. She drifted towards the National Gallery. It was Thursday, free day; she supposed it would be crowded, but she'd just sit in front of one picture. A little way ahead of her, just going in, a figure looked familiar. As he turned going up the stairs she saw it was the trumpeter, Sam Zossenheim, was it? He was wearing an Afghanistan coat, as shaggy as himself.

One foot on the first step, she felt suddenly creeping over her, from face to neck to breasts to thighs, a blush. A great pumping of blood; her heart beating too, wildly. Rooted by surprise, she thought that she might faint, be sick with it. Then a passer-by jostled her. She came back at once to herself, climbed up on. She would go in. She thought, I'd just like to say, 'Hi, remember me?'

'Your bag please, miss. Sorry, it's the rule ... Lovely. OK, pass. Fred, just see she hasn't a bookworm in there, would you?'

So she was through. But where, which way to go? Stupidly, stupefied, she realized: I've lost him. I have lost him.

From Dutch to Italian to English to Spanish: trying not to look as if searching for somebody.

If I go upstairs, he'll come down. If I come down, he . . .

A French family, standing in front of a Velasquez, were engaged in vigorous argument. She wanted to say, 'Stop, look, excuse me, but have you seen a man, a big man, in a shaggy coat?' She had been half an hour looking, searching. He could well be gone, probably *was* gone. In the shop she riffled idly through postcards. She felt desolate, black, disappointed out of all proportion. She was amazed by it. Out on the balcony the cold air struck her immediately. She was cold all the way through, deep down: a damp bleak chill, like the outside world, the weather. It was as if for half an hour, forty minutes, she had had some purpose. And now?

To Leicester Square Underground. 'And don't loiter, as they call it, at Finsbury,' Patrick had said. 'Famous stamping ground. I don't want someone else getting in first . . .'

Chapter 6

It seemed to Tessie very likely that, the day before, Muff had had one glass of Madeira too many. A single one kept her sweetened, gracious, for the rest of the day; didn't affect the morrow. But she, Tessie, had been out; Barney perhaps had been persuaded to stay longer in the room, had pressed on her another and another? There was no doubting the fractiousness. This morning it wasn't clock or grapefruit or noise outside or crumpled *Times*. It was everything.

'Central heating, drying the air. And quite useless against the mist – the fog is seeping through these ill-fitting windows. Barney I know has asked you several times, Teresa, to see about the fitting. He would not grudge the money for double glazing – for new windows if necessary. What he does lack is the time, the leisure to arrange it. You, Teresa, have all day.'

When Tessie said nothing, she said, 'Is that not so?' Then as her tray was put down, 'Has Sandy recovered from her influenza? *Your* influenza, I should say. Very early in the season for influenza. Ask her, would you, Teresa, when she returns, not to sing on the stairs. *Nor* to go about in sabots. Maids should wear soft shoes . . .'

'It's an awful sort of bug,' Sandy said. 'I mean, feels like you've been pissed without knowing – fucking dizzy whenever you bend. I thought what I'd do, come along this morning then I'll maybe kip this afternoon – Terry's got Cubs.'

The Hoover front plate fell off and she jammed it on again, cigarette ash falling everywhere. 'Sit down a sec,' she said to Tessie, 'you look really off.' Then above the noise she called: 'You seen that film *Young Winston*? There's a book isn't there – you read it? Know what happens when he's little? because Terry and me was just at the second half. It's good that – if it's not too like crowded, you've just to wait a bit and that hall place – foyer – it's quite empty. No one in charge.

We're just in there with our hot dogs like we'd been out for the interval. I seen a lot of ends. Only it gets a bit, you know — only seeing ends.' She banged the machine to a halt. 'Don't clean that too good,' she said, seeing Tessie wipe along the dado.

Soon after that they had coffee because neither of them felt good. Tessie asked her about the clogs and Sandy said, 'They're a bloody nuisance anyway, old dear, doing the stairs. Got any old plimsolls I could paint up?'

∞

Polly, sitting in the basement at Hatter's, is being tested in world affairs. She has the right expression on her face: concentration, slight but not too much bewilderment. Lots of pen sucking and narrowed gaze. She's careful never to look around her – above all, not to look at any person. On the paper itself she has written:

'Peter dear, what a lovely evening. I hope you noticed how much I enjoyed it. I can never have enough music, and to listen in such pleasant company,' (but this was overdoing it, grossly, not because he would see through it – he wouldn't – but because she must live with the sort of person who told such dreadful lies). 'The meal was super too. If I didn't talk much it's because I get so absolutely whacked – I expect you did when you worked for "A"'s' (when *ever* could that have been – and didn't they have another name anyway? Cross that out). 'Hatter's really is ghastly. Anyway, belated grateful thanks, Love, Polly.' (Now, casual this, change from biro to felt pen, to show genuine afterthought),

'PS. Did I say, yes of course I'd like to come to that party with you? Awfully afraid I *didn't*. P.'

Ah well, she thought, laying the sheet of half-written questions on top. A shadow was glimpsed coming round the room. Ah well. The end justifies the means.

∞

'I rather think,' Barney said, 'it was about four glasses.'

Tessie said, 'When we were children we weren't allowed to

71

talk about "chills on the liver" or being "liverish" – my father
said it was medically sloppy. He said there's no such thing.
Only, that's what I'd say about Muff today – '

'I think,' he said, 'she was in that pleasant state Father used
to call "buffy". A rather Edwardian turn of phrase. Sort of
pre-drunk. Very difficult to gauge satisfactorily I imagine. That
wonderful moment when they all achieved it together . . . just
that and no more – ' He paused. 'She hasn't the stomach
for it now in any case.' Crossing the room he poured Tessie
a sherry. 'Where is she anyway?'

'I don't know. She went off about five-thirty, in a taxi. She
spoke of going to a theatre. But you know it's as much as my
life is worth, to ask – '

Leaning back, he stretched out his legs. Then reaching forward for his drink: 'There isn't of course very often anything
she wants to see. The unspeakable vulgarity of half the shows,
the tedium of revivals, Shakespeare in the modern style – and
so on. She dismisses them all in a phrase. Yet she doesn't like
the safe things – anything popular is ruled out of court. "Can
you imagine, Barney, there were charabancs unloading into
the foyer . . ." I don't know what we can do for her.' He leaned
back again, arms behind his head. 'Remember that time we
went with her to Graham Greene – *The Living Room*, wasn't
it? Just before our engagement, surely?'

The warmth from the drawing-room fire, from the glass of
sherry, crept outside and inside, so that she relaxed and
thought: if he were only like this every day. Then she wondered
at once why ever she should think this easy talk, this companionable feeling, this reminiscing, had anything to do with
closeness; with a step forward in their relationship. It just *feels*
closer, she thought sadly. He was after all only talking as he
might to an old friend, dropping by for a drink.

What pass have we come to, she thought, when something
exciting, wonderful is happening to him, every day and night
in his heart – and yet I'm honoured that he should sit with me
and criticize his own mother? This is it indeed. We have really
come to this.

Our hold on each other: my hold on him, is so custom-based,
so meaningless. What sort of bond is it anyway? It's not bed,
that's evident, and it's not board (not the way *I* cook). It's just

72

that I'm here and might as well stay. What's the real objection? One man, one wife, one mistress – a serviceable, satisfactory way of life, left unquestioned for centuries. An arrangement after all. And at Edward's death-bed didn't Alexandra send for Alice Keppel? Now though, we are not supposed even to *feel* jealous. And yet I haven't really seen any better solution. Nothing in the 'sixties or 'seventies so far seems to me any better answer. No solution that appeals.

He got up, coming over and filling her glass. 'Look,' he said, 'I shall have to be out this evening. It's a meeting about the St Matthew. The idea is to have it ready for Easter. Ivor Atkins' version – not German unfortunately. But the arrangements for the professionals are through, more or less, bar the Evangelist.'

'I shall be there,' she said.

Looking across at her, he smiled. It transformed his face completely. She would have thought – if she hadn't by now been so wary – that the smile was for her.

∞

All those evacuees ... At any rate that was the excuse, that Easter of 1943, for putting on a show for them in the village. The organization began messily with a host of unrelated ideas: too many people, and not all of them the right ones, wanted to be in on it. Within days the project had been taken over by Muff.

Having drawn up a plan, she issued a few directives and then, with complete confidence, delegated. Stan Barraclough, the local auctioneer, was to be master of ceremonies and entertainments officer. Miss Thackray, music teacher, would do all the serious accompaniments while Mike, playing by ear, would vamp for the choruses.

Rehearsals were held in the draughty village hall where there was a piano, seats and a stage of sorts. Stan, hands in pockets, would stand there, slightly aggressive. Dressed always in Home Guard battledress, he looked at least half ready to stave off the invasion. He and Mike were to do a comic turn together, with patter. Later they were to be Flanagan and Allen, singing 'Down Forget-me-not Lane'. Tessie had a number with

Mike too. Judy Garland and Mickey Rooney again. 'Our love affair, will be such fun, 'twill be the envy of everyone . . .' She wasn't shy when she sang with him. She sang in a talking, shouting sort of voice: Stan said she was rather good, including her in his praise of Mike who he said was the backbone of the whole show.

Several turns however were obviously so terrible that it was questionable whether an audience used to more rollicking fare would tolerate them. 'We're not Works Wonders, you know,' Stan would mutter warningly as an elderly bachelor moved heavily to 'The Floral Dance'. There was a feeling sometimes that the evacuees were to be there by Royal Command: Downstairs, forced to watch Upstairs home theatricals. The query was whether they'd extend to them the same tolerance and admiration factory workers obviously felt for each other's performances.

Then at the last rehearsal but one, towards the end of the afternoon, Barney strolled in, nonchalantly; under his arm a bound music book.

'Squire's son,' Stan said. 'Oh my God.' Tessie and Mike had just finished their turn. Barney acknowledged them distantly. 'I thought I might perform,' he said, carelessly, to Stan.

'Oh yes?' said Stan, eyebrows lifted. But Barney, ignoring him, went straight over to Miss Thackray; leaning forward he explained something to her courteously; for a few moments their heads were bent together over the music. Then he walked back again.

He said to Stan: 'I should think I would come about *sixth* on the programme. Preferably after – or just before something light.'

Mike picked up the list and began glancing down it. Stan, shifting his weight from one foot to the other, looked Barney up and down with a mixture of insolence and diffidence.

'*What* exactly are we being honoured with?'

'Bach. From the St Matthew. *Mache dich, mein Herze rein –* '

'Mark Dick. Who's he when he's at home?' He pulled a face. 'That won't do much for the War Effort. Can't we have it in English, eh? The townies, they'll never stand for Jerry's lingo.'

74

'Oh God,' said Barney languidly. 'Lloyd George, thou shouldst be ruling at this hour.' Then he said, very quietly, so that Tessie was a little frightened, 'No, I think – German. Bach married the words rather carefully I fancy. I shall sing it in the original.' He turned to Mike: 'Time me – would you?'

His voice, which she'd never heard before, was assured, even in a piece so obviously ambitious. Miss Thackray, taken by surprise, was plainly still a little flustered. He stopped her several times, once about three or four minutes in, asking her to begin again. Stan walked up and down at the side of the stage – up and down – occasionally glancing across, as if something had happened to hold up the proceedings.

Two days later Barney was there again, for the dress rehearsal. She heard him tell Mike that he had to report to Catterick in a fortnight's time. He seemed in a jaunty mood almost: didn't seem to mind that Stan had moved him to the last item but one, to come after Flanagan and Allen and before the singsong. He ran through his aria twice. There was a long introductory piano passage, another in the middle. Miss Thackray hadn't got it quite to his liking: 'Faster, Miss T, *faster!*' Blushing, agitated, loving it, her grey curls tossing, she made the notes tumble over each other. Stan, sitting with arms crossed, yawned ostentatiously.

The day of the show was very warm. The audience, restless and enthusiastic by turns, applauded Mike and Tessie. Miss Thackray, playing Chopin's 'Revolutionary Study' – all flying elbows and emotion – went down well; so did Mike and Stan's comic patter.

She and Mike were sitting at the side of the stage, when last but one Barney came on. The aria, which she'd heard three, four times by now, had a familiar sound, an expected rhythm. She feared for him though, knowing the audience. She was surprised too to see his mother wasn't there. But as he sang, she marvelled at his assurance. Someone called out, 'You're not in church, sonnie,' then a moment later, from the back: 'Give us "In a Monastery Garden" – ' Several people took up the chant. Stan, marching down the centre aisle, waved a baton. 'Hey there – you at the back!'

Tessie looked across to where Barney was standing. And

it was then that it happened. One moment he was singing, in German (a language of which she knew only the rudiments), an aria in which she wasn't really very interested. The next, everything had changed. She could see, hear the restive scraping of chairs, the subdued giggles. *'Lass Jesu mein!'* As he called so tenderly upon his Christ: may it never end, her heart said, for suddenly she was bound to him with hoops of steel.

Then a toddler stumbled down the aisle, wide-legged, two inches of damp nappy hanging one side, and began to cry. His mother ran after him, hissing angrily just as Miss Thackray trilling her grace notes played through the final passage. Barney, bowing a little, acknowledged the polite applause.

The moment, for all its intensity, was gone. But it had been one of those indelible, if later scarcely believable experiences. At some point in the pattern, in the finished picture, in the rag-bag that was past, present and future, she was irrevocably fixed, part of him for ever.

Straight after it was the singsong. They sang 'White Cliffs of Dover', 'Roll out the Barrel', 'We'll Meet Again'. After someone had led the applause for Stan, Mike got three special cheers and an encore. In the wings afterwards Tessie hugged him with pride.

∞

Polly didn't have to wait long for an answer. She was telephoned the next evening.

Peter, his voice unpleasantly rasping (although not quite so bad as she'd remembered so that she felt guilty – a little), said, almost patronizingly as if she were a naughty child: 'So you are free, *après tout*? I absolutely *flipped* when I heard . . .'

The party was sooner than she'd realized – that was why he'd phoned. It was tomorrow evening. He hadn't the address on him but she was to come to his place, his *pad*, because it was nearby. 'If you don't mind? If you want to go – ' he added ominously, suddenly in command. Which after all he was.

I have to go, she thought. I must go. Sam must go too. Oh my God, my God, my God, he *must* be there.

∞

At Harrods that Christmas of 1913, there'd been a Norwegian ski expert in the travel department to give advice. Muff herself hadn't been interested; some friends though, keen on winter sports, spoke well of him. For no good reason the detail had stayed in her mind. Like the visit to St Petersburg: something perhaps she regretted?

It had been the end of Con's first term at Oxford. At one of the Sunday evening Balliol Hall concerts he'd met an enthusiastic violinist and now in the vac had asked him to stay. They both wanted to make music it seemed, most of the day. Or Con did. Invited out to luncheon he would never be ready on time: battling with Schubert's *Rondo Brillante* he would have to be dragged reluctant, from the piano stool. David, accomplished, fiery sometimes, was far more sociable, took his much greater talent very lightly: was prouder really of his cricketing accomplishments, lying now in mothballs with his flannels.

A lot of the time she felt moody, discontented. Christmas was in the air and now and then, seeing the decorations about London, she would feel a vague excitement, faint anticipation. The weather, grey, damp, sullen, didn't help. Contrary, a little bored, she was full of a restless, nameless dissatisfaction.

She didn't see enough of Con. To be with him more she would sit in the library while they practised – even though music meant little or nothing to her. David she supposed was pleased to see her there, since he looked over at her often, smiling, sometimes even pulling amusing faces. He was fair like her, but more of a red-gold; both his hair and his moustache were luxuriant and, since his face was never still, it seemed to her sometimes as if he were on fire. She felt always very alive in his presence. Sometimes, just sitting there, she would be aware suddenly of the touch of her own fingers on her arm, electric. A humming. The heavy warmth of the library, the light casting shadows, the thick-curtained door. Once she met him in there alone; it was late after tea, she was just going up to dress for dinner, wanted something to read.

'I came in search of a stodgy novel. Harrods have sent nothing suitable. I suddenly thought I'd read George Eliot – '

'Shall I find one for you?' He walked towards the shelves.

77

'What do you like usually?' he asked; his voice was mocking, affectionate. 'Problem novels? Suffrage novels? Tell me.'

There was a screen in the library. He beckoned her. 'Come and look at this,' he said: he was laughing. When she followed him behind he laughed more, then as she raised her eyebrows, began to question, he kissed her roundly on the lips, seeming to lift her body as he did so – or was it that she floated from the ground a little? Then, as suddenly, he let her go and laughing still went and found *Middlemarch* for her.

The day before he left to go home for Christmas she was alone with him again, a few moments, in an upstairs corridor. Stepping to one side, moving behind her, he cupped his hands over her breasts. She thought that she might faint – at once so alive and yet, where to run, where to hide? 'Shall you tell?' he asked then, laughing, his hands resting a moment on her waist.

Con hoped that she liked him. 'You do like him, Muff?' Worried: 'I wanted you to, so much.'

Me, she thought, my body: that no one told me of. How could I have searched so carefully, penetrated so much speculation, surmise, gossip, hearsay – discovered so much – and known so little? Now she saw the towers, the turrets of an unknown city. They rose from the sea.

A secret. 'Shall you tell?' he had asked, laughing.

What to wear for the party with Peter? What sort of party was it? What paint should she put on? Decisions took so long that in the end she had only ten minutes for the whole operation. In her crayon box the most needed colours were broken, worn or just plain missing; Christopher had borrowed them at half-term. Trying to be quick she grossly overdid it: her eyes staring out at her surprised and too thickly ringed; and wanting to keep the orange silk blouse clean of make-up, putting it on at the last moment, she seemed in the artificial light to flare up, to dazzle vulgarly.

'You'll *have* to do,' she said despairingly.

On her first tentative push of the bell Peter hurried down

the stairs, taking them at the double it seemed, arriving breathless and looking as before at once critical and reproachful: 'Quite an improvement. Only fifteen minutes late. We have the time for a drink before take-off.'

He sat her down. His flat seemed quite wrong: where she'd been certain it would glitter in chromium, all whites and oranges and moulded plastics, it was dark and oaken, heavy Jacobean furniture and flocked wall-paper. This threw her immediately. She'd seen herself managing, coping with the ordeal against or amidst bright noisy colours.

It was a horrible sofa. She sank far far into its knobbly depths. He pointed to an ornately carved corner cupboard: 'Lo I have everything. Please give your order.'

'God, I don't know – I usually just get something pressed into my hand – ' She pointed to a bottle of Strega because she liked the colour. He lifted his eyebrows: 'Now?'

'No,' she said quickly, 'not now. Look, I'm flustered. Armagnac then – '

'Lost your cool, have you?' But Armagnac wasn't what she felt like. She would have liked apple juice. 'Have you any apple juice?'

'I hadn't thought – are you one of those nature freaks, is it? You'll hardly be in the mood, you know.' Without consulting her further he mixed her a brandy and ginger ale. 'Relax,' he kept saying, so that very soon she was all tensed up. 'Now, music. You say what you'd like. No way-out tastes, I trust. There's nothing exciting here – nothing to turn us on, take us for a trip.'

'Oh dry up,' she said into her brandy. He didn't hear. He was over by the record player, putting on Delius' 'Walk to the Paradise Garden'. He brought his own drink over and sat near her on the sofa, stretching out one leg, showing a gap of shocking-pink sock. He rubbed his foot against hers.

'My tights,' she said. 'Last pair – '

'Ah,' he said, then 'ah,' looking at her, head on one side. The drink was having an effect on her: from having been ill at ease, not sure what to expect, now she felt caged inside. She knew that they must hurry. (Already the people were gathering. Sam had looked in – could stay only a few moments.

79

'Sorry, everybody . . .' Once round the room, a couple of drinks – then as she arrived, he would be leaving – had already left: his receding back to be seen turning the corner out of sight, gone for ever, lost . . .)

'Tights,' Peter said. '*Tights*. Do I sigh alone for suspenders?'

'Of course not. Lots of girls wear them – lovely lovely belts. I just haven't got round to any. I'm always late – just grab whatever's nearest.'

'Tell you what – *I'll* grab whatever's nearest. Grab – ' His hand ran expertly up her skirt then over to the inside of her thigh. From terribly near, he leered.

'It's worse when they get ripped at the top,' she said in what was meant to be a warm voice but which came out cold, and small. I must be fair, she thought. After all I'm *using* him. 'Because then you're tempted to go on wearing them all grotty. So if you could be careful.'

'Careful? *You're* in a hurry – we're not that far yet. Of course I shall be careful. When the time comes.' His other hand slipped down her silk blouse then, as he pressed his mouth on hers, she thought, we are never going to go at all. I shall never for the rest of my life see Sam.

Peter's smell was not right: it was some scent or after-shave, over-spiced, not acid enough. She tried to think of the familiar reassuring smell of Patrick as they sat together day after day; anything to distract herself. But too late. Her body had already in its unconscious flinching betrayed what no words would now excuse.

'I feel sick – '

'Cool . . . Why so cool? You just *play* it that way – do you?'

She leaned back on the sofa. 'I'm terribly sorry, I just suddenly felt sick. Perhaps, the brandy – I don't know.' The party seemed suddenly very far away, very unreal. 'We ought to go though, we ought to be off. I feel fine. Honest.'

'Stop here,' he said a little later. 'This is the house.' He pushed her towards the steps. There was a burst of sound as the door opened, babble, music; smoke seemed to be floating down the stairs. The first person to speak to them said: 'Tim and Amelia have disappeared. I think they've slipped out for reinforcements – about double the number they *thought* they asked . . .'

'*Success*,' a voice said behind them. Peter said: 'I've brought along Polly Willingham.'

'Polly, how super. There aren't enough girls. Polly, do you sing? Gareth's looking for altos, sopranos. Let's find Gareth. Drinks. Christ, there aren't any.'

A dark-haired girl said to Peter, 'Darling, take mine. Take it all. I don't deserve any more.' She lurched forward, spilling some on to her shoes. 'Oh shit.' She looked vaguely at Polly. 'Who's she?'

'Some have had too much, some not enough. What a capitalist party,' Peter said.

'Here come Tim and Amelia – lots of *lovely* drink . . .' They moved into a crush. A second later and oh delight – she was separated from Peter.

'And who have we here? No, but really, I'm sober. I'm Rod. You spoke to me when you first came in. Let's go and break some earnest group up.'

'I was supposed to be finding someone called Gareth – '

'Oh Gareth, is very serious tonight, darling, very serious – '

There didn't seem to be an earnest group to break up. She was pulled round, still without a drink; he stopped at each gathering. 'No, no, no.' The room seemed enormous. And no face yet was *his face*, Sam's (pray God she didn't run into Peter again). But in fact there was another room. She was in it now. It wasn't so crowded. A group stood over by the piano: a man with his back to her, shaggy headed, bent listening to a girl in a lemon crochet dress. A small rotund man was laughing, his head thrown back. Rod said, 'That's Gareth.' Then he said, 'Gareth, this is Polly. She's come to say she'll sing for her supper.'

'Oh good, yes please.' And then *he* turned round. It was him, Sam. Oh say you remember me.

'Well, hallo,' he was saying. Rod said, 'You two know each other?'

'Surely. We met in the same watering place.' Then pulling a mock shocked face, he said: 'Seen any good graffiti lately?'

Someone had turned up the amplifiers. 'I gave my last chance to you, Don't pass me up, O bitterblue.' Cat Stevens, deafening.

'God, you can't hear yourself speak. Does she know Morwen?'

The girl in the lemon crochet had glossy black hair massed in a bun. Her expression although quiet was very alive. Polly recognized her as the soprano who had sung so joyfully at those last two concerts.

'The Elly Ameling of N6.'

Morwen interrupted laughing: 'Rod, I can't help where I live.' Gareth said, 'You could help singing quite so beautifully. Who else has got a chance?' He said to Polly, 'Morwen's booked for the 'B minor' you've just said you'll sing in, by the way. And Zoss here's going to blow his trumpet . . .'

'That'll do.' Sam looked at his watch. 'I shouldn't be still here. I'm doing that stupid thing, two parties – '

Morwen said, 'Social type, you never said you were a social type.'

'Younger than you, tougher than you. This one's courtesy. It's another sort altogether. I've got to go home first and dress respectably.'

It could not be, it could not be that he was going when she had only just found him. For once she was struck quite dumb, couldn't think of even the most inane of party remarks. Morwen said: 'Be seeing you then. And you'll send, bring those cuttings?'

'Will do. Bye love. Bye Gareth . . . Rod . . .'

He hadn't even remembered her name; for her, just a bare goodbye. And then he was gone. It can't be all over, she thought, it can't be all over so soon. What do I do now? If he wanted me he could run after me the length of the room and pull me back and say, 'I've got to see you again.' He could do that. And nowadays we're all free and equal – so I should be able to do it too. Only I can't. Nothing but a sickly smile and back to the conversation.

They brought her into it. She liked Morwen: not just because she found her warm and sympathetic but because talking to her, staying in this group, was the feeble next best thing to having him still there.

'I ought really to go,' Morwen said. She stayed a few moments longer when Polly asked her something about the 'B minor'. Gareth jotted down some details. 'An audition, very soon,' he said. 'Polly – Polly?'

'Willingham,' she said.

Morwen said, frowning, a little unsure, 'Willingham?'

'Yes. My father sings with – I can't remember the name. You might – '

Then Peter's face. Peter's voice. How could she have hoped to be free of him?

'Hallo there. *Hallo*. I've been where the decibels are past the danger line – or is it the *Plimsoll* line? Whatever – I've got the whole thing toned down.' He looked around. 'Ah – Morwen.'

'Ah, Peter,' she said, not too warmly. As Polly had feared, he knew everybody: he began at once to take over the conversation. Very soon it had flagged. Morwen took the opportunity to leave and Peter said with a flourish: 'Farewell sweet lass of Muswell Hill . . .'

'Oh please,' she said, without laughing. When she'd gone, Gareth said, 'Lovely girl. Lovely voice – '

Polly slipped away. In the next room the speakers were turned up much louder. 'Sweet Caroline' was all around her. She moved hopefully towards a small group who didn't seem to be talking to each other. A tall fair-haired man came from nowhere and said: 'Hey, I know you! Fiona Wyatt's *ex* – you're a friend of Fiona's *ex*. I *said* I'd seen you. Look how are you, tell me how you are – '

'Oh I don't know,' she said wearily. His hand was on her shoulder. She wondered what could have drained all the life out of her? Any other evening, any other party – a hundred and one ready answers.

His eyes glazed over. His voice was more slurred as he said, 'You *are*, you know – ' She said coldly, hating the voice that came out, 'You're so pissed you couldn't remember anyway.'

'Are you freezing me by any chance?'

But then it was hateful Peter to the rescue: coming up behind, whisking her away. For the next hour she was unable to shake him off. She said she wanted to go then, that she was tired; some nonsense about Hatter's.

Going down the steps, out into the dank November night, she was plunged into despair. Nothing had come of nothing. And she had behaved badly, was about to behave badly again.

'You two,' Peter said, 'Morwen and you. Oranges and lemons

83

I was put in mind of.' Then, waving his arm a bit, he said, 'Well. Shall you come back, shall you come up to my lair again? I have both etchings and girlie photographs, and *Forum* for the last three months. Every sort of entertainment . . .'

'I have to get back.'

'As you wish.' She said hurriedly, 'It's not late. I could get a number eleven from here.'

The bus stop was empty. He stepped suddenly but quite gently on to one of her feet. 'When did you last see your father?' he asked, pinning her down.

'Very funny – '

He removed his foot. 'I could tell you something very *interesting* about him. If you're interested, that is?'

'Yuk.'

He shook his head: 'Poor Uncle Peter. You're being rather vulgar, Polly, don't you think?'

'Incredibly,' she said. A bus came towards them through the darkness and she rushed for it at once, without saying goodbye, or thank you, or even the rude offhand words that later, in the middle of that night, she was to wish she'd spoken.

∞

'I want to help you with Latin,' she'd said to Con. 'You mustn't worry about your Latin. I can't do the Greek, but I could help with the Latin. If I ask . . .'

'We'll see,' the grown-ups said. It was the year before her father was killed in the railway crash. There was a tutor at Corrib that summer and the next. She learned quickly and easily, putting her whole self in it. Even more after her father's death. And she was able to help Con.

There were a lot of bats in those summers. The servants came with big sticks and knocked them from their perches. In a dark corner, the inside of a dormer window, three were hanging, their eyes like red points following the light Con carried. He caught one in his fishing-net. It was a baby, and at once with its paws it clung to him; she tried to prise it off, but still it clung: tiny loving hands. She gazed fascinated at the thick dark membrane of the wings, but he exclaimed in wonder at its small furry body. 'It loves me,' he said in surprise.

'You'll get fleas,' she said. 'Ugh.' To tell the truth it frightened her. 'Put it down.'

'But it won't let go. It loves me, you see, Muff. It *loves* me . . .'

Chapter 7

Polly has been searching. National papers, local papers, agencies, music shops: any place that could conceivably tell her where she might hear Sam play, and twice she's been lucky: seeing his name in diamond, pearl-encrusted words – the type standing out like a message from the beloved. One of the concerts is the same night as a dinner party her parents are giving: she's promised she'll be there; but the other one she hurries to buy tickets for. It's in a church. Probably she will be able to sit right in the front pew.

But when the day came no one else sat in the front at all. She'd hoped, trusted in a few enthusiastic oratoriophiles, amateurs who'd want to watch lovingly the instruments in close-up, willingly sacrificing the whole for the part. She was all ready to look surprised, enchanted, a little taken aback that it should be *him* playing. But – to sit quite so alone; that made it rather impossible. By the time all of the choir and most of the players had arrived there were still six pews between her and anyone else. She tried then to move back, to place herself in the front of the front, but the seats were all taken. Muff would be able to deal with this, she thought, creeping to the side, squeezing against a column.

Oh my most beloved Bach: '*Ach bleib bei uns*'. '*Meine Seel' erhebt den Herren*'. May it go on for ever. And then: I must think of some way, some excuse to talk to him. Just 'hi' again, perhaps?

The interval was a misery. A boy right at the back smiled at her. She tried to remember who he was and identified him as brother of a girl at the convent. If only ... How easy it would be if her passion were for him. ('How *is* Fiona? Haven't seen her for absolute yonks, tell me all she's doing, she must come over...' And she would. Then I'd go back to her and he would be there. And oh God it would be so simple.)

Necessity, mother of invention. All was not lost. After the applause she walked straight towards the orchestra: she could see him talking to the flautist. Pray God he didn't move. She tried to saunter over. Her thighs rubbed against each other clammily.

She smiled before he turned so that the smile would be already there. It froze instead. Then he saw her, in the middle of what he was saying. 'Hallo,' he said, as if in passing. Friendly. Then went back to talking. She stood there.

The other man clapped Sam on the back suddenly. 'See you Wednesday,' then something about beer. He moved away. Sam turning then, noticed her still there. He said in a friendly voice but as one about to move on: 'Did you want something? Can I do something for you?' his eyebrows a query.

Yes, you could fall in love with me, instantly, indelibly, immortally. She said in a rush. 'Morwen Davies. You know her, don't you? It's just – I was trying to get hold of her. I had to see her about something. I wondered, you know, if you had her address – '

He cut in, 'Surely,' he said hurriedly, 'sure. I don't have the number but the address is somewhere in Muswell Hill. Wood something – she's in the book.'

'So many Davies,' said Polly in a flat voice. 'I didn't know the initials, if she lived with her parents – '

'It's her mother,' he said. 'She just has a mother.' Then, 'That OK? Does that help?' He looked very tired and ready to be off. She said: 'That's super. All I wanted to know – '

' 'Bye then.' He added hastily, 'Nice thing to see you again.'

And again and again and again. Couldn't we even walk out of the building together? All day and every day, all night and every night. Together.

She was terrified by her despair. Whatever is happening to me, she thought, whatever is happening to me?

∞

It seemed to Muff that she'd been all afternoon making her way from counter to counter, in search of a Christmas present for Frank. Something she could take when next she should visit the Home. So much to choose from, even confining herself to Harrods' ground floor. Yet she liked nothing she saw. Quality materials wasted on tasteless objects. Useless gadgets to complicate already complicated lives. Linen teacloths with vulgar motifs.

She became irritable with indecision. Stationery. A compendium perhaps? But it was hardly likely Frank wrote letters. A set of named playing cards? Too late now to order. Half-suitable notions, rejected ideas: a box of cigarettes no doubt would finally be the solution (but then she need never have left the house, need never have put up with this jostling, jabbing).

She was tired, jaded still from her theatre visit the other evening. She could not imagine now why she had thought it would be worth the effort, that she would be interested. Hateful admission: it was not what one saw on the stage, but whom one went with, sat with; the story behind the visit.

She could have asked Polly to accompany her. Could have but would not. Polly anyway at the moment was preoccupied: her moods having no shade between dark and bright, glowing. Only a few days ago, dressed for some party, hurried, excited, she had seemed transformed. Hoping perhaps? Hoping to meet the one person, the rare person, who would alter her whole life?

It could be so. She thought that for herself it had been so in a way. But only in a way – because behind the success of that first meeting with Cecil had been Con: he had been the cause, the without which . . .

Letters from him once he had left for France had been something she lived towards. Days made or undone by the vagaries of the post (against all common sense too, for could he not, by the time she took up the envelope from the tray, be already dead?). All that warm September of 1915 she'd felt an ever-increasing sense of foreboding; an anxiety, shared by others: waiting for a battle. In his last letter he had hinted that posts might be stopped soon. Then, 'Two real victories!' shrieked the papers. It had happened. She waited then to hear the worst.

On the last day of September, in the afternoon, a letter had come. He was well, she was not to worry; although prepared, his regiment had not been part of the action at Loos. (And PS. Could she find out if Columbia had made any recordings of the Klingler Quartet?)

That evening she was to go to the Palace for the revue *Bric à Brac*. Thin skinned with joy and relief, she'd taken her perilous ecstasy with her.

During the interval Bim Farquhar brought Cecil up to their box. She recognized him at once. He wasn't as tall as she'd remembered – no one could have been – but if anything more attractive. He seemed suddenly to be part of the happiness of the whole evening. His pale skin toughened by a hot climate looked as if it had been downy once. His eyes – never left her. But she thought later that it might have been his voice, a caressing baritone, very slightly suggestive, which had seduced her. All the time as they exchanged pleasantries she felt his gaze. She was reminded not so much of David but of how her body had felt that day in the library, that time in the corridor.

It was the last night of Bim's leave. Yes, the rumours were true that he was about to become engaged. They intended to marry as soon as he was back again. *If* he came back, hung unspoken.

He should have known better than to be snapped up, Cecil told him, laughing. Bim said that that was interesting – since he'd heard that in India someone from the 'fishing fleet' had been almost successful . . .

She began to worry, sitting there, that he too might be just above to leave for France. But it was not so: at the moment he was safely at the War Office.

All the second half of the show she was restless, feverish almost. The air seemed to her as if before a storm.

On the darkened stage, spotlit, Teddy Gerard picked up her telephone.

    'Everybody calls me Teddy, T E double D Y . . .
    Hanky panky, full of yankee swanky
    And the RSVP eye . . .'

Her hand where it had touched his, formally, in a handshake, burned, tingled. She could not believe but that something momentous had happened.

    'All day long my telephone, keeps on ringing hard . . .
    Are you there, little Teddy bear?
    Naughty *naughty* one Gerard . . .'

Next day she read of David's death. She wrote at once to

Con: wondering already if that would be the letter that would
return, 'Deceased' stamped across it. The daily, nightly,
coruscating worry had begun again.

∞

Tessie wished, at once, that Camilla had never been asked.
She and Rodney had been at a party before arriving. Rodney
was not affected, but already now, halfway through the fish,
Camilla was becoming belligerent.

'Do you I mean, do you really believe that?' she was asking
Jonathan Malling – twenty-seven, likeable, invited mainly to
partner Polly, 'I mean *really*?' Taking up some remark of his
which Tessie, who hadn't heard it, could see he was already
regretting.

'Camilla and Rodney?' Barney had said earlier. 'Must one?
Suppose we were to begin, gently, by refusing their invitations?'
He added: 'Perhaps though – *you* would mind. Camilla does
at least form part of your – how would one define it – your
past. Your rather thin past. In retrospect, why did you never
go anywhere? Do anything?'

He said it idly. He'd said it in one form or another so many
times before.

In any case they had to be invited: together with Max and
Aline Churcher, a quiet couple in their fifties, not easily ruffled.
And of course Jonathan. Muff, formally invited, had as usual
refused.

Polly, dressed weirdly in black lace, looking longer and
thinner than ever, her face almost white, had hardly spoken at
all. Politics, the problems of Edward Heath, the confrontation
with the miners, which had accompanied the crab and avocado
mould, had made her shut her eyes, rudely. She'd been difficult
really for several days now: the shadow side of her warm
loving self; reminiscent of the time four or five years ago when
she would pass whole days at a time without speaking to anyone
but Muff.

And further back. Looking at her now Tessie felt a resur-
gence of that helpless feeling, that hopeless love which eighteen
years ago had threatened to drown her. She had not known
what to do with it. Trying to manage, insisting on managing

90

after Polly was born, she had suddenly one day given up. Years of being Little Mother, and now she couldn't do it for herself. Her milk too had failed. Barney, summing up the situation, without giving sympathy had announced: 'I have sent for Nanny.'

Nanny, sixty-nine by then, had very definite ideas. Armed with Truby King, she came forth joyfully from retirement. 'We shall have everything ship-shape in two days,' she told Tessie. 'Mother must rest.' Polly yelled while Nanny sat calmly until the stroke of ten, of two, of six: when she would sail majestically to the nursery with a bottle at perfect temperature. There was no need, she said, for Tessie to observe or learn: 'I don't expect you will ever be needing to do it for yourself. I'm surprised that Mrs Willingham senior ever allowed it.' The bottles Tessie had bought were wrong: boat-shaped bottles were obtained with difficulty and used instead. There were expressions of horror at Polly's bottom. 'We have not been cleaning her thoroughly,' at what she thought might be going to be thrush around the mouth, at the half-peeled finger-nails, at the rapidly growing cradle cap.

Camilla had been around then and made it worse. She had come to tea and gushed over everything. 'Your luck, your jolly tremendous luck to have a real nanny – Barney thinks of *everything*. When I think of little me – *huge* me now – struggling with the lot, disintegrating paddi-pads – and you just sitting there. What luck.' Her baby in its carry cot had been placed in the nursery with Polly. After tea a visit was paid to them both. Camilla glowed with pride, looking down on the four-month-old Mark, already bearing a sure resemblance to Rodney. She attacked Nanny, in a matey way. 'I mash a banana for him with lots of milk and sugar. He loves it. You should see his face.' Nanny didn't reply. Afterwards: 'Have we been *criticizing*?' she asked; when Tessie looked puzzled, she said, 'Perhaps you don't like the way I'm managing baby?' Tessie looked even more puzzled. 'Mashed banana indeed!' she said. Dr Truby King would turn in his grave, she told Tessie the next day, if he were to see the way babies were brought up now. She had not mentioned it at the time, but the visiting baby had had food, food in the folds of his chin. A *certain* breeding ground for germs . . .

And now as always when least she could cope with it, here was Camilla at it again. She was leaning forward, her low-cut lamé top a little too tight. 'I mean do you really believe that? Be honest. I mean no one's going to mind the teeniest bit if you come out with the truth. I always tell the truth wherever I am. Don't I, Rodney?'

Barney raised his eyebrows. Rodney took an uneasy sip of his Montrachet, and looked for a second as if he were about to speak. Jonathan, shrugging his shoulders, smiled – he had a very clean smile. I think, Tessie thought, I am supposed now to direct the conversation, pour oil on troubled water – except that Camilla has surely a wave-making machine. In fact it was Max who steered them all safely into harbour. He had raised the topic of meditation. Jonathan knew something about this; different methods were discussed. Polly, animated now, queried some comment of Aline's. Max was passionately interested in Sufism at the moment: he had met Idries Shah twice in the course of his work, but before he'd had the interest. Jonathan took this up. Rodney said jovially, re some sorts of meditation, if they were so helpful in decision-making perhaps merchant bankers, bill brokers et al., the way things were in the City just now . . . what did Barney think?

'One would say perhaps, the way things are, help in learning to live *without* decisions. How to possess our corporate souls in patience . . . Less seriously – it sounds reasonable enough. Unless you were going to do it in the streets and frighten the horses.'

Rodney smirked into his napkin. 'Never.' He gave a little-boy grin. Camilla, who'd been completely abstracted throughout the exchange, looked faintly sulky now: concentrating ostentatiously on picking out small bones from under her mackerel, arranging them round the edge of the plate.

Tessie looked at Barney who was not looking at her. Host and hostess. She wondered if it would matter, if anyone would notice if, a grey mess of half-eaten fish lying on her plate, she just walked out? She could feel inside her, like a canker, the unresolved, unanswered question: who is it you're so crazy about? Who is it you weren't going to tell me anything about? (Can't tell, won't tell.) Who is it that's so important I can't even be told? Why not a simple confrontation though – why don't I ask again, and again? Why don't I stand up now, and ask?

She'd removed herself mentally for those few moments, and now looking around she saw that the conversation had flagged again. She realized that it must have done because Aline was asking her, very kindly, about her 'O' levels: 'Your classes – did you manage to get in? What did you decide after all about the German . . .'

She looked at all their faces: it was as if a cold wind had suddenly stripped them of their masks. She saw them all at once, intensely vulnerable. Especially Polly; especially Barney. Reaching out a hand for her glass, saying: 'Well, there've been a few problems, you see . . .' she angrily wished away civilization. She wanted to stand up and say, 'Let's all of us be comforted. Let's all tell each other what the real trouble is. Not our most secret inmost thoughts – just simply, perhaps: I'm loved and don't love back, or I loved once and can't love again, or I loved and didn't know till it was too late, or I'm growing old and am afraid to die – or even, nothing means anything. Only, please, don't talk about the rat race, and high prices, and inflation, and the synthetic quality of everything, pollution, television, violence, Belfast, corruption, the permissive society . . .'

Then suddenly everything was back to normal. Barney was pouring Château Peymartin. The *boeuf bourguignon* smelled delicious. Were there perhaps now too many universities? Quantity versus quality, America, Russia . . . The ball passed to and fro.

But she had wished violence of some sort, willed it from inside, so that it came after the coffee when the men had come back from the port. Jonathan, sitting by Polly, was telling her in detail, but having found an amusing note on which to do it, about a bus trip to Greece. It hadn't been his scene really – some of the types there, some of the characters had been quite impossible. But he'd survived. It was just that it was the sort of adventure more fun in the retelling. There'd been one absolutely sickening woman, older than the rest . . .

Camilla said in a loud voice: 'What's that about old women, Jonathan?' Rodney looked up, then she said, sticking her nose in her brandy: 'Tell me now honestly, Jonathan – how old?

93

You know you never give straight answers – you were positively cagey before, earlier, weren't you? What it is to be young. Well – go on!'

'Oh God,' Jonathan said, laughing, 'I don't know. Sixty?'

'Was this woman sixty? Midwestern, blue-rinsed Mom?'

'No.'

'How old then?'

'Christ. I don't know. Fifty? Forty-five?'

'Oh God now,' interrupted Camilla, tossing her head, 'hear that? Oh I mean honestly. We really were the dreariest of generations, weren't we? Weren't we, Tessie?'

Oh horrors, Tessie thought, she's going to bring me into it.

'And really Barney, she was a pathetic thing when she landed on us – couldn't say boo to a goose and used to weep in her room every day. Didn't I ever tell you that, did I tell you, Barney?' She turned to him awkwardly, slopping her brandy round the glass. She seemed to have quite lost the thread of her outburst. 'I mean honestly, if you could have seen her – '

Rodney said awkwardly, 'That's enough, old thing. You can't monopolize the conversation.' Barney walked across the room with the brandy, his face chilled, pained almost. Had Camilla been less drunk she would have been frozen into silence, but as soon as Jonathan and Max tried feebly to enter the conversation, their opening sentences clashing, and fading at once, she began again belligerently.

'Thank God the Latins still notice me! Divine Greeks undressing me with their eyes, Italians pinching the old bottom – even Rodney pinches it sometimes, *sometimes*, don't you treasure, when you're not worn out with pinching your secretary's.' She warbled, ' "His business is the business that he gives his secretary. Oh I – I – I *hate* men!" That song dates me – I was being courted then, pursued like mad – ' She looked at her glass, then drank the remains very fast, spluttering a little, waving her hand up and down to signal that she was still speaking.

'Anyway *Tessie* loves me. And I really was frightfully cheering, I got her over whatever it was, and I was having the most dreary time myself then, trailing round one party after another. I kept saying, didn't I, sweetie, it'll be all right – *in the end*

Prince Charming will come along. And look – ' She lifted her shoulders, then pulling her mouth in a funny shape: 'Look.'

Barney gave a half laugh.

'Aren't you going to fill my glass?' she said.

Rodney said, 'You've had enough, you know, darling.' He tried to make a move as if to go but he was the wrong shape for sudden movement. Jonathan said then, 'I ought to be leaving,' and Aline said, 'I think, Max, we . . .'

Camilla said again angrily, 'Aren't you going to fill my glass?'

Rodney took her arm. He said to Barney, 'Look, old chap,' then to everybody, 'look everybody, I'm sorry – '

'What do you mean, *sorry*?' she said furiously. 'Are you apologizing for me – worm! That sounds good, I'll say it again, *worm* – I rather like it. Worm. Your eyes, you've got bedroom eyes, running up and down anything in skirts – '

Rather than angry, he looked desperately embarrassed and propelled her towards the door. She was silent on the way, then moving her bosom from side to side she broke away from him and to her mesmerized audience she said:

'How could you Barney? How *could* you do that to Tessie? Worms all of you – I don't know. She's told me everything, absolutely everything, you worm. Fat city worms, thin wriggling ones. Where do you keep her, where do you keep this, this – ' she flailed the air, then when Rodney touched her burst into tears. She was led from the room sobbing.

Wrapped up in a fox fur-trimmed coat, brandy-breathed she tried to kiss everybody. 'Have I been absolutely awful? I have you know, I've been absolutely *awful*. Oh my God.' Rodney, white and red, tried to say, sorry everybody, and thank you, and back out of the room at the same time. 'Tessie, Tessie darling,' she said, as she was led out. 'My poor Tessie.'

In the bedroom Barney said, 'Tired?'

Tessie didn't speak.

'As an evening,' he said, 'it was quite incredible. One doesn't look to spend an evening like that in one's own house. *In vino veritas – in visky veritas*, I should say, I think that was her tipple beforehand . . .'

She choked nearly with not speaking. Wine fumed in her head. His deceptive calm – good humour almost – frightened her. In the drawing-room after Camilla's departure he had even managed to end the evening on a light note. For this she admired him.

She reached out for a cigarette. 'What have you been saying?' he asked, suddenly; angrily.

Versions of the truth – lame enough, God knows – milled round in her head. She thought too of saying: 'I've a right to know.'

'Well, I've certainly a right to know,' she said, lighting up. He had his back to her. He shrugged his shoulders:

'Her name is Morwen Davies. She sings. She has quite a future in fact. Although doubtless I'm prejudiced.' He was silent for a moment. 'One is – I'm very much in love.'

Then he went out of the room, very quietly, closing the door carefully behind him. She heard him go downstairs; then nothing more.

∞

'The happiest days of your life,' they'd said.

And how right they were, she'd thought, drifting contentedly from one day to the next. An undercurrent of joy ran through everything. Patsy was a pinprick only; she could be escaped – *was* escaped – at the beginning of every term. The sheer excitement of returning to school even made up for the sudden feeling of loss that saying goodbye to Mike gave her always.

It was all so perfect, and so naturally so, that she didn't even pray about it: it would have been as presumptuous as praying for a miracle to repeat itself. The prayer of petition was for the bombs to stop, for Hitler to drop down dead, for the Japs to get the worst of it; for Barney Willingham not to be killed.

Occasionally Mother Aloysius, passing with a visitor, would point her out: 'Our little *Teresa* – nearly five years with us now. A doctor's daughter, you know.' (Only why wasn't Barbara Spufford, the dentist's daughter, so praised? Why not, in this game of Happy Families?)

October was the month of the rosary. After chapel and supper the girls would sit about in the recreation hall, with its huge black-out frames keeping the light in, and the moon out. There was a craze for playing jacks that winter of 1943, and all over the hall, bunched into groups, girls tossed the spiky metal on to their knuckles: faster and faster, higher and higher. Tessie was fortune's favourite because her jacks were real bones, a present from Philomena Kelly that summer.

Except for Fridays, when they all listened to ITMA before the nine o'clock news and bed, they played every evening. Looking after them – and often playing too – would be a handful of postulants and novices, and it was they who began the other craze that winter: Irish jigs. Nora McGuire, who with her cousin Kathleen Doherty had come off the boat that September, was the teacher, the champion. Tessie's best friends, Joan and Barbara and Pauline, all learnt very easily. Tessie didn't. Her legs went all the wrong way and everyone laughed – she did too. Kathleen, who was a very bouncy girl, said to her: 'Wouldn't it be grand now if we had your friend Mike here? Couldn't he play his accordion?' She and Nora were always talking about him; they couldn't hear enough. 'Just like another brother, isn't he Tessie? Kelly – that's a good Irish name ... Isn't she the lucky girl, so?'

Sister Bridget, the eldest of the novices, played the mouth organ for the jigs. Her small red face puckered with effort and breath control as she puffed out the quick, quicker tempo: 'Kitty Magee', 'The Boys of Blue Hill' ... Sometimes another of the postulants, Maire Delaney, sang for them all. She had a very young, very pretty face, with sad eyes: her skin was flushed always as if she'd been crying, which perhaps she had for it was rumoured that she was very homesick.

'No, nay never,' she sang, in her high nasal voice. 'No nay never no more – will I play the wild rover ...' In return Tessie and Joan taught them 'There is a Tavern in the Town' and some sea shanties; Barbara showed them the sailor's hornpipe. In November Joan's brother in the Air Force was killed and she went home to be with her mother, who was a widow.

Summer came; and on the feast of the Sacred Heart Nora and Kathleen and Maire were clothed as novices. They were dressed like brides; for a week before they'd been in retreat

97

so that they hadn't played the mouth organ or danced or been with the girls at all.

It was a school holiday and the weather was very hot. Outside the sun beat down and the girls flopped about on the grass courts. Inside it was cool and smelled of beeswax and roses. There were roses everywhere. In the crowded chapel, Tessie at the back with the bigger girls, had been able to see very little. Her hands had stuck to the Westminster Hymnal: 'To Jesus' heart all burning,' turning two pages at once. Afterwards there was a special meal for the nuns, and for the girls a picnic outside, with strawberries, and sponge fingers made with the nuns' rations. Barbara spilt Eiffel Tower lemonade all down the front of Tessie's shirt. Rushing in to change: hurrying not to miss anything, she took a short cut through by the entrance to the nuns' enclosure. She was running too fast: stopping only just in time she almost crashed into Maire. Sister Imelda now. Still in her bridal dress, she looked radiant.

Tessie said, 'Gosh,' meaning both that she was sorry to have nearly bowled her over, and surprise at Maire's radiance. Then she said awkwardly, 'Gosh, you do look wonderful –'

'Oh,' Maire cried, 'I'm so happy! I'm so happy I could die!' Then she ran on, up the stairs, pulling carelessly at the caught veil, the cream satin skirt. 'I'm so happy – I could die!'

The next spring, the War in Europe ended. It was the year of the Hon Teresa. The October after, one of the new crop of postulants went back to Ireland, after only six weeks. She was Maire's younger sister, and Barbara said she'd heard Mother Winifred tell Mother Aloysius she was elevenpence ha'penny and should never have come. Tessie's form had begun their School Cert. year; they didn't play with the postulants and novices any more but sat in corners with Hall and Knight, and Kennedy's *Primer*. There was a craze for being serious.

The day they broke up for the Easter holidays it was Lent still, and fine sharp weather. Tessie had trouble with her suitcase which had a warped rusted lock and wouldn't shut. About midday, coming down to see about it, she went past the dining-room; feeling thirsty suddenly but seeing no water on the tables yet, she decided to go through to the little scullery alongside.

Over the sink a figure was hunched. Maire, Sister Imelda,

holding a wet teacloth was wiping three spoons together and weeping silently.

But when Tessie said, 'Oh, but you mustn't cry like that –' startled, she said at once, indignantly almost: 'I never was.' Putting on a silly smiling face.

Tessie said, 'But you *were*. I saw you.' She felt lost, uncomprehending. She wanted to say then: 'But you can't be unhappy. You, of all people –'

' 'Tis nothing,' Maire said, turning her head away, letting drop the cloth and spoons onto the draining-board.

'*Tell* me.'

'I said – 'tis nothing. Only something Mother Winifred said. I don't know now I've tried enough, if I loved Jesus more – 'tis humility I need. If I hadn't this silly pride,' she turned towards Tessie: 'you've to pray for me, Teresa, you'll pray for me – won't you?'

'Yes of course,' Tessie said. 'Of course I will.' Then when Maire crumpled up completely she said again, 'Oh but don't cry –'

But there was no stopping her. 'It came over me in chapel, I won't have a letter at all not till Lent's past. Tom's gone for a priest and I never said goodbye, then I thought I'd have Bridget all the while only for they sent her back. She's the holy one in our family I'll tell you that – haven't I tried only for I've been so *homesick*, Tessie. I don't like England at all and that's the truth of it. Only I shouldn't say this, I'll be upsetting the others, I'll –' But she'd made herself worse and now, unable to stop, she turned right away from Tessie. Aren't I the silly one? And Mother said for me to offer it up –' Tessie, leaning forward, put her hands on the shaking shoulders, pulled Maire's head towards her. 'Don't,' she kept saying. 'Don't cry.' In spite of the washing-up, Maire smelled sweet. 'Everyone loves you,' Tessie said, 'we all love you.' She was suddenly very strong: she who had Mike, and was happy, so happy at school. She could feel she was giving comfort: the strength she didn't know she had flowed from her: 'We all love you. *I* love you –'

Then suddenly from the doorway, Mother Aloysius said sharply: 'Teresa!'

Tessie jumped, releasing Maire, standing to attention.

Startled, then terrified by the surprise, the voice coming from nowhere.

'Your suitcase, Teresa. Is your suitcase brought down?'

'I'll get it,' she said in a mumbling, inadequate voice, 'it won't shut, I'll get it,' and ran quickly, quickly, towards her room.

The letter came when she'd been home nearly two weeks. Her mother read it first then without a word passed it to her father. When he'd read it, he said to Tessie, 'I think you should read this at least,' then turning to her mother: 'aren't we going to kick up a stink?' But her mother shrugged her shoulders. She looked as if she were about to cry.

'I don't want to discuss it,' she said, 'they have terrible minds. I always knew they had terrible minds.'

The words in the letter danced. It was like the troubles she had had learning to read. Here and there a sentence, leaping out, made sudden sense:

'... after the particular trust we had placed in Teresa ... Reverend Mother and I ... specially chosen as a companion for Lady Babington's younger daughter ... our profound sense of bewilderment and betrayal ... strain under which novices are labouring, highly emotional state ... the peculiar delicacy of this incident ... school as a whole must be considered ... we had no choice ... already entered for School Certificate, possibility of ... nothing to be gained by her remaining with us ... assurance of our prayers ...'

Afterwards her mother said: 'If you ever want to talk about it – Mummy and Daddy would never dream of bringing it up – but if you ever want to discuss it. You know we'd never believe anything of you – '

But it never was discussed. They would have had to start it for her and they were always too busy.

She, too, soon became busy. For three nights after she lay awake: hearing the telephone ring, the teething baby cry, the front door bell at one in the morning. Mike was away, spending Easter with his cousins outside Dublin. She went round to see Philomena. She wanted to weep on her, to sit on her ample lap and be cradled, but she was afraid. She told her only that she'd got to leave. Expelled for being difficult.

'Listen to that now,' Philomena said indignantly, 'isn't that nuns all out! Always the best they send away. There was this girl now, in Dublin, a holy terror she was and even when they sent for the priest . . . I tell you, Tessie, it's the life they lead. They're never right in the head – '

But then Mike was back. When she told him he laughed. 'Oh but honestly – I mean, poor Sister Imelda, poor you – but honestly. Why don't you write them a rude letter?' But she'd thought of that. Lying awake there'd been endless imaginary, false beginnings.

'Anyway,' he said, 'lucky you, leaving school.' Later he said: 'Particular friendships – that's what they're called. They've got a thing about them. If you want a cuddle,' he said, 'cuddle me.'

He'd brought back from Ireland a whole attaché-case full of chocolate for her and Philomena ('the customs man said, "Is that for your tuckshop then?" '). They took some with them when they went up to the farm – half an hour away – to see the new lambs. Afterwards they sat in the loft and held hands. He kissed her all over her face, holding her sideways, their arms linked round each other's waists. She was so big now. He took pinches of flesh and laughed: at the flesh, not at her. 'More and more to love, every holidays.' When he kissed her on the lips his mouth tasted of apples, but something a little bitter with it. He'd been shaving now a year and a half. She'd forgotten how soft his cheek used to be.

And in the beginning there was Mike. As it was in the beginning is now and ever shall be world without end Amen.

Chapter 8

Beethoven's 'Archduke' Trio. Con had been determined to learn it. It was the vac before Trinity Term, 1914, and now as well as David he'd a cellist, Marcus, a Harrovian up at Queen's.

The early spring afternoons and evenings were full of the sound of Beethoven. It seemed always to be practice time. She minded this desperately, for ever since the autumn her longing and need for Con's company had been growing and growing. Years later she was to tell herself it had been premonition, but at the time, if only occasionally, she had been more honest: he was growing away from her. Not obviously, through university, new friends, a different life, but in some more real way, as if he were finding an inner self. Certainly it was not an outer one: he dreaded formal social occasions, attending them with reluctance, ill at ease. Except for these easy contacts through music he never sought any company outside the house.

Often, he sat bent over the piano, for the whole morning. The Trio was too difficult for him. Lured originally by the rhythms of the second movement, he found now that the variations were harmonically too complex. There were half a dozen passages which like a juggling act he could never get quite right, never quite sustain. He was showing a determination he showed towards nothing else. All morning she would hear from the library his impatient, determined attempts *this* time to get it right.

One afternoon they had arranged to go out together, the two of them, as a treat. It had been her idea. They were to have tea at Rumpelmeyers and then visit the exhibition in New Bond Street of Ponting's photographs of the South Pole expedition.

There was a practice beginning immediately after luncheon which David and Marcus had come over for. Coming down the stairs, already dressed, she heard the first movement ending triumphantly. Hurrying, she tried to get to the door before they began again (how many times had they played it already?), but she was too late. Even as she crossed the hall they had gone into the second movement.

She crept in. David noticed her at once. She sat down uncomfortably on the edge of a chair. Marcus acknowledged her with a friendly lift of the eyebrows, Con, his back to her, hadn't even noticed her entry. There was a long passage between him and Marcus now, and in the lull David smiled more thoroughly, pulling clown's faces at her, shaking his head: signs that were almost a private language. Conspiratorial, she might have said: the shared secret.

Then it was his turn and the grin fading slowly he'd already picked up his bow and leaped into a passage of great sweetness, carelessly played. Those lovely sounds, while all the time he clowned with her.

But the sounds *weren't* lovely to her. As they slipped without a break into the third movement, the sheer jauntiness of the piano part inflamed her. She sat there, tapping her foot impatiently, interfering somewhat with the rhythm. Occasionally she tossed her head. Ready to go out, she looked very well. Knew that she did. Her hat was new: of chiffon net, stiffened. It had on it one red rose and one black.

At intervals she looked meaningly at the library clock picking up her fob, shaking it. But Con, his back to her, could see nothing. He sat hunched over the piano, taut with concentration, clumsy sounding in his intensity, his will to get it right. Suddenly, she wanted to hit him. She was infuriated, possessed by rage. That he should ever, for so long, so completely separate himself from her; be so totally, utterly absorbed. Her presence, indignant or not, could surely be felt, surely filled the air? But he was not one to tease or play-act. He had merely – not noticed. The words, indignant, flashed into her mind as if spoken: '*And I am so beautiful!*'

The scene ever after was one of shame: she could not bear to remember the stone wall against which she had beaten. Beauty was something she took for granted, had never consciously used before: now, on this occasion, like her petulant inner cry, it had been useless.

They went off together, only half an hour late in the end. It was a pleasant outing, a happy one even. But she had for a short time been afraid, and because afraid, angry. That was how she saw it.

Later, she saw it as another premonition of his going away from her – totally. Then too, her beauty would be useless. The hat became hateful in her memory: its black rose an omen.

'And I am so beautiful . . .'

∞

It was easy enough for Polly to find Morwen Davies' mother in the telephone book. She should have remembered anyway: the Elly Ameling of Muswell Hill. But making the call reminded her unpleasantly of brave acts at school. ('I'll go and ask Sister Francis, *I'll* do it. Oh Polly, you wouldn't *dare*, honestly . . .') And what a complicated way it was of going about it all too: waylaying one person to get another's number so that that person could be asked for the other person's. There must be simpler ways: Lat Think, Polly, Lat Think. But she hadn't come up with anything better.

A squeaky, rather querulous voice answered the 'phone. Elderly. 'She's not here.' Then pause: 'She's not here, she's in the north of England.' When would she be back? The voice said suspiciously: 'Just before Christmas,' and then as if regretting the revelation, 'she'll be resting then, completely resting.'

She supposed from the Welsh lilt that it was the mother. Try again then, Polly – if you can wait that is. And indeed the days did drag, Hatter's seeming quite intolerable. Patrick was away with 'flu and she missed a concert they were to have gone to. Twice she went over to see him. She bought him the Pink Floyd as a Christmas present, and took along the family backgammon set because they hadn't one. They played, along with his sister; when she was out of the room he took Polly's hand and pulled it under the bedclothes. 'Here's something that hasn't got 'flu.' 'You never give up, do you?' she said, 'it's gorgeous.' 'Well?' Then she said it was super and the best hard-on in Fulham at 4.45 pm, *but* . . .

(What did I ere I loved? Some work – possibly.) She did a little, as much as she could bear; mostly maths because it was impersonal. The days did pass.

She prepared her speech: she was to be an aspirant singer,

104

wanting advice. But when the moment came she dried up completely. The number was repeated, twice. (I must speak now, at once. Say anything.)

'You won't know me my name's Jane Sullivan I'm writing an article for a student mag some of us just started and I was really hoping to get some material from you if that's possible – ' her voice sounded bright, a little hard – she could hear it by delayed action. Then the answer she could hear by delayed action too: '. . . won't want to trail out here. I'm rehearsing at Smith Square tomorrow, two sessions, so if in between – '

Oh my God. She said hastily that no, she could do it quickly now if that was all right; and then was cursed immediately with another attack of tied tongue.

'What part of the world do you come from? I mean with a name like that – ' No, that won't do. She grabbed a pencil and scrawled: training, hours of practice, aspirations, whom do you admire . . .

It went quite well in spite of the bad start. Only a little way more up the hill, and we're there: 'It's really super of you but there's just one more thing we'd thought of interviewing another person an instrumentalist flute or fiddle – or *trumpet*. It's such a difficult instrument.'

Then, oh joy, it was all right. 'Where do I find Sam – *Zossenheim* is it? You don't happen to know where he lives?'

'. . . can give it you if you'll hold on. He's not in the book . . .' Her head was muzzy, tick-tocking; her hand shook so that she could hardly hold the pencil.

But she had what she wanted. Or a millionth part of it anyway. And talking like that had been almost like talking to him, at one remove. It was only in the middle of that night that she had the silly thought. Why ever should she have supposed him heart-whole? Why ever? And if not heart-whole ∴ . . She ran over again the film of the party – had there been any sign between him and Morwen? But the film was suffering from too many showings and she couldn't remember much at all. They hadn't left together – sure, and yet? Something niggled at her memory: a word or gesture that had made her think, I'll puzzle that out later.

Getting out of bed she walked round the room, arms clasped,

boobs pressed hard. I'm going mad, she thought. She felt certain that her guess was right. Why else suddenly wake up with it?

Mirror, mirror on the wall, she thought, who is the thickest of them all?

∞

Camilla had rung up twice already. Weeping down the phone: 'Sweetie, you must tell me what I said – Rodney just won't discuss it at all – was I absolutely *ghastly*? Was I? You know what it is, sweetie, I'm sure it's an early change – I feel absolutely terrible, you can't imagine. I'm asking my doctor for something. I need hormones, don't you think, sweetie? Those new ones that everyone's having. What has Barney said, Tessie? You must say if Barney said anything – I shall never *never* be asked again. Tell me what you think, sweetie, do you think hormones will help? I mean I'm just absolutely *certain* it was some sort of glandular mix up with the alcohol . . .'

It seemed to Tessie unlikely that anything she might say would help or even in any way stem the flow. She knew Camilla: it would be months before it was all forgotten and buried.

She herself would have liked it out of the way at once, immediately, completely. It was too vivid a reminder of the whole unresolved problem. It brought back the end of the evening: Barney, in the bedroom, coming out at last with a name, with the truth: 'I love her.' (That, she thought, I never doubted.)

And since then: nothing at all. She hadn't asked any more. She wouldn't have believed, except that it had happened so many times before, that it could be so impossible to speak to someone. 'And so I told him,' people said, 'and so I told him what I thought of him, I said, you can just answer when you're spoken to, I said . . .' But although she could envy she couldn't imagine that raising of the voice, that confident chiding: open only to the uninhibited and the righteous. She was neither. She was timid, tongue-tied; and in the wrong. If she had been right, would this ever have happened? A woman who could not keep her man, all the magazines had said, all the books, a woman who could not keep her man had only herself to blame. *Mea culpa, mea culpa, mea maxima culpa.*

Where do we go from here? As ever it was surprising how

106

normal, how cool, how composed a front could be shown to the world; how a night together, even touching – even once, being fucked – could happen too: to her, to them both. It was as if he'd come up that evening after the dinner party, and written large and obscene in white chalk on a blackboard: 'Tessie is a cunt. I love Morwen.' Written it in chalk for the evening; then rubbed it out. Whenever she, they, looked now, lying in bed together (again, whenever else do I see him?) the blackboard was bare. Neither of them had anything to write on it. It was as if it hadn't been – except that it had.

And now Christmas was coming, the geese were getting fat. Even this year, obstinately, she loved Christmas; finding in the miners' strike, something Dickensian about the half gloomy, gaslit shops. She would like to forget herself, or rather realize herself: bathed in something between German sentiment and simple prayer and piety, mediaeval reverence and gaiety. As a season it spoke to her of new beginnings, clean endings, tidying up, in a way that the New Year couldn't.

But in fact there was too much else to think of. The sheer mechanics of the festive season. All those groaning platters which each year only groaned because someone reminded or actually did for her what was required: remembered the nuts, or the stuffing, or even the goose itself.

And then there were relatives to consider. Uncle Theo. Barney's sister, Prue. Her own brothers and sisters, scattered about the globe, barely kept in touch with. Each year she invited her mother and each year her mother refused; Patsy, equidistant, had claimed her already. 'She needs my help,' her mother said. 'And then there's Dominic, I promised them – I'll come to you in a year or two, Tessie . . .' In the meantime what would Polly like? Money? – she couldn't manage much of course. A length of material perhaps, or one of those funny shawls she'd seen girls wearing? What did Tessie think? And for Christopher?

Then the tree. There had to be a tree. 'You want to *buy* it, Tessie?' Sandy asked.

'Meaning?'

'On account of I was behind this old duck last night – over Fulham way, I never been in the shop before. She paid up for a whopper. Gorgeous it was. I can't carry it now, she says,

107

the name's Deacon. Okeydoke the girl says, I'll put it there my love, and Mrs Deacon says I couldn't get in before five and the girl says I go off dinnertime, I'll tell the girl that comes after . . . I could go along now Tessie. Want it back here?'

'No,' Tessie said. 'No. You have it, Sandy.'

∞

'What absolutely splendid news!' Con wrote. 'Although I suppose I should have guessed, with the name Willingham half a dozen times in every letter – and then your visit to Yorkshire (which you haven't told me very much about, by the by!). Only, I so much don't want to lose you, and, "*tarde quae credita laedunt, credimus*", is not that perhaps it?

'Truly though, Muff, I'm tremendously happy for you. And if you're happy (and you do sound it, you know) then that's good. It's just that no one, I suppose, is half good enough for my sister! But by all accounts, Cecil is a splendid chap and will take good care of you, and that's all that matters.

'I had rather wondered though at one time, and I can say this now, if it wouldn't be David? Because I thought, though neither of you said anything, last year in London that he was rather sweet on you. It was just that, if it had been you and he, then I would have lost you just a little less, if you take my meaning. But anyhow, Loos put the kibosh on all that, and I couldn't wish it now because you'd be more sorrowful still and that I couldn't bear.

'Anyway Muff, it is good about you and Cecil. And it isn't after all, is it, as if anybody (or anything) could ever come between you and me, and our love for each other?

'Now for the nice surprise. Our new company commander is an Etonian who knows Cecil. They were in Lubbock's together. He seems an awfully nice chap. Dear Muff, do you remember that game we used to have? I know the man who knows the man who knows the man, and so on, sometimes! Well now, I know Eddie Straton who knows Cecil Willingham who's going to marry my sister – It's rather a short one that time, but it's rather good don't you think? And doesn't it bring us just a little closer, dearest Muff?'

∞

108

It's like a drug, Polly thought. This need to see him, talk about him, read about him, hear him. For a while after I think: well that'll do, that'll have to do – just one more and then I'll stop. Like that last concert. Like telephoning Morwen. Because the awful truth is he's had every chance, every possible chance to get off with me. And hasn't even looked remotely like taking any of them . . .

Perhaps I should just go up and say, 'I love you – is there any chance?' The sort of way men have behaved through the ages and we can behave too nowadays, in theory – only you don't see too terribly much of it. I'd like to have *style*: the sort of woman who can just stroll up and unzip a man (but wouldn't it be just my luck to get the zip stuck?).

This evening though was to settle it once and for all. Absolutely. Here she was in Baron's Court outside his flat, quite by chance, meeting a friend. How surprised I'll be when he comes out – or comes along. 'We seem to run into each other everywhere,' I'll say, 'are you meeting a friend too?' 'No,' he'll say, 'I live here.' And *then* . . .

I grow sillier by the day, she thought. I'm younger this December than last: because then I knew it all. Mad she must be, because the rain which had been coming down heavily before had now turned to sleet.

From time to time she glanced at her watch. The hem of her coat had trailed in the mud, the weight of damp cloth had settled on her shoulders. To passers-by she gave brave little smiles, looked meaningly at her watch, brought out an old letter; then an *A to Z*. To two people she'd already said: 'Oh but thank you, I'm just meeting someone – ' What time, what exact hour, should she give up? She wasn't quite sure which way to look. And cold – she was so *cold*.

Then suddenly it all happened. Nose throbbing with cold, eyes stinging, mouth frozen, she was about to give up, when there was a clattering sound, the banging of a door, a sudden apparition in the cold.

Quick, quick, my story, my set piece, my little cry of recognition –

He was wearing his Afghan coat; it was difficult to tell where his hair ended and the coat began. She hurried forward, prepared surprise fixed on her face. But he'd seen her already.

Coming right up to her, 'Look here,' he began – the tone weary, exasperated, 'look here, are you by any chance *following* me?'

'Yes,' she said, and burst into tears.

The café was very full. He sat down, not alongside her as she'd hoped, but opposite. She looked about her, above her, anything but at him.

'Your coat's wet,' he said. 'Throw it back across the chair.' When the girl came for the order, he handed her the coat: 'Be a love and see to this.' Polly expected her to say, 'We're a café – not a bloody airing cupboard – ' but she just smiled at him. 'OK,' she said, 'for you – yep.'

He didn't speak then till the coffees came. She was shaking and still unable to look at him because he was looking at her quite obviously. She watched to see if he took sugar – he put in three spoonfuls. On such small details she would soon have to exist. She blew her nose, then spooned some sugar in herself.

'All right,' he said, in a patient voice. 'Now tell me – no, I'll tell *you*. An hour ago I saw you standing out there. I thought, that's odd – that girl's everywhere. Then I have a bath and come through for some nosh, and you're still there – and when I've finished, vulgar curiosity and I look again. Sight of your back view, in emergency lighting. So – ?'

'It's a project,' she said firmly, afraid she was about to cry again. But her voice came out decisively. 'A survey if you like. That's all I'm allowed to say.'

'If I believed that, I'd believe anything – '

In the warmth of the café, sipping the coffee, she felt more confident. 'A project. It's the truth.'

'OK, OK. My persecution mania showing. Let's cry quits shall we?' He smiled, slowly. '*I'll* interview *you*,' he said. 'Get rid of some of my feeling mad at you ... Right. Name, age, sex. Birthplace. We'll scrub all that. What do you do for instance?'

She told him.

'And then?'

'Oh, university. I don't know. Anything. Anything but *marriage*.'

'So? What's wrong with it – out of date?'

110

She shook her head. 'I think it's all wrong – I was brought up that way, religion and all that sort of thing, but I couldn't. It's just what it does, what it can *do* to people.' She said passionately, 'To be fettered like that – it's like a death.'

'But – some people . . .' He looked surprised.

'Love,' she said, 'that's something alive.' She twisted her hair round her forefinger, looked down at her coffee cup. 'You should see at home.'

He asked gently: 'What's wrong?'

What was wrong? Complicated emotion choked her and she said in her throwaway voice: 'Oh awful. They're awful. She does nothing all day, absolutely nothing – except get on his wick. Although she's supposed to be doing some sort of exams. I don't know – she's just such a mess. And they never have anything to say to each other. But *once* – I mean it must have been love . . .'

It was not how she had meant to speak. She wondered if she couldn't now just say simply: 'I love you,' and wait to see what happened? But he must have taken note of her tone of voice because he said lightly, 'Now, what's next? When you're not out on secret projects late at night, what do you do with your time?'

His voice was so beautiful to her that she wanted just to sit and listen. 'Oh, parties,' she said, trying to sound casual still. 'Too many of them. The odd concert, you know.' She could not, would not mention music. 'All a bit sickening. I often get – oh silly, fed up, bored. Too rich maybe. I'm spoilt to be honest.'

'Yes, that's honest. It sounds true too. Still . . .' He finished off his coffee. 'More? I'm spoilt too – I'm doing what I want, as much of it as I want – how many people can say that? I don't do it as well as I'd like, and that's good too. I'm lucky, I'm a lucky person – '

Now there was a lull in the conversation. She couldn't ask for more coffee; she hadn't finished the first cup. Terrified that he would get up and go, she said hastily: 'And you – are you married?'

He shook his head, looking very serious.

'Someone said . . . I thought, Morwen – '

'Morwen? Why ever, who ever?' He looked puzzled. 'It never

111

was, either. She's terribly tied up anyway.' He glanced at his watch, pulled a funny face at her, then said: 'What do you say I give you a few more facts – then we both go home?'

'I'm sorry,' she said, her hands enclosing her cold cup. 'Of course. Well just – hobbies, that sort of thing. And age, and so on – '

'Twenty-seven. Twenty-eight on the twelfth of March. I'm big, and one day I'll be fat. Spare time – I read a lot, sit about a lot, in the sun if I can. Biography, poetry, and fat nineteenth-century novels – Russians mostly. I never get bored – And where work is concerned I've got terrific patience. Not so good like this of course . . . Is that enough? How many words do you need?'

'Oh, look – sorry again, sorry to be so secretive. You'll understand, one day.' He was getting up to go, walking off in search of her coat. 'Then if I need to know more, can I get in touch?'

He'd brought back the coat, was helping her into it. Oh undo me, undo me, she said inside. Be my undoing.

'You *could*,' he said, looking doubtful. 'I'm off on tour though, after Christmas. Three months.'

Suddenly then it was all over. He'd walked along with her to West Ken station because they were nearer it. She had made a mess of everything, a confusion – annoyed him but not really aroused his curiosity. Why had she not told the simple truth?

She said jauntily, 'Oh by the way – a "B minor Mass" you're in – months ahead – don't get a shock when you see me grinning from the sopranos . . .'

'Not to worry,' he said easily. She was getting out her money for her ticket. 'I won't be sent an octave higher . . .'

∞

'And all the bells on earth did ring . . .'

Christmas Day, 1915, and Con was home and safe and (middling) sound. Wounded in the leg while out on a wiring party and on an extended sick leave now, he walked stiffly: often his leg would refuse to obey him. He would need massage and treatment for many months to come. Even after sick leave was up he would be for a while in England. So that perhaps

112

by the time he was due to go back, perhaps – oh, almost certainly – the guns would have stopped.

'Why on earth should men be so sad, Since our Redeemer made us glad?' Try to forget, or rather, try to accept David's death. Because Con couldn't. She was unable to protect him from that; or from news of people she'd never heard of and now would never meet; or from worry about Marcus, now finally passed fit and out in Mesopotamia.

He spent as long as his leg would allow seated at the candle-lit piano in the long dark evenings. She didn't, couldn't grudge him this. No jealousy now: only a deep content that he was in there, playing, *alive*.

In January she was to be married. She'd given up nursing a few weeks ago: later she would involve herself in various good works, but for now she could be with Con. Cecil had a staff appointment: red tabs and little need to worry about him. Not a hero perhaps, but were there not enough heroes amongst her family and friends?

Crisp cold weather for the wedding. Three bridesmaids, two of them Gore-Lewis cousins, Con the best man: she worried that he might find the standing too much. Then to the East Riding of Yorkshire for a ten-day honeymoon in the small village of Aislaby. They went over to Whitby, Scarborough, Redcar; a deserted Saltburn: Cecil remembered from an earlier holiday a girls' school playing hockey on the sands. 'How windswept, how *cold* they all looked.'

Some days were grey – what else could they expect of January? – but others like the wedding day were suddenly piercing blue, sharp tingling air, clear bright colours. Caught in the sleet one afternoon they went into the Skelder Inn and made themselves sick on 'fat rascals', succulent, dripping with butter. Opposite them the house was supposed to be haunted: she never saw anything; but the other way, from their bedroom window, the view, sometimes misty, sometimes clear, stretched out over the moors, beyond and beyond.

Everything was strange, yet simple; at times, it was hard to believe in the War. The strangeness stretched to her new personality. She was no longer Margaret Gore-Lewis – should not have expected to be – but the strangeness struck when after

113

three, four days Con wrote to her: 'Mrs Cecil Willingham'. She wondered, who is this person?

But it was her body that was most happy. She often thought of it as 'her body', a being separate from the real her. Above all it was something owned, that she hadn't known she had – not in this way.

Although she'd known, from the engagement, from the courtship, really from that moment in the box at the Palace Theatre (even, was it not true, from the foyer of Drury Lane, months before that?) that she was dealing with that same fierce excitement which had so surprised her, two years ago now. David, behind the scrapwork screen in the library, upstairs in the dark alcove. (Ah, David.)

She'd known so little really. Emily, dead nearly ten years now, had told her nothing. She had no sister. Aunt Victoria somehow could not be asked: probably her knowledge was scanty, possibly even incorrect. Friends who had married (acquaintances rather – for what close friend did she need, having Con?) spoke only of social excitements: freedom, change of status, their own establishment, and now staffing problems.

In the end a girl she'd been nursing with, a widow after only three months, had enlightened her. She flushed in the telling:

'It gets better, I mean, it's of course the first – it's rather a *shock*, you know. Even when you have a pretty good idea. But it gave him – gives men happiness. And you sort of get looked after in return – I can't explain, the sort of feeling, the way they show gratitude without saying that's why they're grateful . . .'

Only one person's experience, but at least she'd been armed with a few facts. And it hadn't after all been so bad because mixed with her natural curiosity and its satisfaction (the 'so that's what she meant') was an undercurrent, a murmuring of the old excitement; showing so clearly where it belonged. Pride, and novelty, and what seemed an insatiable longing for Cecil's body: surprise that it was at once like and yet unlike the heavily clothed one she had touched, caressed only through layers of khaki, leather, cloth. The leap from hot kisses to all this – well, it wasn't the frightening leap she'd been told. Only another step: a little strange, but only another step.

Then the third night: the room so warm from the peat fire.

114

His mouth, very loose, kissing her – and impressed on her memory the way he had stood when she'd first seen him, mouth open in laughter, swagger stick touching his thigh – a moving, warm image. As he kissed her now she let go. No longer trying to hold in her head this reserve, this worry, habitual, about Con (is he safe? is he alive?). Released of it, she was released into herself. 'I could forget everything else' became: 'I can forget, I *will* forget'. Surprised, every way: by the hardness of nipple, the glow, like a blush spreading, now breasts, now thighs, fiery. Little light in the room; just the turf smell, reminder of Corrib and security, peace.

He was hot, eager from his excitement, haste to be in. As he touched her thighs to open them, it was then that it happened. So much feeling, bursting through, flooding almost so that she thought in terrified joy that the bed, the sheets, must be part of this damp delight. Then it died down as, leaning too heavily, he came in. But a mere minute and everything was back: so intoxicating her, so fixing her, that as he thrust to and fro, to and fro, she cried out.

'Oh my God,' he said, withdrawing at once, talking into her nightgown, 'I'd thought – you should have said. If it hurts, if you're still tender – '

They had sorted it out the next day, standing on the cliffs high above Whitby, pretending to look out to sea. They had skirted round the subject; she had not realized it was possible to discuss something without really talking about it at all. For no reason that she could think of, unless it was to launch the topic, Cecil told her about a school friend of his, who had been sacked for sleeping with a chorus girl at the Paddington Hotel during Long Leave. It appeared later that what he wanted to say was that since the War many girls, of their own class, had become very bold. Some were even experienced. Distracted by seeing on the horizon what he thought might be a battleship, he had later gone on to say that he appreciated deeply that she was all he had thought her to be. (And what was that? she wondered.)

But discussed or not, it was a delight to return to again and again. And they did. She supposed that for some it was like that; and for some it was not. She felt little real interest in finding out.

'All this and Con too' – the words slipped into her mind one night, unasked for, from outside. She knew of course what they meant. All this happiness – and Con safe at home too. (That was what they *must* mean.)

They travelled south again. Cecil was to be at the War Office for three months. After speaking to a friend in hospital, she went to a doctor in Wimpole Street and had a stem pessary fitted.

Chapter 9

Christmas was over. And Boxing Day too – or nearly: they were sitting over drinks now, Christopher out of the way in bed. He'd been sick twice. Even at eleven, Barney had pointed out, he should have had his sweet presents rationed: Tessie should at least have kept an eye on him. 'Oh, Mum,' he'd said, 'Amazin' Raisins, I never want to see another Amazin' Raisin – When they're spewed, you see . . .'

Muff was with them, also Polly. Prue and her husband, Charles, over in Europe for six weeks, had spent most of the day with them. It had seemed to Tessie a very long day.

She'd always been ill at ease with Prue, even though, or perhaps because, she hadn't met her till she'd already been three or four years married to Barney. There had been time to dread, for her fear to grow of an updated version of Muff: rack her brains as she might she could not remember seeing her in the old days. Dimly she recalled a figure in WRNS uniform: 'that's the Willingham girl on leave,' but she could attach no face to it. All she had to go on was a 1938 deb photograph (Margaret Willingham had so much wanted to present her in the Coronation season, someone had said), pushed behind a potted plant in the Knightsbridge flat. She had looked like a coarsened version, a caricature almost of Muff's brother, Con. Even the gauze had been unable to soften the arrogant, nearly insolent, false sweetness. Later and probably more authentic snapshots taken in South Africa had been unable to alter this image.

Then she'd met Prue. Here was someone who far from trying to intimidate or negate her, Tessie, was trying constantly – and largely unsuccessfully – to impress Muff. Tessie had noticed it with a sort of ashamed delight – why, I don't need to bother! – at the first real family gathering. Uncle Theo had been there, she remembered. Prue had made some rather bossy remark, and he had been dryly sarcastic. 'You lack your mother's charm,' he'd said, 'for what it's worth.'

117

Perhaps unconsciously Prue had put all these miles between her and her mother, had looked deliberately for someone who would say, 'I'm afraid we won't be able to live in the old country, you know.' Now she had something of her own. Charles. Tessie could sense Muff despising him. The Fat Boy, Polly called him. Beside him, Barney's elegance was almost frightening (as was Barney himself at the moment. Over Christmas he had hardly spoken to her. A present, of money, without a smile).

'Everyone grumbles so now,' Prue was saying aggressively. 'Not like during the War. In a boring way – you must have noticed it, Mummy.'

No one could address Muff as 'Mummy'. And yet it must have been so once. Prue, pinafored, must have run to her with precious news. Or rather, in *crêpe de Chine* or starched lawn, all pleats and frills, down at five o'clock for a privileged glimpse of the exquisite mother. Would she not probably, a quivery eighty, still speak unselfconsciously of 'Mummy'?

She had coloured with the drink, with the day's over-eating: 'Charles, bear me up. No other country carries on so about the cost of food, and getting the dustbins collected. And education. You'd think from the way they go on that England was finished – '

'Isn't she?' said Charles, turning his feet outwards. His black shiny toes reminded Tessie of her childhood statue of the Little Flower.

'Really, darling, I don't think that's awfully funny. What I mean is, heaven help us, they don't need to carry on *all* the time. I think – '

'What you think is quite evident,' interrupted Muff. 'We have heard a great deal of it. Home truths from abroad perhaps?'

Prue was made irritable by this. She felt obviously that she must prove her point and unable to get off the subject she appealed for help all round; but threw her argument all the time at Muff. Charles, needling her, said:

'No more booze.' He wagged his finger: 'Tears before bedtime as Nanny used to say.'

Prue said indignantly: 'You never knew Nanny! Nanny

118

Buckley, she always made sure there were tears. Ghastly, awful woman. Sickening woman – '

Barney said, 'Well, I didn't see her like that. And Tessie was not a little grateful to her.'

Muff asked, 'Can Polly remember? Polly, surely not?'

'What's that? Remember *who*?'

'Nanny,' Tessie said. 'But you were only tiny. You couldn't.' It was apparent to her that Polly hadn't been listening. That most of the time now she wasn't listening. Not difficult, just abstracted; and odd too; a week or so ago she'd flung her arms suddenly round Tessie's neck. 'It's going to be all right!' she said, 'I can't tell you how, but you mustn't worry, because it is!' And for a moment Tessie had thought, my God she knows. And she's sorry for me. Oh my God. Then she'd realized, just known, that it wasn't that at all. Only, what was it?

The topic of Nanny had run out. Muff announced suddenly, 'I shall go up.' She rose immediately and bestowing kisses graciously, in strict order of precedence, went out.

Barney said: 'More drinks? Prue, Charles?' then as if he hadn't noticed her, 'Tessie?' But Prue and Charles thought really they ought to be off. An early start tomorrow: they were going to spend three days with Charles' family. 'Mother hasn't been too well,' Charles confided. Prue, legs wide apart, said that the holiday seemed to be all duty visits. Ireland meant seeing Uncle Theo in his nursing home, and so on.

She gave Tessie a pecking kiss. Charles as he kissed her patted her a little, as if to reassure himself that she was still a big girl. 'I like big girls,' he had said admiringly, the first time they met, gazing fixedly at the blouse button which wouldn't do up. She feared sometimes the notion of being alone with him, fantasizing that on some desert island perhaps he might suddenly grab great handfuls of flesh, squeezing them sensuously with his buttery hands.

'You're gorgeous,' he said now, giving her another pat. 'Lucky Barney – aren't you?'

Polly alone, they'd all gone up: Muff, her mother, even her

119

father, although she hadn't seen him go. Her aunt and uncle had left a little earlier, after much sparring and an imperious: 'Charles, fetch it at once. Of *course* I left it. Otherwise I should have it, wouldn't I?'

'I'll just clear,' Polly had said. Gathering up glasses, emptying ashtrays, wanting of course to be alone, to make the actual journey upstairs alone.

She was happy, still. That was it. She was living on the little – no the immense wealth, of only a week or so back. It shut out everything else. Niggling worries, like the amount of maths to be covered in the holiday, and larger worries: like Alice's silence. (Not knowing her whereabouts, and then her own natural reluctance to telephone the family and ask. That bright compensating voice of Alice's mother: 'No we haven't heard from her *just at the moment*.')

She could shut all this out. Or rather, all this was shut out by what she'd achieved in that one meeting. Truly, it hadn't been a great deal – but it hadn't been nothing either. Joy bubbled inside her obstinately, unreasonable joy. She thought the better of it for that. Unreasonable, against all the odds. *Real.*

So upstairs in her room now, she wouldn't play Bach. Superstitious reluctance to taste the fruit, to associate, to overdo it. I might hear it, hear the highest note of all and have that feeling, that terror: it can never be mine. It is not for me.

So I play – what? The whole army of records, ranged: the left flank, the right flank, Beethoven, Britten, the Slade, Handel, Fauré, the Who, Moody Blues, Mozart.

Mozart. *Sinfonia Concertante*, yes. From the sleeve, Oistrakh father and son beamed down at her. A record she didn't remember buying, one of half a dozen passed on by her father; he bought too many.

Curled up on the floor now, hands over soles of feet, head on knees, the music starting up: going, going out of the world. Only something had gone wrong. She tried to crowd out the sound. She was straight back in the hated convent days – back like an arrow. It could have been that she was reminded of Alice, but she thought that it wasn't. Although Alice certainly had been there, had been sitting on the other side of the class-

120

room: they'd been separated two terms before, for passing notes and incurable whispering.

It was an English class. Sister Scholastica, who was elderly and difficult to please, had just been replaced by Sister Perpetua. Their lessons were going to be fun, she promised them.

Going over to the record player, 'Now,' she had said, 'I want you to listen carefully to the music – make little notes about it if you like – but try to relax and see what it suggests to you. We shan't do anything easy or obvious like Delius and his cuckoo – ' A hand shot up at the back of the class: 'Please, Sister, Mahler and the cowbells.' Sister Perpetua looked rather blank, then said quickly, 'A good remark.' Alice muttered in a giggly voice, just loud enough to be heard, 'Cow pats, cow pats, country pancakes.' She was dismissed from the class.

The music was the first movement of the *Sinfonia Concertante*. Polly didn't know it. It came at her from all sides of the room. Unable to bear such perfection, such beauty – and something else too, that she could not define – she moved uneasily, pushing her chair back, chewing at her pencil, so that flakes of paint filled her mouth and had to be spat out. She caught Sister Perpetua's eye and received raised eyebrows. At once she smirked in nervous reaction. The music went on, unbearably. She made a few pencil patterns, savage stabs on her rough paper, shapes that could have been words.

They had twenty minutes, the remainder of the lesson, to write up their notes. The best exercise would be considered for the school magazine. She was paralysed sitting there. She had nothing whatsoever to say. It was all of it there in her head, but it had nothing to do with words.

Next to her a girl called Nicola was scribbling industriously, hardly looking up, sometimes smiling to herself. Polly glanced her way once or twice. Then catching sight of a sentence, leaning over a little, she read on, horrified:

'. . . behind the tree two elves are hiding. One peeps round the tree trunk. Here he comes! Now he's dancing, skipping in rhythm to Mozart's joyful music. A little dance of joy in the greensward. Soon he is joined by the gnomes, with their heavier steps. These are not bassoons but the voices of the denizens of elfland clad in . . .' Nicola had paused to think.

Polly went back to her blank paper. Five minutes dragged

by. Then she thought, simply, that she would write the truth. In block letters she wrote the one word PAIN. Then for the next ten minutes she surrounded it with a garland of ornate flowers and thorns, running and triumphing over the lettering.

The work came back three days later: on the whole the class had made a really good effort, had understood the spirit of the exercise. There had been a real response to music. One girl, showing a good historical sense, had had a most interesting mental picture of an audience, periwigged, listening to a performance, projected back to more gracious times But the best example of a lively, well thought out reaction had been Nicola's. She had used her imagination and then conveyed it in crisp prose: her clever use of the historic present had conveyed *immediacy*. The thirteen-year-olds listened respectfully.

Polly was sent for at the end of the lesson. She turned her head away. 'Look at me,' Sister Perpetua said. Then: 'This,' holding up the paper, 'I can only suppose this was done for *effect*?' She shook her head sadly. 'What shall we do with you? You *and* Alice? Thirteen and quite irresponsible. First you tried to copy someone else's ideas, and then . . . Try and cultivate your imagination, Polly. It shouldn't be used only for impertinence. I shall tear this up and *not* speak to Reverend Mother – this time . . .'

She hadn't wanted to talk about it with Alice. In any case Alice, because she'd missed the lesson, had had to write a composition on 'My Favourite Museum', or 'A Nature Walk in Spring'. She was busy getting up steam about that.

All the rest of the term, Polly spent a great deal of time in the chapel. She didn't pray (Alice had teased her though, about turning holy), but had just knelt. It had felt sometimes like prayer; but mostly like peace.

She moved the record off now. It was no good. Nothing was any good. She had once again been incredibly, unforgivably stupid. All right, so he had gone abroad, so he was away, so she couldn't run after him – but one day he would be back. And then she would see, yet again, that there was nothing doing: and that there never would be. That was reality. But she could have done, for a little longer, with the silliness.

She said the word 'silliness' several times over, to impress on herself that she was silly, silly, silly. But then she spoilt it by remembering (from Chaucer was it?) that once the word had meant 'helpless', 'defenceless'. She ran her fingers through her hair, making it stand out either side, and thought: that's me; except that it isn't – I could quite well manage, if I just faced up to the facts.

She couldn't bear to go over it all again. She would go downstairs and make a drink. Something warm and despairing: Ovaltine, cocoa, some despised taste or flavour.

Coming down the stairs, she met her father. He looked grey, with work-worry she supposed, since she'd thought that earlier in the evening he'd looked preoccupied, worn. It flashed through her mind that like that, he looked old suddenly. One day he will die, she thought.

He had stopped on the small landing.

'You look enormously weary,' he said. 'What have you been up to? Parties, Christmas parties?'

'No. I'm great. Great. It's just I couldn't settle – '

'Hatter's all right, not too ghastly? They are getting you through?'

'Oh my God. There'll be a report soon. That'll give you the latest forecast – ' she pulled a face. He smiled, slowly. As always, it transformed him, light coming into his eyes, his mouth made gentle. She felt a small, violent upsurge of tenderness. She would say something; the right thing.

But he spoke first. 'Still, I don't know – you don't look yourself. Have you got everything you want? The allowance, would you like a rise? Money. Is money all right?'

For no reason at all she thought she was going to cry, as if tears had been waiting all evening, building up, dammed, for this moment.

'I'm fine, *really*. It's just things, sometimes, they get a bit – I don't know . . .'

She thought he was looking at her, but when she turned her head back he was gazing at some point beyond her. 'All right then, that's good. And the room's all right, I suppose – the gramophone still good?' She nodded. 'If you should want – if you feel it would help at all, a television? A small portable perhaps . . .'

No, she didn't want that, she wouldn't hear of it, but of course it was a super idea. 'Now I really must go to bed. Just get this drink first – ' She did the rest of the steps in doubles to show that she really was in a hurry.

She found herself crying in the kitchen, stirring the undissolved granules of Ovaltine – she hadn't warmed the milk enough – and thinking, in an angry muddle: I could have talked to him about Sam, about Morwen, about all of them. He knows them, must know them. I love him, surely I do? Couldn't we have just sat down on the stairs and talked?

Chapter 10

It was unusual to meet Barney for a meal – unusual really to be going out with him at all in any way other than social obligation.

'I want to talk to you,' he had said – announced rather. 'A restaurant would be best possibly. And if you could be on time?' (said courteously) 'I do have work to do.'

It was a fine clear January morning, and to calm herself she was walking for the last half hour. She'd allowed herself time. Standing on a corner waiting to cross the street, she stood back suddenly as a lorry, turning, nearly mounted the pavement. She stopped still, quaking.

All these years of living in London and she still wasn't accustomed to the clanging and clashing, the bustle, the hootings, the vibrations from the road. She'd been brought up in a village and her convent had been in a small market town; the Marchants had lived in the country.

But anywhere, in any place where there was traffic, it was the lorries she feared. Roaring towards her – even when they passed they seemed still to be coming towards her – their black tyres gleaming evilly in wet weather, their great bodies throwing up pale, blinding dust on windy days. Deafening, rumbling, twentieth-century dragons. They belonged surely in fairy tales, horrific fairy tales: how could a mere human being – skin, bones, hair, warm blood – control such a fire-breathing monster?

But a year or two ago her fears had been, after a fashion, explained. Her mother on one of her rare visits to London had suggested: 'I suppose it *could* be . . .' Apparently, in her pram, Tessie had seen – but of course without remembering – a lorry out of control, hurtling down a hill, crashing into the sweet shop at the foot. 'Right through the glass, right inside. Three people were killed. Such a *mess* . . . his brakes had gone, you see . . .' Nowadays, in the face of this simple explanation, Tessie dismissed her terrors; was rational. Yet felt exactly the same.

125

Glancing at her watch now she was certain that it had stopped. She shook it: then saw a shop clock just ahead of her. She was over ten minutes wrong – would indeed be late.

In spite of her best fitted coat, in spite of the wide green hat Camilla so admired, she didn't look good. Late, flustered, worried ('and what is wrong with the London taxis?' he would say), she would not be welcome. Twenty years ago – more now – she had hurried once to meet him. Been easily on time.

'*I want to talk to you.*'

It was menacing in its simplicity. She thought, felt weakly certain, that it was to announce his departure. It must be.

∞

1953: Camilla was married now (married from the house in 1951 – austerity still, and lots of tears). Those two post-war fruits, Amanda and Simon, were nine and seven. Simon was to go to prep school in the autumn.

Life was nothing. It was living with the Marchants; knowing them so well; recipient of their worries: Was Rodney really suitable? Which school was *best* for Simon? Was there no way to stop Amanda biting her nails? She had become so much a part of their life that whereas once it had been: 'when Tessie goes somewhere more exciting/gets married/goes round the world . . .' now it was: 'after us, you're going to be snapped up by Mary and Colin – they've got their eye on you for their youngest. When nanny goes.'

She had cut off so much, such a brutal slashing away at the past. Isolated memories, escaping, would make her twist in anguish. But it had been possible – although she would never have believed it so – to parcel them up into boxes, to stow them away, emotion-proof, out of sight and – out of mind.

Every now and then, it seemed, Pam Marchant would obviously think: 'We must do something about Tessie . . .' And some thoroughly uninterested, and often uninteresting young man would be invited to drinks, or to dinner, or to tennis on Sunday. Twice, Camilla's cousin Anthony, just called to the Bar, took her out, most expensively. Conversation died with the sherry.

She felt somehow that deep down she didn't know how to

126

behave. It wasn't externals: with a little effort these were manageable; but rather, sudden inappropriate reactions. Introduced to one Nigel Bewke, she'd misheard 'P' for 'B', laughing suddenly and loudly. Some of those invited, when they found she knew no one they knew, had been nowhere they'd been, didn't ride, hadn't been presented, would try at first to find common ground. 'Are you sure you weren't at Felicity Mayhew's? I could have *sworn* I'd seen you there . . . You mean you don't know them? Oh, but – ' and a great laugh ' – you *must*!' Incredulous. Once, possibly in despair, one of them said, 'But what *are* you interested in?' and she answered, perfectly honestly, because the truth had just come to her: 'Nothing.' 'Oh but really,' he said, 'no but really, that's awfully good.' He repeated it with delight, 'Nothing. That's rather good, you know. Nothing . . .'

But although they seemed in memory to have been hordes, there hadn't really been above seven or eight of them in all the years she'd been there. Now, by 1953, the Marchants didn't bother. They said things like: 'Tessie, our man hater,' or 'Tessie loves children but not the men,' or 'Tessie, our home bird.'

She had one whole day a week free and every third weekend. She went home very rarely; it was too much of a journey. Her father was semi-retired now. A bad heart attack had forced him to give up his practice and they had moved to the coast, to Filey. He worked two days a week; her mother, fourteen hours seven days a week.

She spent little money, putting away most of it in the Post Office (she wasn't sure what for). Now and then she bought clothes, because she had to. Her day off was a problem. Usually she slept late, then took a bus into the town and went to the cinema, whatever was showing. Afterwards she had tea at the Tudor Café, looking at her watch at intervals until she could set out for home, and burst into the house, breathless: 'Had a lovely day!' Very occasionally she went up to London: walking or bussing from department store to department store. Sometimes she would arrange to meet Joan or Barbara from convent days. But both were married now and with small babies were increasingly tied. She was invited to stay, but never went.

Then one morning, just after the Coronation, waking up

127

to her day off, she saw that it was going to be perfect June weather: looking at the blue sky, at the depth of green everywhere, she thought of leafy lanes. She would pack a meal, and take a bus into the real country and ramble. Then she remembered that she had to buy a birthday present for her father. It had to be posted tomorrow. She would in fact have to go up to London.

Dressing to go, she fretted in front of the glass, not liking what she saw. Usually she scarcely looked. But today, impatient with herself, with the wasted weather, she began all over again. Her tired blue suit did nothing for her, and would be too hot; the hem of its boxy jacket needed mending. She had one good dress which she wore when people came to drinks: poplin, peacock-blue, sleeveless and full-skirted, it looked luxurious. Putting it on now, with the lace cotton gloves Camilla had brought back from Italy, she felt she was altering something, acting out of character. And what to wear with it? Not her ageing tan gaberdine, or worse, the puce-coloured cardigan an aunt had given her for Christmas. She would be – would have to be – warm enough without.

Strangely enough on the journey up she was almost happy. And once arrived, everything went right for her. It was something to do with the Coronation perhaps. At Harrods, she went straight to the Gifts Department and at once found the present. A pigskin brush case with a zipped compartment on top for studs. She was delighted with it. From there she strolled through to Hats. The summer stock had been well sought into, but with the same feeling of near happiness she caught sight suddenly of a hat, Italian straw, black, and knew she had to have it. When she was trying it on the saleswoman said, almost as astonished as Tessie: 'But it suits you. It looks *really* good . . .'

She moved, glided almost, on to Fabrics. She didn't often look at materials, she couldn't sew. But today she wandered among them sensuously: great rolls of velvet, purple, emerald, gold; glazed cottons, stiff and shiny, all leaves and flowers; folds of oyster satin catching the light.

Suddenly, from just behind her, she heard a penetrating voice: 'I fear we shall have to see the buyer. Frankly, I don't think my dressmaker would handle this quality. Would the tussore be better?'

128

Memory knocking, she turned. Margaret Willingham, one ungloved hand fingering material, raised her eyebrows, hesitated, frowned a little, then smiling, said: 'Teresa – my dear!'

Barney was standing to the right of her. 'Barney – you remember little Teresa.' She paused. 'John Fletcher's daughter.' Then in an irritated stage whisper: 'The *GP*, darling.'

He was very tall. She had forgotten how tall he was, how long and thin. He looked at her with polite lack of recognition, pretended – she knew – that he remembered, and said, 'Hallo, Teresa. How nice.'

Margaret Willingham began to talk at once. 'We miss your father so,' she told Tessie. 'The village is quite lost without him. But such a well deserved rest . . .' There were questions about the house in Filey, about the children, about the new work.

She hadn't changed, not perceptibly. She must by now be sixty or thereabouts. But the beautiful bonework, the fine skin, the very blue eyes were the same; only the hair, what she could see of it, was more silvery. As she questioned on, Tessie looked at her dress: silk, in a rosebud print, with a matching jacket. Barney, standing still beside her, didn't join in the questioning. Every now and then he smiled a little distantly.

'What are you doing now, Teresa?'

Tessie started to say, 'It's a sort of job, well – it's a job with children,' but not a word had come out when Margaret Willingham said: 'At any rate, whatever, if you have the time to spare, my dear, perhaps you could have luncheon with us?' She turned to Barney, 'I think so, don't you?'

Then, as Tessie said, without really believing it was happening: 'Yes, I'd love that,' she turned again to Barney. 'Your shoes,' she said. She looked at her watch.

Tessie found herself attached to them: it was twelve-fifteen, hardly worth their separating. She sat on a little chair beside Margaret Willingham, while Barney, six pairs of shoes about him, walked the length of the department. Margaret Willingham kept up a running commentary on the quality of life today. Once, he disappeared from sight. When he returned the assistant commented mildly: 'Perhaps – we don't really allow – really we prefer customers not to walk *off the carpet* – '

Barney ignored him. 'Something with a little less obvious

stitching, I think?' Another pair was brought, and found satisfactory. 'Charge them – would you?' he said.

Over the meal, she learned that Margaret Willingham was up for a week, staying at Claridge's. She'd come to see her solicitor about the purchase of a mews flat in Knightsbridge. It would be more convenient. She was selling their home in Yorkshire, would probably buy a cottage in Somerset. Yes, it was sad, but the house had not been in the family so very long. Neither Barney nor her daughter were interested. Barney was in the City now, in banking. He had a flat in Chelsea.

The conversation generally was easy. Inevitably, they touched on the Coronation. 'Thank God for a return to normal,' Margaret Willingham said. The agony column had become so boring, all robes and coronets for hire. And if only this absolutely gorgeous weather had come at the right time – wasn't the Queen of Tonga quite marvellous – that open carriage ... Barney had found Everest, the conquest of, far more exciting. There were a few remarks about Kenya; the *worry* of it all; someone whose son was out there. Then, holidays: the day after tomorrow Barney was going to Greece for three weeks. 'The cheapest country in Europe,' he said. 'A nicely devalued drachma and double your money.'

He talked freely, easily, relaxed perhaps by the drink. He even laughed at some of Tessie's remarks. Something about Camilla. It appeared he knew Rodney slightly, had met him once or twice.

All the time she could feel Margaret Willingham looking at her, watching her. At first she was uneasy, but there seemed something so benign about it that she lowered her guard, began really to enjoy herself: she looked well, and knew it.

The meal ended. Barney who was having visa trouble had to go and see about it. Margaret Willingham had a dentist's appointment at three o'clock. Tomorrow she would go back to Yorkshire.

'What do you usually do then, Teresa, with this day off?'

'I get the six o'clock train back,' Tessie said simply. Adding: 'From Waterloo.'

'Ah,' said Barney, raising his eyebrows, smiling, 'it's a creature of habit, is it?' But Margaret Willingham, cutting in, announced: 'She must dine with us,' and before Tessie could

130

speak: 'no, I *insist*, Teresa. We shan't be late. Shall we say seven-thirty, at Claridge's? In the foyer.'

How to pass the rest of the afternoon? The feeling of unreality, which the evening wasn't likely to improve, was overwhelming now. Restlessly, she wandered about for a while, unable to stay still long enough even for window shopping. Then on impulse passing a post office she went in and cashed the maximum allowed, ten pounds, and went back to Harrods. Up in the hairdressing department: yes, they could do her hair – if she cared to wait; there had been a cancellation.

'I want to look just right,' she said, but the girl understood at once. Her hair, easily manageable, the pins out, fell into place. Then she went downstairs and bought a linen dust coat from a special inexpensive range carrying a Jean Patou label. It had deep-cut dolman sleeves and a cardigan band and cost seven pounds.

She walked along Beauchamp Place. It was still decorated, hung with banners of previous kings and queens. There in a small shop she saw a large rush bag, hand-made, and bought it to put her hat in. She had spent all her money now, except for her return ticket and about ten shillings. She thought she'd like a bath but didn't know how to set about it. On the way to Claridge's she tried to telephone Pam Marchant – but no one was at home.

Only Barney was sitting in the foyer. Surprised, she stopped where she was. 'Mama asks to be excused,' he said rising, uncoiling. 'Mr Libbley made her suffer rather more than she'd feared. She's having a meal sent up ... Perhaps we could have a drink and then go on somewhere?' He signalled a passing waiter. 'What will you have?'

She'd thought that conversation would be at the very least halting; she couldn't imagine how if she were around it could flow easily. But it did. She found out that all was well with the visa. She asked, and was told no, he wasn't flying – he hated it – he was taking the Orient Express, the slip coach to Athens. The friends he would be staying with had just been over for the Coronation; it had all been most amusing. Tessie, who'd watched it all on the Marchants' television, said she'd liked to have slept out on the pavement for it.

'Ah yes,' he said. They'd all had seats near the Dorchester.

131

Oddly enough, his father had watched Edward the Seventh's funeral from Dorchester House. He'd been on leave from India. 'A rather sadder occasion. He mentioned it quite often. The last blaze of sun before it set. Contrary to the myth, they felt the storm clouds, he said, all during those wonderful summers after. It seems to be women who are so nostalgic about the summer of '14 – it was all over long before then . . .'

She asked him something about his war. While he was telling her she remembered suddenly the girl who'd jilted him. Looking at him curiously, trying to imagine the welter of arrangements, a dress hanging up, announcements made, a hall full of presents, letters, cars ordered, food piled high – then towering, tottering at the height of the pyramid: Barney. She tried to imagine the figure toppling. But – what had the girl thought? How did one, how could you push Barney out of your life? In idle sequence, she thought – if it hadn't happened, then I, Teresa Fletcher, the doctor's daughter, wouldn't be sitting here in Claridge's, drinking a Pimm's – she couldn't imagine what boldness had made her order that. Under its influence fantasies flowed easily.

There was a silence. She was surprised to find herself at ease in it; as if she'd known him for years and years. And indeed, although not a friend, he had most of her childhood *been* there. It was strangeness with the sting taken out.

'Where would you like to go?' He was easing the knees of his trousers. She noticed how long and thin his hands were. 'The Café de P? Probably you're bored with it, and we're hardly dressed . . . but Coward's excellent I hear. If you're a fan.' He looked over at her. 'Another drink?' When she refused, he said: 'What about the Pheasantry?' She hesitated; she had never heard of it. 'Let it be the Pheasantry,' he said, getting up suddenly.

They took a taxi to the King's Road. She felt unbelievably calm and collected. She thought: this isn't happening to me. A magazine – or was it a book? – had said, to be attractive it's only necessary to feel attractive. And so it was – with a little help from Harrods, and Jean Patou.

She chased new peas round the plate, speared new potatoes, ate asparagus, drank claret.

'Would you like to dance?'

His hand as he clasped hers was very cool, very dry; his other touching her dress, was hard. She would not have expected so firm a grasp. Her dancing – rhythms patiently instilled years ago by Mike – was all right if the other person was above average. Barney was. It was true then, it was possible, what she had sometimes heard said: they moved as one.

'If I loved you,' sang the vocalist, 'words wouldn't come in an easy way. All I'd want you to know, how I loved you – *if* I loved you . . .'

A very large man, almost lifting off the ground a tiny gauzy girl, crashed heavily into them. 'What a fine figure of a man,' Barney commented ironically, looking after him. The man was waving, grimacing, it could have been apologizing. 'Do I know him?'

'There's enough of him,' Tessie said.

'Beefcake. Inordinately admired by some, but a condition to which I can't possibly aspire – '

'I'm not madly attracted by it anyway, I think. You look very nice, like that,' she added lamely.

He looked down at her, he couldn't have been used to such naïve remarks. 'Oh me,' he said affectionately. 'I'm just a weed with a good tailor.'

She ate ice cream; he had only cheese. Then they were dancing again: the music was 'How About You?' That she didn't like. It stabbed. She had lumbered about the sitting-room at the Kellys': their Garland and Rooney act. She had to speak at once. 'Heavens – this is an old one,' she said. Then to cover up her emotion she sang with the vocalist: 'And Franklin Roosevelt's looks give me a thrill . . .'

'Aren't the words of these things curiously dating?' he said. 'And the devil to change I imagine. "Dwight Eisenhower's looks give me a thrill . . ." The rhythm's not right at all. Nor the sentiment, I fear . . .'

'Yes. He hasn't at all the same sort of face.'

He bent down to hear her better. 'I don't remember the tune, actually. I'm never very up in them. The odd number sticks – if it was played a lot at a Commem Ball or always on in the Mess. Otherwise – '

'. . . holding hands in the movie show when all the lights are low, may not be new, but *I* like it – how about you?'

133

'I'm not very musical,' she said. 'Just honky-tonk. Popular stuff like this. Anything with a tune.' She asked him: 'Do you still sing? You know, serious singing?'

He looked surprised but also, it seemed, very pleased. 'Actually yes. Quite a lot. One has no difficulty here of course, I belong to a small society – a very pleasant crowd. One – gets some solos occasionally. At minor performances. It's very charming though you should remember . . .'

'You sang, you see, at that evacuee concert – just before you were called up.'

'Ah that. Yes – '

'It was, must have been awfully difficult. At least, I thought . . .'

'Yes. I suppose in retrospect, all things considered, one did it rather well.' And then, as if recollection came through a fog: 'Didn't *you* do something?'

She nodded.

'I remember,' he said. 'That Irish boy. A song and dance act, wasn't it? He was a demon on the ivories – quite remarkable. Whatever happened to him, what was his name?'

'Oh, Mike,' she said. There was a thundering in her head. Her legs had gone weak. 'You must mean Mike. Mike Kelly. We lost touch years ago. He became a priest – I think. Or he's becoming one. He – '

'Ah, of course, he was a Roman. Ampleforth wasn't it?' He led her back to the table. 'Mama has a great respect for your faith – I expect you noticed. It can't be because of the Irish, it must be in spite of. A large part of the family is Anglo-Irish, you know. The big house was burnt down but the dower house, which is Uncle Theo's, is there still. We were often there before the War . . .'

It was an easy conversation again now. She had been down to the depths, and risen again. Survived.

They danced again after coffee. He asked her about the time of her train as they jogged to a Guy Mitchell number. Then he asked, did she like revue? Had she seen *Airs on a Shoestring*? 'Max Adrian does these wonderfully dotty old men. You'd be amused, I think. You should try to see it – '

She thought that for all of her life she had been held like this, had moved so easily, so naturally. The evening seemed to be without beginning, without end. She had only to stay like this, going his way, and everything would be all right for ever and ever.

'You're looking very seductive,' he said, suddenly, but in a tone of voice as who would say: the weather's mild today. They were dancing to another tune from *Carousel*; slower now. 'What's the use of wondrin', if he's good or if he's bad?'

He put her in a taxi to Waterloo. She caught the last train, barely. She was cold on the journey and slightly sick. No one heard her come in and the next day, rather than exhilarated, she was exhausted and flat. A cul-de-sac, a torment. A dig into the past: it was as if everything of which after all Barney didn't form any *real* part, had been resurrected and hung balefully before her, saying, 'we *dare* you to look . . .'

But time healed it: time and busyness. Amanda was a bridesmaid, the Marchants had a stream of visitors. The weeks passed. And that, she thought (about the odd lunch, the even odder evening), that is that.

Only it wasn't. When Pam Marchant called her to the 'phone, she thought it would be her mother. He said: 'Barney Willingham here.' But why? she thought at once.

'I believe you wanted to see *Airs on a Shoestring*!'

'My day off – ' she began. 'The tickets are for Friday,' he said. 'I shall have to come straight from the City. Shall we say – six-thirty, at Bentley's?'

She had to look Bentley's up in the telephone directory. He was very tanned, very confident. She supposed the evening was a success, since he invited her to the Eton-Winchester match. Margaret Willingham was there and embraced her ardently; she introduced her everywhere as 'little Teresa'. Barney said: 'She won't be cheering for us – Uncle Con was a Wykehamist, and Father came on the scene too late to change her allegiance.'

They went to Henley. The sun shone on them. She had bought two more dresses, but wore the Italian straw whenever a hat was needed. She spent money too on shoes and new gloves. At the Marchants' they had begun to talk: Camilla's cousin, Anthony, knew of him. 'A bit of a cold fish – but he can be quite a charmer, I believe.' Camilla mercifully was abroad: Rodney was working a year in Kuwait.

For their engagement that Christmas he bought her a watch:

135

eighteen carat gold, Vacheron and Constantin. She saw that it cost more than two hundred pounds. Her ring she never saw the price of. Everyone, her parents, the Marchants, Margaret Willingham ('you must call me Muff'), was absolutely delighted. The wedding was to be in July.

Although she remembered the venue – a hunt ball – she didn't remember saying 'yes'. She felt then and for a long time after as if, travelling on a railway line, she had come to the station marked 'marriage'. And yet: on the morning after she'd accepted him, before the social flood came, she woke up with the words in her head – clear as if she'd heard them spoken: 'I have come home.'

PART TWO

And still she cried
I love him the best
and a troubled mind
sure it knows no rest
and still she cried
bonny boys are few
and if my love leaves me
what will I do?

Irish traditional

Frank was sitting in the sun. He looked pleased to see her. It was her fourth visit: the daffodils were out now, some miniature iris too, round where his chair had been placed.

She sat down beside him slowly. The aches and pains, the twinges, to be expected in winter, affronted her in the sudden warmth. Spring was a time of renewal. She was not renewed nowadays. The busy efficient Margaret Willingham who could always be relied on, who had not given herself time to notice the spring, whose wounds could be healed by activity. The later Margaret Willingham, leading such a pleasant sociable life from her small Knightsbridge flat (so wonderful for her age, so *energetic*). When had the downhill journey begun? It was the move to Barney's house that had done it: she had had little arthritis before that, she had had mobility, it was then the journey had begun. I ought to be thankful, she thought, that as the road slopes down it *seems* to be level.

Frank said, 'I don't like *General Hospital* like I like *Callan*. I like *Callan* best.' He had stopped calling her ma'am. 'I watch it Tuesdays. Afternoons – '

Some visitors walked by in the spring sunshine. A wheel-chair passed with another old man pushed by a very young girl. She winked at Frank and smiled at Muff: 'Well, hallo there.'

'There's this one called Gladys,' Frank was saying, 'she's in the nick. Then Flo's really called Sevet something – she's really Russian see and these others they're flaming about the chap's been visiting her, that's Callan, she's supposed to have done him in see . . .'

In her dream Con had asked her: so she had come and would continue to come. Lest we forget. Manifestly, many had forgotten: there had been much else to remember. But now – since the 'sixties in fact – this reassessment of, fascination, obsession sometimes with Con's war; acted, written, talked about by people who weren't alive then. A thin but tough thread bound her to this old man sitting in the sun. He had been there.

'Fourteen years in the nick and she doesn't want that because she's got this little kid in Russia, where she come from, she's a spy see – she puts one over him acting ill in the toilet so she gets the pistol off him . . .'

The garbled version of *Callan* dragged on. She'd lost the train if ever she had had it . . . I don't want to die, she thought suddenly. Even my not caring doesn't make me want to die; I don't believe that Con and I will be together. We will cease to be. He exists now only because I am still here.

'. . . the deal is she's to shop Richmond, he's the one old Callan's after but this geezer's trying to get a radio call, one of them trawlers in the North Sea . . .'

She smiled and bowed and looked interested, all the time pushed farther and farther back into the confines of memory. Frank was pleased, honoured: his account a success. Sister, nurse, hadn't the time to listen – and who else in the Home wanted to hear the plot of something they too had watched?

∞

Con went back the first week in June 1916. The electrical treatment and massage were over; a final board had passed him. A temporary respite, an officers' course in Hampshire; and then the inevitable.

He went in the evening. The next day she was to be a helper at the War Fair in the Caledonian Market. She felt numbed, sick with worry already. Although often, staying in Kent or in Surrey, she'd heard the guns (had *had* to hear the guns), today in the London traffic – motor-cars, heavy engines, thrumming, jangling of horses' tackle, all the throb of a busy weekday – she heard them the most clearly of all: an inner ear that could not lie.

She worried about him all the time (should she not be doing the same for Theo, in Egypt now?); that he might be cold, hot, tired, dusty, thirsty and she not know; that away six months he would find too many changes. He had said he thought Eddie Straton was still his company commander. Shadowy Eddie: Cecil had not seemed particularly interested in him; talk of meeting him after his convalescence in the Highlands had come to nothing.

July. After three days at base hospital Bim Farquhar died of wounds. She went to console his wife who was expecting a baby at Christmas. News came of Marcus' death. Almost every night she would wake suddenly, and unable to get back to sleep she would be at once certain and comforted that somewhere Con needed her. All her senses alert, she hedged him round with her body, her loving care: I will, I *can* protect him. Only sometimes, lying in Cecil's arms – August was it or September? – she forgot him; betrayed him.

Just after Christmas he came on leave. He was odd, she thought; depressed probably. She could not reach him. He wasn't sleeping well he told her, almost irritably. Often he would go in to play the piano but twice when she went in there he was sitting, hands on his lap, looking at the keyboard.

'Are you all right?'

'Don't I look all right?' Of course, she said, yes, yes, of course.

Well then? Was there something odd about him? What had she meant? Could she not perhaps – just leave him alone?

She had come to Hill Street to be with him. Aunt Victoria, running a sewing circle and several other concerns, had little time to notice him. Theo was still her favourite. 'Well, that *is* a good idea,' was all she said when Muff told her they would be out at a concert, a theatre. But often Con would cry off at the last moment, going up to bed early, not even coming down to dinner.

On the last night but one, half-waking, she heard the opening, banging of the heavy lavatory door. It would not be Aunt Victoria. Without fully waking she listened for him to go back to his room.

After a while she got up. The lavatory was empty. The bathroom, next door, was shut. She tried the lock: Con's voice, muffled, said: 'One moment.'

'It's only me,' she said. He opened the door at once: 'I'm sorry.' When she came in she could smell sick. 'It's nothing – it's all right.' He leaned over the basin suddenly: 'I'm sorry,' he rinsed his mouth, 'I'm sorry, I didn't expect – I've just been in there.' Even in the thick Jaeger dressing-gown he looked cold, drained. The bathroom, vast domed with its geyser, its complicated array of pipes, struck chill. The bath had a huge mahogany rim nearly a foot wide: she sat down on it. After a moment he joined her. He was very hunched, his head bowed.

'What is it, darling?'

He didn't answer; a muscle in his face twitched, on and on. She watched it sadly. Every now and then he shivered.

Then, 'Oh Muff,' he said suddenly, turning to her, 'Oh Muff.' She put out her arms and he came into them, burying his head: it almost touched her breast. She could feel his heart beating. Above the smell of sick was the clean scent of his hair.

He sat up slowly.

'Is it – about going back?'

He shook his head. 'No. It's – I never thought of feeling nothing. I never thought of that. That it would be so terrible – nothing, not feeling. Not funk or wind up. Just nothing. It's all grey you see – the whole world.' His voice was very thick. 'I wish – ' He said flatly: 'It's all grey, everything's grey, or dark – some dark colour. Sometimes – it's as if I'm dead already.'

He turned to her again: 'So tired,' he said. 'So sad.'

She took his hand. They sat quite still on the bath's edge, holding hands. She wanted never to move; she felt still at one; the closeness when he had nearly wept in her arms. We should have touched more often, she thought afterwards. We should always have been touching.

'I wish,' he said slowly. 'Corrib – I get so homesick for it. Though I never did at school. If we could just go there, if I could just disappear, be part of the place – '

'We could go. If that's what you want – next time, your next leave.'

'Yes.' His hand in hers felt cold.

They could not stay there for ever. They would have to go back to bed. 'Will you be all right? We could sit in your room. Or play the piano – why don't you play the piano?'

'No,' he said, tight-lipped again. 'No, I'm all right.'

Then in the doorway he turned back to her suddenly: 'Oh Muff,' frightened, puzzled, blank, despairing: 'I only wanted to make music. That's all . . .'

The rest of the night she was haunted inexplicably, not by his face as it had just been, but by a memory of the young Con. Walking about, a velvety bat baby clinging to his hand. She had been so afraid. But enchanted, he walked everywhere with it: 'Look, Muff, it won't let go!' as it clung to him, and loved him.

Chapter 2

Polly thought: odd how I always manage to be late, for every-thing. Yet when it was to do with the 'B minor' rehearsals there she'd be: arriving sometimes even before the doors were open.

It was the nearest thing to being with Sam.

They'd been rehearsing for some months now. Their usual conductor, bald, fat and very jolly, was away for three weeks: his place had been taken by a very earnest young American. Up on the rostrum now, a slight figure in jeans and roll-top sweater, he was looking irritatedly at his watch.

There was a last straggle of latecomers. And then they were singing. They began with the *Credo*. Although she'd arrived before anyone else she couldn't find the page. They began badly and the conductor, already impatient because so many had been late, pulled a face, held up his hand. They began again.

Is Sam back? The question ran along underneath all the time. So vague: his 'sometime in April'. His coming back was the spring. That was what spring meant. The cherry tree in the garden, burst into a froth of pink, gave her hope; her voice, rising, rising.

When they all stopped, the traffic in the sudden silence seemed to shake the building. The conductor said resignedly: 'If we could just maybe – get this right. *Forte, fortissimo*, then,' his hand lifted, '*piano, piano*. Basses alone please.'

The elderly woman sitting beside her yawned very thoroughly so that Polly thought her jaw would click apart. She waited their turn. The tenors rose, and she fancied (and oh please God make the day come soon), almost heard the entry of the trumpets.

She stood up automatically but she'd lost her place again; coming in several bars late. Now they were being talked at again. 'Stress here on *resurrexit*. I guess we'd better all have the same stress. Else . . .'

Et ascendit in coelum. Then the door opened and, oh horror

of horrors, it was Peter creeping in. At first she wasn't sure –
he'd grown a beard, a Solzhenitsyn one (he *would*). It did
nothing for him.

In a gesture of survival she held her score high against her
face; then realizing that was more likely to single her out put
it down again.

She was safe now because he had his back to her: during
a pause he'd changed seats with the pianist. Thinking about
it, she was surprised that she'd managed to avoid him for so
long recently. From where she stood she could see his hands:
she hated the way he touched the keys.

She wondered if perhaps she could steal out before the end,
to be quite sure of avoiding him. They'd stopped singing for
a few moments. The conductor was puzzling over some comment a long-past conductor had marked into the score. 'I can't
figure this out – some kind of warning I guess . . .'

Sanctus, sanctus, sanctus. Too late to escape. She thought
too she'd been seen. The rehearsal came to an end – then a
few moments arranging for next week: 'Altos – I guess we'd
better have you in early. How about, say, twenty minutes?'

She'd gone fifteen yards down the road when he caught up
with her.

'Long time no see, I think,' he said, almost blocking her
way. Her trousers flapped in the breeze, she could feel her
hair blowing out either side. She felt like sending out arms,
legs flailing, a windmill to drive him far away. But he was
much too substantial. Already he'd taken her arm: 'I'm going
to get you a drink. Whistle-wetting needed after singing, *always*
– and accompanying too really, even half an hour. I definitely
need a snifter. Any particular rendezvous you'd like or *not* like
perhaps? Or shall you leave it to Uncle Peter?' Her arm was
held just under the elbow so that his fingers tickled her funny
bone. She hated his touch.

Handing her a drink, and he hadn't asked her what she
wanted, he said: 'And what are you *into* just now?'

She affected not to understand him. 'What do you mean –
"into"?'

He sipped his gin. 'Don't tell me you lead the quiet life. The
dull life. Come on, blow my mind with your revelations . . .'

145

She said in an offhand voice, barely concealing her irritation, 'I'm not going to blow any part of you.'

He looked shocked, quickly glancing around to see if anyone was listening. 'Naughty, naughty,' he said playfully. Even when he wasn't touching her, she felt from his look as if he were lifting one layer of skin, irritating a layer below.

He peered at her: 'What about another night out? Would you like me to take you to Carrier's? Stringalong territory of course, but – '

'Why should you want to take me out?' she said rudely. 'I didn't behave well before, I'm not behaving now. And I – '

'All these put downs,' he said. 'Is this the big brush off?'

Oh how I dislike you, she thought, letting the feeling grow and grow. Rejoicing, not minding. Accepting it. It was so positive that it assuaged the other lack.

'You come on like royalty, old style.'

'I'm sorry,' she said wearily. 'Let's just call it quits, shall we?' She launched at once into the topic of the 'B minor'; it was safe. Curling and uncurling her toes, she felt one clog fall to the floor. Pray God he didn't notice and do a Walter Raleigh-Prince Charming act. 'It's gone right out of my mind who's singing – the contralto I know I think, but – '

He reeled the names off.

'Trumpets,' she said casually.

It worked. He came out with the beloved's name; and – extra bonus – it appeared Sam was back.

She wanted to take that piece of knowledge home. 'And yours truly, harpsichord,' he said, 'possibly. Although that means I won't be able to see the luscious Morwen.'

She said with a sudden ray of hope: 'Do you fancy her then?'

'*Hardly*,' he said. 'I don't poach on other men's territory. It's your *father* to whom she's so immensely attractive.' He peered at her again. 'In fact, I'm not sure they don't have what used to be known as a love nest. I'm surprised you didn't know that – it's common knowledge. *Vulgar* knowledge one might say.'

'I'm not desperately interested,' she said.

On the way home: 'You're not upset,' he said, 'I hope?' He looked pleased.

'Not in the slightest. I just want to go home.'

146

His hand was on her arm again: 'You'll let Uncle Peter take you to Carrier's then? *Please.*' He put on his little boy expression. From that sort of beard a face of integrity should have peered. 'You will?'

'Oh shit,' she said, 'shit. Get lost – can't you?'

'Now tell me for the nineteenth time, am I forgiven, sweetie?' She had her spectacles on to read the menu, and looked distracted. '*At last* I've got Rodney to tell me what I said. I was absolutely *appalled.* Sweetie, it's no wonder I haven't been asked again, is it? And those other people – and that boy – I should absolutely *die* of shame if I met them. Everyone must be talking still. And Polly – '

'But it was ages ago,' Tessie said (what was it? three, four months? it seemed years). 'We never think about it,' she said exasperatedly. 'Just forget it, Camilla. Please.'

'Sweetie, how *could* I?' She looked shocked, reproachful, hurt. 'Doing a terrible thing like that to you. I just couldn't make myself into one of those hard sort of people – I've just gone on feeling absolutely *ghastly.* And Barney – what he must think . . . Sweetie, what does he *say* about it all?'

How to tell her that she never entered Barney's thoughts (except as an occasional irritant)? 'Thank God, with a clear conscience we need never invite her again,' he'd said – apropos of what? – as months ago now (oh glorious New Year) they'd sat, by appointment, in a restaurant. 'Thank God, yes, we are clear of Camilla.'

She'd said then, tartly: nervous still and flustered; 'That's surely not what you invited me out for. To say that.'

'Ah, no.' It had not been indeed. It had been so that he could deliver a statement, an ultimatum.

'The affair with Morwen,' he'd said. 'What we'd prefer – what I should like, is just to continue exactly as we have been. No questions asked – no reproaches.'

'Really?'

'Tessie, please.' He spoke sharply; precisely too, as if their time was limited, which it was.

'Do you visit her in the afternoons like a courtesan – and

147

then have to tear back to the City for the five o'clock meeting? No, but do tell me how you square it all with your work – '

'I was saying, before you interrupted – that is what would suit me. You may suit yourself, please yourself also of course. If anyone is interested in you, that is . . .'

The tables on either side were unoccupied. An expanse of white linen, hovering figures, hushed voices: only in this atmosphere of total correctitude – where a state of undress was unimaginable (leave alone tangled limbs) – only here could he talk to her in this preposterous fashion. She felt immediate, massive, cooped up indignation.

'How *dare* you talk to me like that?'

'What do you mean "dare"?' White cuff showing, hand crumbling bread. 'I think I can say what I please, where I please.'

But surely he had chosen a restaurant because there she could not touch him, because here words like 'cunt' and 'come' and 'you're no good at it' were not only unsuitable but unlikely. She could be asked to stop if she raised her voice. Nowhere at home would have been so safe. In bed least of all.

There had been a hiatus then while they were served with sweetbreads; mockingly not lovingly (how could it be?), he had chosen the same as her.

'You haven't finished what you were saying – '

That was all evidently. It appeared that the alternative was divorce. 'Either solution is perfectly agreeable to me.'

'Does she want to marry you then? Would she marry you?'

He didn't answer. 'A divorce would hardly be ideal,' he said. 'Polly would of course be little affected – Christopher is another matter. The more so since he's adopted.'

'What nonsense,' she said, 'I expect half his friends come from broken homes – '

'That doesn't mean those are the conditions one would want him to grow up in . . . And your religion – but that's scarcely relevant here. I suspect the remnants of it would hardly constitute a barrier . . .'

And so on. Circular conversation. She remembered it now as circular: reaching the coffee and having to take another turn. He had a grim, committed look. In anyone else she would have called it purposeful.

148

She had been asked simply to choose. He'd used the obvious formula, a gracious 'think it over, would you?'

There hadn't seemed to her to be any choice. Nor had she thought any differently in the months since. Both were humiliations. She'd found it unbearable to be trapped so formally.

He'd looked then at his watch: 'I'm glad,' he'd said, 'we've been able to discuss it so calmly. Such unfortunate things can be said in the heat of the moment – '

Now Camilla's voice, mouth full, pierced her thoughts: 'You never said, sweetie, you know if Barney was furious with me – I mean he *must* have been. I should think he's absolutely *splendid*, sweetie, when he's furious. I just can't imagine being angry with him though – that's why I can't believe I was so frightful . . .'

This greyness, this darkness since. Sadness. Where are all the unfaithful wives? Sad – because I don't even wish to set about it. Don't wish really to do anything – and that's a great sin, isn't it? The only sin. The noonday devil. I am in my noonday.

'What we suffer with our glands, sweetie – I know it was just glands. If men had any idea – honestly, sweetie, if you can imagine what it's like to do things, to *say* things so absolutely shaming – honestly so *frightful* . . .'

The noonday devil. I am in my noonday. Camilla at least had *felt*. When last had urgency driven her to do, say something never to be forgotten, for which she'd unreasonably ever after ask forgiveness: of God, of herself, of anybody?

∞

There was an elderly walnut-cased wireless fixed up in the kitchen, tuned permanently to the Forces/Light programme. Her mother had it on all day. *Music While You Work*, dance band programmes, Sandy Macpherson at the theatre organ. In that hot summer of 1947 the sounds floated from the open window: 'And when she's weary – women do get weary, wearing the same shabby dress – and when she's weary, try a little tenderness . . .' Whenever afterwards Tessie heard that tune it conjured up an image of her mother standing over the ironing-board (the pile of clothes never grew any less), pushing back with her wrist stray wisps of hair; she was almost completely

149

grey now. What was she wearing? In Tessie's memory they were just – clothes. Mostly shabby. Button-thro's with stretched buttonholes, skirts which had been let out and then pulled in again, unsuccessfully. There was a dirndl – bought for Tessie but rejected by her; she remembered that it had looked odd on her mother: not so much peasant as jumble sale.

And it was so hot. Mrs Braithwaite, scrubbing down the waiting-room, said: 'Oh aye, it's hot enough – it's that all right, *and* we'll pay for it . . .' But after the terrible winter everyone thought it was the least they should have.

She'd been home nearly sixteen months now. Ideas of taking School Cert. had gone: never deliberately scotched, just allowed to die, fade away. Now they were never mentioned. There was threatening talk of 'doing something' perhaps in the autumn; but she, and they too, had for the time being put it out of mind.

Mike had been in the Army since the end of April and was now in Catterick for six weeks with the RAC. He wrote quite often. At the end of August probably he would come home for two or three days. Later, after OCTU, if all went well, he would be home for longer. Philomena was arranging to go back to London, two years now after the War: the village had welcomed her, she said, she felt warmly towards it but, well, now it was time to go back. London was her adopted city; she spoke of all she would do, see, the friends she'd catch up with again. Now Mike's schooling was finished there was more money and so on. But her going, their going, didn't seem real to Tessie. Something would happen; she didn't need to think about it. It was not as if time, or place could separate her from Mike.

All that hot, hot month of August: Joseph, Dominic, Katy, Nicholas, Martin, pushing and fighting, spilling out of the twin pushchair, toddling and falling. Take them out for the long hot afternoons, armed with sticky sandwiches, dilute government orange, plums (not too many): get near a stream, let them try to dam it, look for sticklebacks. No, *never* swim in the beck. Sometimes they went as far as the moors. Quite an expedition. She would lie back and watch them, neck cricked in the heather, dreaming or reading. Joseph would wander too far off and she would pretend to be angry: at the farm they'd promised him a part in the bracken gathering – it had gone to his head. ('You don't know where *I'm* going soon!') Dominic, like a small bull, butted him continually.

She read *Wuthering Heights* twice through. Butterflies hovered, linnets trilled, larks sang, not in carbon copy but in confirmation. Her sense of time was lost. She knew herself to be, against the odds, about to be healed. She wondered why she had ever bothered with wanting to stay at the convent. Realizing that no one could touch her – nothing they said, or had said, or would say.

In bed at night – she often went early up to bed – it would still be light, the air still smelling of summer and heat. She left the curtains open: soon moths would flutter round the bedside light as darkness fell. She read till late often. Poetry. Emily Brontë again. Often missing the meaning, twisting it dreamily to suit herself. 'In summer's mellow midnight, A cloudless moon shone through Our open parlour window . . . The wanderer would not heed me; Its kiss grew warmer still. "Oh come!" it sighed so sweetly; "I'll win thee 'gainst thy will. *Were we not friends from childhood? Have I not loved thee long?"* ' . . .

Once, downstairs in the sitting-room alone, she heard a talk on the wireless, a lecture really. It was about Emily Brontë.

'. . . and almost certainly she would have heard talk of, more likely read of, Irish waifs, emigrants from the terrible famine of 1845. Branwell, visiting Liverpool, would have brought her back accounts of these little savages. The tongue no one could understand – Erse . . .'

Heathcliff was Irish. Celt, fey. This knowledge satisfied as she had never imagined anything would. Everything that summer fed her; it was as if the shock and upset of last year had existed only to bring about, to underline this coming of age, this flowering.

∽

Seventy-two hours' leave. He was due in the village about five: the train came from Richmond to York, then he'd get the local bus. As soon as he'd been in to see Philomena – he'd be up.

151

It was the evening surgery. The children were in the garden, swinging, riding pedal-cars; Nicholas could be seen poking plants with a stick. Tessie was washing up their tea things. A cottage pie was already in the oven; next she would stew the plums. She could hear a baby's high-pitched wail coming from the waiting-room – it wasn't a Fletcher cry. Her mother said: 'He's running late tonight.' She was folding a pile of rough-dried nappies. She removed a stray attached clothes peg: 'I'd hoped to get the meal over – I ought really to get down to the mending, I thought I'd do it with a play on the wireless – I do love a good play, Tessie.' The door banged behind her. Then a moment later her voice: 'Coo-*ee*! Someone to see you, Tessie!'

He was in uniform, battledress: she couldn't think why she hadn't pictured him like that. In his hand he carried a black beret; her eyes went straight to his highly polished buckles, the slides of brass on his belt. His hair, always short, was close-cropped now at the nape, standing up a little on top.

'Well?' He looked so hot: it reminded her of how the first days of the summer holidays he would rush up to see her: 'Oh Tessie – I'm so hot – I ran all the way . . .'

'Did you run all the way?' she asked now. He understood at once, pulling a face, laughing. Then letting his beret drop, pushing his hands out: 'Well – don't I get a kiss?'

She had an aunt who always said that. As she put her face forward awkwardly, her mother coming back in said: 'Tessie, you are hopeless. Do take Mike into the sitting-room.' She looked round the kitchen. 'I'll do the plums. Mike must have a sherry, darling.' She told Mike: 'John won't be a moment. He's just a baby to see now.'

It wasn't going right. It wasn't the reunion of her dreams. Already, sickeningly, she didn't know how, it had gone wrong. They sat, formally almost. He said again: 'Well?' And then, 'How's Patsy been?'

'She went to France on this scholarship thing. I told you.'

'You did. I'm an idiot. Nice for you though, without her.' There was silence for a moment then: 'You did a show?' she said, and 'Yes,' he said; and told her all about it. He'd been in charge of the dance routines, played the piano too: while he was telling her he seemed enthusiastic, eager, natural. 'And you? What about you? What's been happening to you, Tessie?'

How terrible; how do I tell the real person – here in the flesh – what I have been breathing, dreaming, all summer long? But she didn't have to answer because just then her father pushed open the door. 'Hallo there – welcome to the warrior!' Then, 'Has Tessie got you a drink?'

He flopped down in a chair almost at once. Mike said, 'What about you, sir? What would you like?'

'A whisky. The usual. Tessie'll get the water.' He looked over at Mike, 'Sure you don't want one? That sherry's terrible. Cyprus. I must say something – Peggy gets more and more distracted . . .'

They talked politics. She couldn't believe it afterwards. Some of it was about the National Health Service and how it would affect them all. Her father said he hadn't a lot of time for BMA politics. Mike asked was it true foreigners would all be rushing over to get their free false teeth and glasses? They spoke about all the poor people who'd had to buy their glasses at Woolworth's or use someone else's cast-off false teeth. Good and bad would come of it all.

Then her father got up. He said to Mike: 'Well, your mother – I expect she's got the fatted calf ready . . .' And Mike getting up too, said: 'I must go. I only looked in – '

She went with him to the door. 'Silly,' he said suddenly, digging her in the ribs. Then: 'Tomorrow morning I've promised to Ma – but in the afternoon let's go up to the farm. Or up onto the moors. You'll be able to get away?'

The weather will break, she thought. Indeed there was a shower, and in the early afternoon it was chilly almost. But because she was determined to, she wore her new cotton dress with the red and white stripes – although she wasn't quite sure about it: the stripes, banded in different directions, made her look fatter, a violent misdirected wasp. With it she wore some Clarks sandals which Patsy had discarded because they hurt her back.

On the walk up the weather changed, sun coming from behind the clouds, blazing. In the new sandals her feet rubbed, one of her toes blistering; but she didn't want to say anything. They were going to stay out till six or seven and had a picnic with them: jam sandwiches and a Thermos and some queen cakes made by Philomena.

153

He lay back in the hot sun, shirt sleeves rolled up, collar undone, arms above his head. 'Nice, these clothes, Tessie, after so much khaki.'

In the cut-out of memory, in the heather where she'd lain (how many times this summer?), he was the missing figure. The blank was filled now. And with that for the moment she must be content: I ask too much too soon, she thought. His leave was so short: there was scarcely time to be natural with each other. So tame your longing, she said to herself, and be patient, and everything shall be added unto you. For a start she had not prayed enough. Her mother, storming the gates of heaven for another child, had (God knows) been answered.

An aeroplane roared above them, dying into the distance so that it was like thunder in the hills beyond. She looked up at it idly; then fell to stroking his hair with a blade of grass. Nearby a sleepy bumble-bee tumbled from bell to bell of heather.

'It's all right, is it,' she said. 'The Army. Or are you longing to be an officer? Go on, say.'

The Thermos and their shared cup with its dregs lay on the heather beside them. 'Fine,' he said, 'yes, it's good. I like it, Tessie.' He lit a cigarette. His eyes crinkled up with the smoke: spirals of it went over his hair so that she could imagine it when it had gone grey. 'Tessie,' he said, 'there's something I ought to tell you – '

In the pause she went on stroking, tickling his hair with the blade of grass.

'I want to be a priest.'

For a few long seconds she went on automatically waving the blade of grass.

'Tessie – what do you think?' (This was what it was to be struck dumb. A lump from chest to throat to mouth.)

'Say something, Tessie. What is it – wouldn't I make a good one?' In a voice almost frightened he said, 'I thought you were going to laugh.'

She said shakily, deliberately casting around for the right, the safe language. 'Regular or secular?'

'Heavens, you make it sound – I don't know. I hadn't really decided, Tessie. I shan't I think try to go back to Ampleforth.

154

I'm still a bit odd, a bit uncertain about it. Not about being one – I'm sure of that. I mean about *telling* people.'

Her voice which she could hear sounded very odd: not her own. 'Tell me all about it.'

He blew smoke up into the air, curling patterns: 'You sound like a doctor, Tessie darling. After all these years,' he said affectionately, 'some of it rubbing off on you. But I'm not ill at all – awfully happy really. But sad too, in a human way. If you understand – '

She wanted to say, I don't; but knew that she did. She cursed the ready understanding that came from her background.

'You never said anything before. Is it something new?'

'No. Not really.' He paused. 'I didn't say – it wasn't anyone's business but mine then. When I was about fourteen, fifteen. It came and went, sometimes very strong. But at that age . . . Of course I could be wrong now, have it all wrong. You know what it is with vocations.'

'When shall you go?' she asked in a tight voice.

'When I get out of the Army – I *think*.' He had turned his head away a little. His cigarette was finished and propping himself on an elbow he stubbed it out in the packet.

'Have you told your mother?'

'Mm. Last night – '

'How did she take it?'

'She's – well she's proud of course, though I mean she's upset, as who wouldn't be, but she said in a way it's what she'd always hoped for. In a way. The honour.' He added a little uneasily: 'That's what she said anyway – '

And well she might, Tessie thought, well she might since she will never lose you. You won't be hers but you won't be anyone else's either. She'll have you *and* she'll have sacrificed you.

'A hundredfold,' she said into the chilling air.

'Sheep,' he said in a false light voice, 'talking about sheep – Just look at the amount of wool that's got caught round here – remember, Tessie, how we used to collect it and wash it and sell it to Ma for her bad feet? Mercenary pair – though I think it was *my* idea. The original wide boy, Tessie.' He turned to her. 'Maybe I'd have come to a bad end. Perhaps it's just as well.'

She could feel his face questioning, half-amused, not quite sure. She didn't answer but just looked straight ahead of her.

'Oh well,' he said, 'now I've told you.' They lay without talking. It was as if he were waiting. She reached out for his hand and for a while they lay hands held; then she placed her head, as so often, in the crook of his arm.

'I *am* happy,' he said. 'You mustn't think, you mustn't worry – '

But you *can't* be happy, she thought: not when you have hurt me beyond reckoning, beyond remedy.

She ran her fingers idly down his chest, then her hand moved for her and came to rest lightly between his thighs; in a second it seemed, he grew beneath her touch. It was unbelievable to flower so rapidly, so beautifully: in a terror of delight she felt the hard heat.

She couldn't move her hand. She thought afterwards that she would never of her own free will have been able to. He moved it away for her. Then he said in an odd voice, 'Do you think that's really fair, Tessie?'

She turned her head so that she couldn't see him. Her sense of loss: she felt that she had fallen not one step, or two, but down some cliff, some ravine, to bottomless depths.

'It's all right,' he said. 'I didn't mean. Look, Tessie – '

Her mouth tasted of metal; she swallowed, it was full of silver, lead, iron. Getting up suddenly she rammed the Thermos into the haversack, then taking it out again, opened it and splashed the dregs out onto the heather. There were three of Philomena's cakes left. She trod them into the ground.

'I know all about it,' she said. 'You only got this idea because – it puts you in the clear, doesn't it, you don't have to do it so no one can say you can't – ' She had never before had such a weapon, so big, so clumsy. She terrified herself, shouting: 'You're not interested, not in a *real* way, it's a sort of "book" sacrifice, it's something you read about. You just don't know, because if you knew – you don't have any passion, you're just brotherly and sing silly songs and dance about, why don't you go on the stage? All stage people are pansies, often they are, I know they are. It's worse, it's worse you've no *passion* in you – '

156

She went on and on. She couldn't imagine stopping. He had gone very white.

On the way home they didn't speak at all. Near the house Joseph and Dominic came out to meet them. Joseph had cut his knee: too big for a plaster. He showed off a bandage proudly. 'Look, the blood's *still* coming through . . .'

Mike said, 'Tessie, if you want, you know – I could come over after Mass. Or you could come – '

'No *thank* you,' she said. He said nothing. He came into the house. With the children, with her mother, he was perfectly contained, relaxed, so that she wanted to cry out, take it back, undo everything: feeling already, fearing, that she could never, would never touch him again.

She heard him say, 'Goodbye, Tessie.' She looked up from fastening Dominic's sandal, but he had already gone.

Next morning she had a sick headache and by lunchtime a temperature. It was a virus it seemed, a summer 'flu; it was to be hoped the little ones wouldn't catch it. Too much for her mother, running up and down so: 'Please leave me alone. I'll be all right. Please.' She was a wounded animal, just wanting to lie in the shade and get better. 'Tell anyone I can't see them.'

Afterwards she was unable to ask if he'd been round. Her mother said later, 'You hardly saw anything of Mike on his leave . . .'

She meant to go and see Philomena, or rather she told herself that she meant to. By October she was at the Marchants; when she came home for the first Christmas Philomena had already moved back to London. Mike wrote sometime in the November. He had sent two postcards earlier which she'd ignored. It was a stiff letter in many ways: so deliberately cheerful, so full of news. He asked for *her* news. 'You know I care what happens to you.' She thought he must have had trouble in writing that. But she never answered. Nor the two or three letters that followed. Years later she received an ordination invitation sent on through her mother. But she was already married then, and expecting Polly. She ignored it.

Saturday breakfast. Polly couldn't think what she was doing up so early, unless it was the postman's ring. A birthday present, three days late, for her mother – from her sister Patsy. A crystal glass (broken). Her father, raising his eyebrows, had said, 'Don't we have enough glass?'

Looking at him, she thought perversely: well done. Thinking suddenly, as she'd done a lot these past few days, about his affair with Morwen. Well done.

He didn't see her looking; he was deep in *The Times*. Her mother was smoking, reading the letter from Patsy (smoke, smoke, smoke). Christopher wouldn't be down for ages: passing his door after midnight she'd heard his engines going round the bend; his voice said: 'The train now coming into platform four is the six-fifty for Nether Wallop . . .'

What does *she* think about it all? she wondered. If she knows, that is. Camilla's outburst that night (middle-aged ramblings of someone pissed out of her mind – that's how I saw it) must have been about that. And if she knows does he know that she knows? (Does he know that I know?)

Here we sit: vintage marmalade, crisp bacon, Grapenuts, smell of coffee percolating: round the round table. A family circle. And what's being done about it all? Most likely everything's to go on as before. Enough in its way to make one puke. Their madness was ever to get married.

I'd like to bang, crash down on the breakfast table, shatter the crockery; shatter the clichés. ('Another spring day, thank God. By the way, I shan't be in till quite late.' 'All right – what do you want me to do about the Lennoxes?' 'Answer their invitation I should think . . .') She could shatter them of course most easily with her tongue: 'Well, Daddy, is Morwen a good fuck – do *say* . . .'

Her mother had got up from the table. Polly was moved suddenly by the bruised, shadowed look of her face. I'm older than her, she thought. Then: what a mess, what a mess she's made of it all.

'Shall I clear that glass for you?' she said. 'Straight in the bin?' The present had rested in crumpled newspaper. She picked the whole lot up. The paper was *The Scotsman*. She straightened a few pages, looked them over idly: some book reviews, the Edinburgh cinemas, theatres; concerts.

It couldn't be, it couldn't be. Except that it was. A 'B minor Mass' next Saturday. Who cares who, as soprano, contralto, tenor, bass? But there (trumpet), the magic name, Zossenheim.

It was a long way to go – but not difficult to arrange. She got on with her aunt well and found her easy to talk to. She liked Hamish too, and her small cousins (Patsy had married quite late). Twice a year at least she went up there to stay.

'. . . exam fever seems to have got hold of me,' she wrote. 'It would be such a change. So if you're sure it's all right? . . . PS. Someone I know is playing in a concert . . .'

Crazy of course – but it just *seemed* more hopeful. In a foreign country wouldn't she be a familiar face? And then? And then . . .

The Saturday was a blowy day: an icy wind came off the Forth. The sky was uniformly grey. In the afternoon she took the children up to Princes Street Gardens. Calum had seen a rabbit there on New Year's Day: 'I did! I did!' It appeared that during the buttressing of the Castle a warren had been disturbed. She thought, all the time, that she couldn't live until seven-thirty in the evening.

Patsy said: 'It's terrific your liking that sort of music. I'm tone deaf – Tessie was rather hopeless too though she used to sing pop songs with this boy – Mike, what was it? She had a voice like a dying corncrake.'

And then the concert itself. It was possible never to take her eyes off him (next month when she sang, it wouldn't be so). Then afterwards, pushing her way straight up to where he was standing, talking to the second trumpeter. 'Hi,' she said, trying to make it sound natural. 'Look who's here.' Her hands in her coat pockets were damp with sweat.

'You!' He looked genuinely surprised. Almost but not quite pleased. 'What are you doing up here?'

159

'Staying with my aunt, till Wednesday – I got quite a shock when I saw you out there. I – ' But what had she been going to say?

The second trumpeter was looking at her all the while. She could feel his gaze. He said suddenly: 'But this is great. We're just away to drink at Andy's. Will you join us then?' He waited confidently for her reply, saying: 'That's Andy,' pointing to a bearded man who'd played the flute.

Sam hadn't spoken. She was unable to look at him and fixed her gaze on the second trumpeter. 'I'm Finlay,' he said, 'by the way.'

'Polly,' she said. 'I'm Polly. And I'd love to come.'

Andy's flat was in Stockbridge. Sexy-Coburg Street, he said. They all got into one car: Sam in the front with Andy, while she and Finlay sat at the back. Very soon after they'd arrived some more people came up the stairs: another man, small with glasses, and two rather plump girls, twins, with flaming red hair. She found herself sitting the other side of the room from Sam: once as he passed to get his beer mug filled, he said: 'How's the project?' She had only to reach out to touch him, but he didn't stop for an answer. From the general conversation she learned that Finlay and Andy knew him from several years back. They'd all been at the same summer school in Switzerland. 'The only bloke who could spout two of the lingos – not counting our own . . .'.

Finlay had the idea they should all go to a disco. They went in two cars because his wouldn't fit seven, and they stopped off at Finlay's place and Sam's hotel so that they could get out of their penguin outfits.

Strobe lights flashing, warmth, womb, deafening mind-obliterating sound, oh comforting known scene. Sam was dancing with one of the twins – she couldn't tell one from the other – she had Finlay. He had a round amused head which he nodded a lot. When they were sitting out drinking, he asked her where she stayed? What part of London? He came down quite often, he said . . .

But then at last, at last – she was with him: he had really asked her; she was alone with him and only perhaps a hundred other bodies, twisting, shaking, jerking. Her hair flew every-where: she was near him, far, near him again.

160

'What sick lyrics these,' he said, his head close to her ears. ' "See my baby die . . ." '

'Silly,' she said easily. ' "See my baby *jive*." It's an oldie, rock.' Her heart was suddenly riven: his mistake making him so vulnerable. But he didn't laugh at himself as almost anyone she liked would have done, but said almost earnestly: 'It's all that trumpet blasting – my hearing done in . . .'

Here was where the noise was: Rolling Stones now. 'Jumpin' Jack Flash', 'Honky Tonk Women' . . . Then it was old again, Buddy Holly: 'Every day it's a getting closer . . .' The music went on. No one now was changing partners. Her eyes, her mascara ran a little, smarting in the smoky dark.

Why should the night ever end? More old tunes now: 'Like a bridge over troubled water . . .', *'Eine Feste Burg ist unser Gott'* and suddenly into her head in joyous counterpoint, running strongly underneath, Bach: *'Und wenn die Welt voll Teufel wär, und wollten uns verschlingen . . .'* All those trumpets rising, rising; so that she hardly knew where she was.

Oh Bach and Garfunkel how gloriously are you one, oh such happiness on whisky and lemonade. I drank only a little but I am heady, on fire.

They were pushed so close together that she thought she would die from happiness and desire. How to tell one from the other? Her heart breaking, about to break, she thought, she said below the music, 'I love you, I love you . . .' *'So fürchten wir uns nicht so sehr, es soll uns doch gelingen.'* 'I love, I love you . . .'

Con lasted a full eight weeks; till two days before her birthday. The telegram told her little, but Eddie as his company commander wrote. He had been with him. Con had been shot through the heart: the place of his body was marked, but when they had come back it was missing. He himself was writing from hospital.

Expected, awaited – and utterly unbelievable. Impossible. For days she felt separated completely from her body, walking about, feeling nothing: a lack of sensation such as he himself had complained of. Her mouth all the time had a taste of death or dust, an ashy taste, flavour: she kept rinsing it frantically, fanatically trying to swill away the reality.

Cecil came on leave. He comforted her. A pity, he said, that Con had refused a new portrait: if she liked he could get someone good to paint him from one of the studio photographs. 'As large as you like – say how large you want it.' But she refused. It was the Con of childhood, the young Con, the private Con whom she wanted. She moved to their bedroom the portrait of 1909, painted at Corrib. Con in semi-profile (he'd had to be very still that summer: he'd told her that all the while in his head he'd been playing a Mozart sonata).

Inevitably she tried to get more news. But when she'd had letters also from his colonel, his servant, and two fellow officers, she knew there was no more to come. Cecil, contacting Eddie, found that although he was physically better his nervous state was such that he was now in a special hospital in Edinburgh. Calculatingly, despairingly, she thought of some friends living up there, in the New Town. She went to spend a week with them and got in touch with Eddie. He was well enough it seemed to come over to tea.

In an abstract way she noticed that he was very good looking – Cecil had pointed him out earlier in a photograph of fellow wet bobs, c. 1908. He was better looking than the picture. At the same time she saw that her visit was hopeless. She had come up for nothing. Wooden, stiff in demeanour as if holding himself precariously together, he answered her questions mechanically, looking away from her. She knew it was wrong to press him, and did so; looking for assurance that 'shot through the heart' was not the euphemism it so often was.

They discussed the Scottish climate. (The last person Con had seen on earth: the last to have seen him.) Removing the cover from a dish of muffins, she said that in the south the spring had already arrived. He said politely that Con had invited him to stay at Corrib. How nice, awfully nice, they both said. They spoke a little of Cecil. When he did look at her, he seemed not to be seeing her but to be gazing obliquely at some distant object. He had a nervous tic which each time it came altered his looks.

That night after seeing him, she dreamed of Corrib. Bats outside screamed, crying to be let in: it was dusk and their bodies banged and swayed against the glass of her bedroom window. Swooping, despairing.

Chapter 4

'She comes for me,' he said, 'almost when I touch her – '

'That's her good fortune,' she said, 'isn't it? Lucky Morwen.'

'It's my good fortune certainly . . .'

Barney was sitting on the velvet chair in the bedroom, his hands behind his head. Half lying, half sitting in the bed, she felt the conversation had been going on for months, not minutes. She couldn't think how it had started, why even he had come upstairs so early.

'I hope it doesn't make her over-fertile,' she said nastily. 'You can't want that.'

'Where do you get that rubbish from? It sounds like Sandy. Lore of the old fishwives . . .' He looked across at her: 'Didn't we have her to thank for that idea about buggery? A Russian sailor told her, or some such nonsense. It always worked I remember. A baby nine months later. I'm tired of having her half-baked opinions in the bedroom – in any case something even more dramatic would be needed for your barrenness.'

'Take it easy.' She was angry for Sandy. 'I did have Polly – '

'One wasn't at fault oneself,' he said. 'At least we proved that.'

'You're never at fault,' she said tiredly. 'About anything.'

And indeed about that he had not been at all in the wrong. It had been her, entirely. Fertility and pleasure weren't linked. But to fail at both? She thought with a dry tiredness of all those years of effort, of hope. Theory learned, theory applied. The cold voice of Barney: 'What was I meant to do now? Ah – and if *that* doesn't work? Quicker, slower, more to the right? Such detail *cannot* be necessary . . .' And in lighter mood: ' "Teach yourself sex" – but that can only be for solitary achievements. It should be "Teach yourselves". . .' Impatient though still, and she impatient in her despair. It was as if, stir the mixture how she might, some magic ingredient was missing. The years had slipped by. Surely, in this world of split knickers and vibrators and psychedelic sheaths, it was possible to do a little better?

'Why don't you have a baby by her?' she said. 'Why not go ahead and do something irrevocable for a change?'

'That's *enough*. It would hardly help her career – if you're really so concerned.' He leaned forward. He was grey with fatigue: she had forgotten how easily and suddenly he tired. She said angrily, 'Any sensible girl would want your baby.'

He said drily: 'That wasn't the point at issue.' Half smiling: 'At issue indeed. Word play not intentional.' He got up.

'Are you coming to bed already?'

'Any objections?' he said coldly. He went through to the dressing-room. When he came back his face was set, still grey. She'd been flipping through a magazine he'd left in the bathroom. Now with a sudden gesture he knocked it out of her hand, then leaning over pulled off the light switch.

'Thank you,' she said, 'thank you.' She slid down into the bed. She saw then as her eyes grew accustomed to the semi-darkness that he was sitting up. She could hear only his tense breathing. Raising herself again, she brushed against his thigh – flesh so cold that it burned. She moved away.

'What is it you want?'

'Me? I don't want anything,' she said. 'It was you pulled at the light switch.'

'It's ridiculous, the whole thing. What *do* you want?'

'It's certainly rude, pulling off the switch – and all that baiting earlier. None of that was necessary – '

He put a hand across her mouth. Then, as he took it away again, she said, 'If something's the matter you could say, instead of taking it out on me. I'm going downstairs, out anywhere.'

Turning, moving as suddenly again, he buried his face, cold-nosed as an animal, burrowing between her breasts. He lay on them, very still. She felt unable to move, her hair right over her face, her body weighed down by his: as they touched he grew gradually warm.

After a great while, his hands moving, cool tipped, touched her, sought.

'Now for one of my failures,' he said.

∞

165

A London wedding: Margaret Willingham's idea. Nothing about the elastic Fletcher house – overrun with children, and smaller than the one Tessie had been brought up in – suggested that it would be a suitable venue.

So many arrangements. She remembered Camilla's wedding and the frenzied behind the scenes preparations. Why could one not simply get married? Lists, lists, lists: luncheons, conferences, telephone calls to her harassed mother. ('Let Margaret Willingham decide, Tessie. I'm sure she knows best . . .') Snowed under mountains of paper, she forgot that she had ever said 'I have come home.' Barney, she scarcely saw at all.

But it was after all a success. St James's, Spanish Place, in the July sunshine. And the same alchemy that had made a beauty of her last year was here now: everything she did or said or looked was right. She floated on champagne.

Camilla, sans Rodney, bore down on her suddenly. 'Just a moment, sweetie, while you're alone. He's absolutely *gorgeous* – didn't I keep saying someone quite wonderful will come and sweep you off your feet – you can see he's suffered.' Her face, pop-eyed, came up close: 'How any girl *could* . . .'

Everyone had studiously avoided mentioning Anthea. Muff – and she must remember to call her that – had referred to her only once during the preparations: ('It's not, Barney, as if we have to fear a repetition of *last* time'), so that Tessie wondered if she'd been chosen, as chosen she surely had been, just because she would not run away.

It was only later when the reception was nearly over and she felt suddenly tired, that she noticed he was tired too. Grey with exhaustion. For him, it had all happened before.

They were to stay the night at Claridge's even though they had their own house. He preferred it that way, he said. He ate little of the meal. Fatigue, washing him of what little colour he had, gave him a curious beauty.

Camilla, just back in England, had chosen Tessie's going-away nightdress and negligee for her: when Muff had tried to shop with her she'd had to say, 'Oh, but I have that.' The nightdress was an odd pink shade in frothy frilly nylon; the negligee was covered in blobs of a paler pink. She would have liked something with lace, lace insets perhaps: she would have liked to have chosen for herself. Upstairs now in the big room,

waiting for Barney, she'd grown cold, shivery – although the
air was warm, the night warm.

What happened? What went wrong? What did I do wrong?
All those tales she had heard: grooms coming drunk to their
wedding bed, falling across it in an alcoholic stupor, asleep.
Only what was this? 'Such utter, absolute, unbelievable exhaustion,' he was saying, then a moment later: 'what a panto-
mime. I can't think why one puts up with it. A society
wedding . . .'

He was beautiful; it was to have been so beautiful. Some
discovery would be made, a journey through uncharted territory: 'Tessie, you're so lovely, those breasts, your breasts – and
this, oh *this*, but this is the best of all, what do you call it,
what shall I call it, Tessie?'

'So tired,' he said, 'damn it. So sleepy, darling, I had thought,
if one . . .'

It was an instant and complete falling into sleep. She lay
awake, for how many hours? He smelled clean and sweet;
breathing deeply and gently, as if placed there by nanny. The
early morning traffic started up and still she was awake. Then
gradually she felt herself go. She could only have been a
little while asleep, was still sodden with it, when he woke her:
she thought at first, half in a dream, that she was trapped
somewhere, in the sea, in a lake, struggling among thick weeds.
In her dream she gave up; I will drown, she thought, what else,
why ever not? and at that moment woke. Very soon after,
prodded, pressed, rubbed, mute with pain, she had been entered,
the city taken, the castle beseiged. 'Tell me if it hurts,' he said.

'I'm sorry,' he said later. 'One can't really expect much
enjoyment without experience.' He was collecting his shaving
tackle. 'We shall do better in Ireland no doubt. Do you want
the bathroom first?'

No one had asked her where she would like to spend the
honeymoon. She would have liked to go to Greece; or failing
that, Italy. She couldn't remember a discussion, only an an-
nouncement: 'Mama has most efficiently laid on three weeks
in Connemara.' To her own family, the wedding already taken
out of their hands, she said, 'We shan't need to bother with

167

hotels or abroad or anything, Barney's uncle has this house . . .'

It was a surprise then to find Ireland so lovely. After staying three days with friends in Dalkey they had driven west, stopping over at Tullamore and coming through the mountains to Lough Corrib late in the afternoon.

The house stood on a rise above the lake. It was whitewashed; around it hydrangea bushes. Otherwise the garden had run wild; purple clematis trailing. Long wet grass fringed a brook running at the bottom. What had once been a walled tennis court was overgrown.

She didn't like it; couldn't like it. It was nothing she could exactly define. Something about the dark twisting passages, sudden unexpected rooms. Barney had stayed here often as a boy, she realized; certainly up till the War. But the house, welcoming him, wanting him maybe, didn't want her: that was how she translated her unease. Yet the house was let regularly: people came for the fishing, the duck shooting – they wrote in the visitors' book about their luck. The loud voices of uncaring strangers should by now have exorcized, even neutralized the place.

But it had not been so. Suddenly down a corridor she would come upon some water-colours, wishy-washy, faded attempts at capturing Corrib – *failures* to capture Corrib – all dating from the turn of the century. Bound copies of the *Badminton* magazine in glass-fronted cupboards; and around the walls, groups: Oxford, Winchester; 1909, 1911, 1914. Odd, forgotten ghosts.

And the bats. How she hated the bats which swooping, exultant, woke up each dusk to haunt the corridors. There was the ruin of the big house too: a cracked faded hulk, chipped paint, falling masonry. The dower house had once been in its happy shadow. Now from the windows at the back, she could see its burnt out corpse. When they'd first arrived she'd feared some family retainer who would bear down on her with memories of Master Theo, Miss Margaret, Master Con. But Nora and Tim, tenants of the farm nearby and caretakers of the house, were only in their early thirties; Barney remembered Tim as a boy but that was all.

The bedroom was the only room she liked. From its window she could see fifteen, twenty islands, seeming to float on the lake: the watery green, the shadowy purple, mauve haze of the mountains indistinguishable in the mist, the gentle light of outside. Leaning on the sill, gazing and gazing, she would be suddenly full of hope.

Not that it got any better. Nothing stirred in her; it was as if a stranger touched her. He didn't want to discuss it. She never wondered if he felt a failure, or wondered what he felt at all; she was wrapped in her own sense of doom, as if she'd lost her way, or was heading for death. She blamed it on the house and its atmosphere. She blamed the bats. When Barney drove her around, passing where the slabs of peat had been cut and stacked by the roadside, the great squares were like tombs.

What to do in the house all day, all night? The place was to large to be cosy, too small to be gracious. By day they were seldom in it. There was the lake to bathe in, to row on – she would have liked to swim at night but Barney, disapproving, said they might be noticed. The weather was good and sometimes they sat out in the sun at the white cast-iron table above the lake. She tried to sketch. In the evenings the trout rose for Barney. He was angry that he'd forgotten to bring his gun and thought of buying another. When it was not so fine they went for excursions: to Galway, to Clifden; they took the turf boat to Inishmore and spent the night there.

Once they went to dinner with some people who'd known Muff and the family in the old days. They called her Margaret. In Barney they saw something of Theo. How beautiful Margaret had been; she had kept her beauty. The old grandmother, eighty-six, said: 'If you could only have seen them – Emily's two youngest. The one so fair and the other so dark – ' Con had been such a beautiful child, but 'a little disappointing grown up, wouldn't you say? A fine looking boy, *but . . .*'

She bought presents for all the family and for the Marchants. 'Buy anything you want,' Barney said. She bought them all bog oak crosses and lucky leprechauns. She didn't want to buy Patsy anything at all so she chose for her the most expensive gift: book-ends in green-veined Connemara marble.

On their last day it was misty and drizzling in the morning. Nora was told they would be out till late. They drove around, stopping for Barney to pore over the map. But by two or three there was a brilliant washed sun; they were near the coast and spent the afternoon swimming and sunbathing on the near-deserted beach. A family of four boys came and built a tunnel in the sand. There were hoppers everywhere. She sat up on her elbow watching them, listening to the sound of the Atlantic. They left late, after the boys, only just clearing up before the tide came in. They drove inland looking for a hotel: hungry, almost happy, they ate T-bone steaks with an egg on top, brown soda bread. Barney said during the meal that he missed music; he found it hard to imagine, he said, more than a given time without it. He was singing in the *Missa Solemnis* in the autumn: it was possible he might have a solo.

They drove back leisurely. 'Tessie, it's been rather good.' Then, still twenty-five, thirty miles away, passing the lighted half-open door of a pub: 'Shall we? I *think* so – '

They hadn't been drinking locally. Too much notice was taken of them. Tessie was looked up and down. But here in this crowded pub it was different; in the murky light, the smoke, they could have been anybody. Barney, tanned, a scarf at his neck, looked relaxed. She felt suddenly close to him. A group of women in one corner looked him over as he went up for the drinks, passing remarks, nodding approvingly.

A man was playing the accordion. When he stopped, a girl with a great mane of blue-black hair stood up and sang a song about the Boyne, in a nasal high-pitched pressing voice. Barney said: 'Those are fighting words.' But the feeling was happy. Afterwards she sang: 'No, nay never, no nay never no more – will I play the wild rover . . .' Everyone joined in. Even Barney. Even Tessie. Gaiety grew: a red-faced man, working through the crowd, called out: 'Is there anyone here at all will give us a song?' He touched people, touched Tessie: 'Will you give us a song now? Give us a song?' To Barney.

A young boy with a crooked face and great fringed eyes went up on the dais. 'Where's your mammy?' shouted an old woman. He sang 'The Beggar Man'; then, 'What's it to be now?' ' "O'Reilly's Daughter"!' someone called.

They all joined in the chorus, 'banging on the old bass drum', clapping, swaying as they sang of the one-eyed Reilly. She was warm: the air thick, heady; not sleepy, but alive, relaxed. She was off her guard; that was the only explanation.

'What's it to be now?'

' "I Know My Love",' called out an old man. A voice cut in with ' "The Lowlands of Holland"!' The old man said again, ' "I Know My Love"!'

The boy sang: 'I know my love by his way of walking, I know my love by his way of talking, I know my love in his suit of blue – and if my love leaves me what will I do?' There were three verses that the boy knew, and three times through with the chorus, and once more for luck. Linking arms, Barney swaying against her; a stranger on the other side. Here in the smoke, the companionship, all was possible, all the worlds would merge.

'And still she cried, I love him the best! And a troubled mind, sure it knows no rest. And still she cried, bonny boys are few! And if my love leaves me, *what will I do*?'

Outside: 'Did you enjoy yourself now?' a man asked her, shaking her hand, shaking Barney's. Surprisingly it was midnight already, everyone spilling out. 'Come again,' he said to them, 'come again. Come again so.'

'Come' was a slang word. Back at the house again, downstairs, he took her in his arms, before the turf fire. He had revived it and smoke rose with a sweet smell. There was no other light in the room. 'Our home,' he said.

That which had awoken with the boy's voice remained now. It will be all right, she told herself, certainly now it will be all right. All that, Mike, everything, that is in the past. The mistakes I made, the nuns made, this is a new life. Me reborn, a second birth.

But two hours later, lying awake in the bed, her body burning: such tension, such disbelief. Mistaking her cry of pain, he had said: 'But that was splendid.' Laughing, encouraged: 'Tessie, one has *arrived* . . .'

In the room next to theirs there were twin beds a little apart, covered with dark patterned Indian bedspreads. In her dream Mike and she sat opposite each other. He hadn't changed at all, and she was seized with such happiness and relief: 'You haven't changed at all!' she said. He smiled and said calmly: 'Why ever should I?' He was so near that pushing her foot

171

out she could touch his. He was impossibly desirable. 'Then it's going to be all right? Will it be all right?' He nodded. Coming forward, flying forward, legs widening, widening, she was on to his knees, 'I *knew* it would be all right,' sobbing her fierce excitement, her arms almost breaking, clasping him, urging him higher and higher, deeper and deeper. 'Of course it's all right,' he said, as flooding painful delight she knew she was about to die.

She woke as the waves receded: unbelieving, horrified, querying this stranger beside her. Her arms were tired, aching, stretched as if she'd forced open a door, carried some enormous weight. She lay a long time without moving, desolate.

Then she got up, the first one up, and began to pack. The honeymoon was over.

Chapter 5

The sunlight teasing her, played on her bones: warming her even through the glass of the windows. Oddly uneasy, restless – she must *do* something – she waited with irritation for her breakfast tray.

'Order me a taxi for eleven, Teresa.' Hauteur masked her frantic impatience: 'Is Christopher about? I should like to take Christopher with me.' He'd gone round to see a friend; evidently he'd been up since seven. 'Fetch him back then, please. And leave a message at Hatter's. Polly must lunch with us.'

She would go to Harrods. There she could rest if sudden exhaustion came. She knew too exactly where the lavatories were.

Now already here she was. Christopher (perhaps he had had other, simpler, end of holidays plans?) washed, combed, suited; she was proud of him here in the Beauty Hall, walking amongst the creams and lipsticks and false eyelashes and promises of disappearing wrinkles.

Taking Barney out. Ah, but that had been tedious, fitting him out for school. Thin and querulous, inclined to yellowish-green after journeys, he would stand, shoulders sagging (at least later the Army had made a better looking specimen of him), although what had she cared anyway – since it was the wrong school? (Cecil's sudden confident obstinacy. 'He's already down . . .' 'It's not too late to change,' she'd suggested. He, Cecil, balding, a little stouter now: 'Why ever should it be changed?' And of course it wasn't. It had been some distant cousins, not Barney who, "strat" doffed, had walked daily through War Cloisters, seeing but not noticing: leaping from the stone, his name, Francis Conran Gore-Lewis . . .)

Christopher walked at her pace. 'Have they got wigs in here? One of the chap's sisters has a blonde bubble. I tried it on.' She thought he was going to pick up one of the creams and put out a hand to stop him. Her eye caught some lotion. The shape of the bottle, the black, the gold, something about

173

the packaging decided her, although it was unlike her to buy without first sniffing. The girl who was very pretty said: 'It's new. We've just got it in. It's absolutely fabulous.'

Handing it to be wrapped, looking for her account card: 'Good – *perhaps*,' she said. 'But new? I hardly think so.' She thought suddenly of the years of slapping and prodding, massaging, chinstraps – had she worn even those? – masks, depilatories, waxing. The in-between years when she had feared her easy beauty might be fading. I needn't have bothered, she thought now, feeling a sudden panic amidst the scents and colognes. Decor on decay. My own, everybody's. Receiving the package and moving on she could feel her earlier mood disperse. A very little time, and I shall be dead. (And what then?)

'I shall buy you a present,' she announced to Christopher. 'You've been most patient.' She offered him sweets first but he chose nuts, cashews, eating them there and then. She said nothing. It was for Teresa to teach him manners. He wanted then to go up to the zoo – someone had said there was a bush baby. They could buy some fruit for it: 'Though you're not meant to feed them of course, I think,' he said solemnly.

He could be sent up there while she went to the lavatory. She went always to the marbled, ornate (and surely original?) ladies' cloakroom. There she felt safe. She had for years now this recurrent fantasy of dying in a lavatory: the ultimate indignity. But if it must be – then here (and practical, humorous thought almost: where better than Harrods? A place where the whole process of dying – undertaking, funeral – could be attended to on the premises. Charged posthumously).

When out these days she rarely saw people that she knew – so many dead, so many bedridden. She thought now that she saw Patricia Palimpsest, moved her stick slightly, then thought, I'm not sure that it is. And – what if it is anyway? I never liked her when we were younger.

Polly was late, rushing in breathless. 'Sorry, Muff darling.' Kissing her, smelling of patchouli. Looking tired too, as always these days (but with more excuse than Teresa). Examinations probably. Watching her pick at her food, some salad only, she thought: I see her already, a bird released from a cage,

174

soaring away, out, out of sight (if she goes, when she goes, shall I *bother*?).

Christopher was eating well. She summoned the sweet trolley for him again. Polly had already had to leave. Throughout the meal images of death and decay had pursued her. They went upstairs for Christopher's present: she bought him a record of the Bay City Rollers.

Coming out with him into the April sunshine she felt a mood of increasing, inexplicable sadness. The doorman got them a taxi. Girls were out and about in summer frocks, in billowing trousers. The taxi came down Piccadilly, up Half Moon Street, Curzon Street, Shepherd Market, Queen Street – no need to look out of the window. All changed, and yet unchanged. Everywhere, on a Friday afternoon, busy, busy; and alive.

∞

Eddie had a flat in Half Moon Street. Their affair began in the spring of 1919 while Cecil was in Paris for the Peace Conference.

She had never been unfaithful before – and perhaps, if this had not been so easy and so inevitable, would not have been so often after. Certainly a pattern was set.

It had been wonderful to meet him accidentally at a party at Christmas. Frightening too, a little: a reminder of unfinished business, of unhealed wounds. He had recently been demobilized. The charm that his wooden convalescent's manner had successfully disguised was now very evident; and all part of his frantic gaiety. Hardly drawing breath between remarks, dark hair finely flopping, head on one side; a glass in his hand was how she remembered him now: pouring from a bottle, pouring for her, for anyone. Party time. It was always party time. 'Let's have a party,' he said.

With surprise, with terror almost: it was David in the library again. She had thought herself satisfied, amused, excited enough – so why this? But why not? They happened upon each other so often – always by chance – but so often: at parties, more parties, at the theatre, one afternoon in Liberty's.

The affair was managed without gossip, discreetly. It was

175

she who visited him. The flat was an upstairs one. Harrods had furnished it for him; one day it had not been there and the next, he said, it was complete.

One warm afternoon in May; a light breeze just moving the net curtains. Lying in the big bed, Eddie nervily sipping champagne – Ayala, it had always to be Ayala. 'Suppose I lose my strength? I mean, the *perfect* reviver . . .' She drank it too, why not; all part of that quiet hour or so after, when they lay and talked and sipped, and maybe slept a little, lightly.

'It sounds a trifle alarming,' she was saying idly, about some face lotion. 'It's supposed to be made with "rare herbs and radium water" – I think I would be just a little frightened to put it on. I mean, *radium* – '

'Perhaps that explains Connie Vernor's complexion. Not just pock-marked, crater-marked. I think really – '

'Don't say her name,' she said tartly; but trying to keep her voice light: 'it sounds too like – I don't want to think of Con,' she said suddenly, 'not when we're in bed together.'

'Oh,' he said in a small voice. Almost as if she had hit him. There was silence; she was about to speak again when leaning over he laid his hand on her stomach: a blow, a slap almost. Too far removed from the act of love to be sexual. He was shivering slightly as if chilled.

She thought at first he might be joking. His head was turned away: 'I told lies,' he said suddenly, swallowing loudly. He swallowed loudly again and again; then his tone raised: 'Lies, they were all lies – '

'About us? Oh Eddie, surely? I mean, my dear – '

His voice was like a scream: 'Blown to pieces,' he said. 'The heart, why did I say shot through the heart, why did I say it? Tell me *why* I said it – ' She was unable to speak, lying rigid beside him. He said in a whine almost, 'Blown to bits. Everywhere, pieces everywhere. Blown to bits, spattered, the pieces, on me, pieces – Oh my God – '

'Eddie, stop,' she said, her mouth thick, cottonwool, her voice distorted. But he continued, tonelessly now: 'Oh my God, oh my God . . .' Then just as suddenly stopped and lay there, every few seconds giving a small animal scream.

On her stomach where his hand had lain her flesh felt ice cold. After a while she saw that he was shivering again, long

176

body shivers shuddering right through him. There was a small vase of freesias on the bedside table: their smell seemed cloying now, sweet and sick. She got up, dressed again, and left the flat. He seemed to have fallen into an uneasy slumber. She couldn't have borne to touch him.

She heard nothing for several weeks although at third hand she learned that he was on holiday in the Italian lakes. Then, as if nothing had happened, he got in touch: some joke, something frenetic. They began again; neither of them ever referring to the incident. They even had fun.

Gradually the affair ended. But no faster, she thought, than it would have done naturally. It just faded away. Over the years she saw him here and there; sometimes thought about him quite a lot. He died young, at forty-four, of cancer.

But some time on that May afternoon a splinter of ice, something like that, had entered her. Its outward manifestations were odd but startlingly apparent when two years later her daughter was born, and then her son. She felt little stir of affection. Babies bored her, she told herself, glad of nanny and the social arrangements.

She had been waiting, she thought later, for Con to be reborn. But in its way would that not have been a worse mockery? The same flesh inhabited by a different spirit. Yet when it came to grandchildren, she was waiting and watching still: that he might even at this late hour reappear.

Sandy asked: 'Where's Mrs Willingham, where's Muff?'

'Harrods,' Tessie said. 'She was in a great fever to be off. Late spring fever. She was there only the other day – in the travel bureau. She even made an appointment – I heard her. "Is Mr Blank still in charge? No – well then I'll have – who is your best man at the moment? I should like to be seen at *eleven*..." What'll come of it, I don't know – she's so moody nowadays.'

'Torquay,' Sandy said, lighting her cigarette from Tessie's. 'That's where ducks like her go.'

'I'll be the last to hear.' Perhaps *I* have spring fever, she thought. Yesterday suddenly full of energy, this morning over-sleeping, hardly able to open my eyes. And tomorrow I have to face Camilla.) I can see myself at Muff's age *still* lunching with her.

'I found some more photos of Terry's dad – me Mum had them all the time, she don't never tidy nothing, I was wanting photos of him, Tessie.' The kettle was boiling; she got up to make their coffee. 'Whatever, he is his dad. Terry asks. I can't say nothing really – like I don't remember. It's all that time, I *don't* remember, honest. Lots of that mob – there was lots flashing their whatnots at me. Steve, it was just – we was all different then, Tessie. If it hadn't been him . . .'

She put the cups of coffee down. When she saw hers Tessie wasn't sure she wanted it; her head throbbed so; one leg felt heavy and dragging. Low back ache too so that she thought she must surely be expecting a period – if 'expect' was ever a word she could use of her hormones or glands or whatever. Lately they were so infrequent, so without any pattern at all, that she thought that sympathetically perhaps with Camilla, she was to have an early menopause. Perhaps I've caught it off her in the way you get whole villages suddenly full of pregnant women . . .

Sandy had some aspirin on her. She took one herself too. 'Purple hearts, they was a bob then. When I remember – it's things like that. Can't remember real things – '

Tessie said: 'What do you tell Terry?'

'Pictures, I show him them photos. Steve in his rocker gear. He's real impressed. And I tell him two things, Tessie, about his dad, because they're important. He didn't fight dirty. And nobody ever sold him a wooden nickel.'

∞

She could hear the 'phone ringing as she came up to the door. Her mother would be out: evening classes; Christopher in front of the box. And Muff – well hardly . . . Hurry, hurry, because at the next ring it would stop, give up.

It was as if she'd known. His voice. 'Could I speak to Polly, please?' And her own silly one, breathless now, heart pounding, 'Polly here.' Then: 'How did you know my number?'

178

'I looked it up,' he said patiently, 'I looked up Willingham.'
The television was too loud – gun shots and yelling came at
her. Then, 'Oh well,' she said. There was a pause and she
panicked, thinking, he'll put the receiver down.

'I'd like to see you. Can do?'

Confusion, a different panic: clasping the 'phone as if it
were him himself; 'When,' she said, 'which day?'

'Now – when you like. This evening?'

She wasn't late: even though she'd tried three different outfits – smart, flowery, and what she'd finally settled for, jeans.
All the time with wet purple nails held against the hair blower,
her mind wouldn't settle; with wild flights, she thought he'd
somehow discovered her love and was angry.

He smiled at her as she came into the pub. It was the first
thing she saw. He was alone, half sitting on a bar stool and
turned towards the door.

When he'd got them both beer they went and sat in a
window-seat with cushions. 'I wasn't late,' she said chattily,
terrified already of a silence although there hadn't been time
for one. 'I'm nearly always late everywhere but tonight – I
made it.'

'You did,' he said. She was very near him on the seat; she
could have placed her hand on his thigh, between his thighs.

'Well,' he said easily. 'What have you been doing?'

'With my time – since Edinburgh you mean?' What had
she been doing indeed? (When I'm not with you, nothing I do
is anything: I do nothing.) 'Oh – work. Too much. Exams . . .'

He looked at her closely for a moment, so closely that she
evaded his glance. 'Why didn't you tell me your name was
Willingham?'

She said indignantly, 'You never asked – '

'True.'

'Why should I anyway – I can't see what it's got to do with
anything.' Her heart pounded all the time, with the simplest of
statements.

'Sorry, badly put. Start again. You know a character called
Peter Kyrtle-Murray?'

'*Do* I – '

'OK, I had the great good luck to meet him on a train last
week. "Zoss, my old Zoss. Mind if I sit with you?" and so

179

on – you'll know the style. I can't remember exactly how we came to talk about you but you must be a bit of an obsession with him. He got on to the one note – I must have met you, he said. That party, I couldn't forget such a face, such a figure. *True* – so I put two and two together.' He stopped for a moment to drink. She said:

'So what if I am Willingham and he carries on about me? I don't see him you know – '

'No, but he's mighty proud of what he's done. Your father and Morwen – he says you knew nothing about it. He did the telling and you went all to pieces, he said. Pale and faint. He really shattered you, he said. So *pleased* about it he was. He'd a fucking great grin. No he hadn't – it was small and pinched . . .' He paused, finished off his pint. 'All that gloating. I told him where to put it.'

She said in an attempted off-hand tone, 'I didn't give a damn in fact. I bloody didn't care.'

'Surely. Sure thing. Maybe. After though, I don't know, I got to thinking about you. Worrying really. That's what I'm here to say – one way and another I've met you around often enough, well, felt I knew you enough to say, ask – OK, are you? Truly?'

'Truly.' She wanted to cry suddenly.

'Let's forget him then. He's a shit.' He gathered up both their mugs.

'I expect he's in love with my father and that explains it all – '

'You may be right . . . OK, food, nosh – you'd not eaten, had you?'

He came back with two plates of shepherd's pie, then went for more beer. He asked her how her mother had taken it, what she thought would happen? 'He's going to miss Morwen, by the way. She's off on tour. Lengthy.' There were bits of gristle in the meat and she wasn't very hungry either.

'She's remarkably placid for an artist really. It's not Callas-Onassis stuff at all. She ought to be married though, she'd be better off married – '

'To you?'

He laughed. 'Just better off married. Seriously. Everyone

180

is – ' He stopped: 'Wait a moment – I remember you on that subject. Sitting holding forth in my favourite caff. I remember. And being mysterious generally. You can just tell me about that some time, will you?'

'Your parents,' she said, 'their marriage, how did that go?'

'OK, that went OK. I got a good impression of that.' They sat a few moments in companionable silence. There were other people in the pub. She had not noticed there were other people. An old man with a retriever lying at his feet sat near. Two women were stroking it.

'Pud?' He brought over bread-and-butter pudding. He ate his at once with obvious relish. 'It's good,' he said, 'so good. And hardly a bloody place left that serves it.'

'Why are you so crazy about it? Didn't you get enough at school?'

'No, not really I didn't. School dinners stopped around eleven when we went abroad.'

'Where was that?'

'Greece.'

'But you're English?'

'With a name like that? Yes, sort of. I just had a wandering father – although not to begin with. He was one of the ones Hitler didn't manage to get rid of, *nearly* got – he said for years he was a mixture of thanking somebody or something for getting out, getting through and an opposite feeling of being there by accident, not really belonging, some sort of mistake. They got my grandparents you see and a horde of aunts and uncles and cousins. Most of them there aren't even photos of. But my mother's Yorkshire – they married when I was on the way, and he got to be fantastically solid and settled. All those first eleven years or so I couldn't imagine living, us living, anywhere else. Oddly enough she was the ambitious one then – her grandfather had been in the colliery band, and an uncle too. There was a cornet – and not an ice-cream one either – stuck in my mouth the second they'd decided I'd the chest for it.' He imitated: ' "Listen to the lad blow. Just listen . . ." She was after me to play it all the time. Nag, nag. Then bursting her guts with pride when I was about ten, just winding up at primary, and Sunday evening in church leading

181

the whole congregation in "Who Would True Valour See". She had it all planned . . .'

'Why'd you go abroad?' She felt terror – conditioned by all her unsuccessful chases – that he would suddenly get up and leave. 'What happened?'

'He seemed settled enough – he was full of projects, all to do with staying put. Then one day he just came and announced that he'd handed in notice for the house and we'd all got passages through Brindisi to this island. He was manic almost, full of some wild idea about making a fortune. It was hell because my mother shut up like a clam, wouldn't talk, just packed us all up – I really felt the boat rocking then, the only time. For me all the novelty wore off in a month or so. I was just bloody homesick. All that sun, I thought it was going to be great, but none of us seemed to settle. Even my father. He kept saying "Israel then" and my mother said "no". Then suddenly we just changed islands – and everyone settled beautifully, just like that. The tourist trade started up and my mother got some work to do with that, then oddly enough my father actually made money – quite a bomb and for quite a while. School – that was rather bitty, one of those places for exiles, all races and creeds, except you're somehow all white and a bit pseudo-colonial. I went over to Athens one day a week for trumpet – it all went on being serious. But then later, when I'd just come over to the Royal College, my father had a coronary. They said they were surprised it hadn't come earlier. He was young enough, not fifty. My mother suddenly upped and went off to Majorca – she saw really big tourist money. She runs two agencies and a hairdresser's – loves the work out there, wouldn't be back in Yorkshire for anything. She's changed a lot. She still pays the odd state visit and has a good gossip and feels sorry for people not making ends meet, and not getting their washing dry in the unreliable weather and so on . . .'

He'd finished his beer. 'More,' he said, 'I'll get more. My trade's a thirsty one. Like anything different, anything stronger?'

She shook her head. When he came back they went on talking about families. He had cousins in Yorkshire, a good supply, otherwise no one over here. She said:

'My life should be stiff with cousins – my mother's family was *huge*. But somehow they don't add up to many. I don't really get to see any of them – they're mostly too young anyway. Some in New Zealand, some in Canada, some in West Africa. Two in Edinburgh that I go up and help look after.'

'But friends,' he said. 'You've lots of those?'

'Not really – I don't know – after school I got a bit turned in. Party friends yes, names I could reel off. And I'm very thick with someone called Patrick at this crammer's – we talk our heads off, and he'd like to lay me. But it won't get to that. I had a very close friend at school, Alice. I seem to have rather lost her.'

'Lost her? Real lost?'

'Yes, real lost.' She told him the history. 'Latest sighting was busking in Amsterdam outside the American – genuine accredited one. She sent me some message. All a bit vague though – just that she'd made a Krishna marriage only it was all off again. And that she'd write. But nothing since. Not a word . . .'

'That's bad.' She saw that he'd been watching her all the time she was talking. She coloured, felt the flush crawl up and down her body, growing, growing.

He said, 'Drink up. Beer'll fatten you nicely.'

'For the kill?'

'For the kill,' he said, 'if that's what you're dressed up for – no, *to* . . .' He looked down at his empty mug. 'We're getting stupid – '

The old man and the dog had gone away now; the two women earlier. Picking up her mug she drank some beer: too much too quickly; she had to swallow hard. He said: 'Polly?'

There was a long pause.

'I bought this print,' he said, 'a little while back. Gustav Klimt – 'Lady with a Fan'. I like it a lot. The trouble is – I can't think whether I like her because she looks like you or whether I like you because you look like her . . .'

'*Have you got problems*,' she said.

'Have I. But it's good, that's good. I thought – I can look at her whenever I like.'

'Yes, that's good.'

183

'But looking at you whenever I liked – that might not be so simple.'

'It should be simple,' she said, colour flooding her again. 'It should be. Because I love you.'

Chapter 6

'What sort of a dinner?' asked Tessie, as if by rote.

'Run of the mill. I spoke badly.' Getting into bed he bumped against her.

She'd been going to make some other polite remark ('What was the food like? the other speeches?'), but she said instead: 'Something's wrong, isn't it?'

'I should think there's a *great deal* wrong with everything. The world's not in a pretty state.' His tone was dry, off-putting. She persisted:

'You've something on your mind – That at least I can recognize – '

He switched off his bedside light, turning over with his back to her. 'Could you be quiet?' he said.

Silence. After a few minutes he said suddenly: 'Oh, *God* – ' She waited too long to say anything, choking on non-words. Then putting out a hand she touched him – immediately he gave a great shiver as if of revulsion. A moment later she realized from the nature of his breathing that he'd been already asleep.

She was afraid now to knock against him, to wake him, to move suddenly in the bed. She began to wish he'd slept in the dressing-room. I want no part of his misery, she thought, why should I know about it? Downstairs she heard the clock striking three.

She must have fallen into a heavy sleep. It seemed though that she was still awake. She felt in her dream an overwhelming tiredness, a great reluctance to get out of bed, yet a nagging feeling that she must: dragging herself out wearily and down the stairs quietly, very quietly. For some reason she must wake no one, no one must know that she was up and about and that it was morning. The post lay downstairs on the mat, a great pile, scattered. She rummaged through it, knowing even before she turned the big white envelope over that it would be from him, that it would be from Mike.

His writing had not changed at all, the same small firm hand with the backward 'd's that had written all those years from Ampleforth, from the Army. She tore it open standing in the empty kitchen. Pages and pages: with the nonsense of dreams she could not read them, they didn't make sense, were in fact addressed to someone else whom she couldn't recognize. Perversely though she didn't at all mind. One line was darker than the others; it stood right out. She knew with joy that this was addressed to her. 'Send me some news of yourself.'

She woke slowly, stirring in faint unease succeeded by sudden happiness as she remembered her dream. '*Send me some news of yourself.*' So real was the memory of the written word that surely, she thought joyfully, unbelievingly, surely this was in reality a message – a great sending through the unconscious, an acknowledgment, a cry now after all these years.

We should never have lost touch, she thought. How could I ever, *ever*?

∞

Muff sipped her Sercial, bit into a dry biscuit; tried to ignore Sandy's presence. The drawing-room was to have been ready by midday but dusting and polishing was still going on. And with the stupid unreasoning obstinacy which afflicted her so often now, against her will, she had determined to sit in here as planned.

Cigarette ash gathering, about to fall. Stained torn plimsolls. I do not like thee Doctor Fell ... Often nowadays she saw Sandy, and Teresa, as some sort of malevolent pair, teaming up to make an even greater discomfort of her old age. Yet at times there would steal over her, unsuspected, a sensation of admiration almost, a sneaking respect for the style with which Sandy handled a life which she, Margaret Willingham, would not have thought worth living.

The lid of a Limoges trinket box rattled dangerously. Sandy stubbed out her cigarette and threw it in the fireplace. She sang, 'I'm on the top of the world'. Her voice was croaky, painful ...

I don't have to tolerate this, Muff thought. What is she after all but first cousin to the stage parlour maid, defunct now but so important once? The one who in lovable cockney, lawks-a-missus, waved her feather duster over the china ornaments, setting the scene for the audience; filling in those awkward moments while those late after oysters at Bentley's, champagne filled, trooped noisily into their seats ...

She thought of going back to the haven of her room but she felt suddenly too tired, and too obstinate. Teresa could do this work, she thought, she has nothing else to do. Matriculation is hardly a fit occupation for a forty-three-year-old woman.

'I don't have to tolerate this,' she said aloud.

'What's that?' Sandy said. 'What's that you said?' She sprawled in one of the velvet chairs. 'Eh?'

'I didn't speak,' Muff said, leaning forward and picking up the *Spectator*. She hadn't her glasses with her.

'I'll tell you something,' Sandy said, lighting up. 'Nearly finished, my love – about getting old. Something I read. I can't rightly – about things in brain cells it was. Fuck I can't remember but about *changes*, some sort of pattern thing written in when you're born. Made me think of you, don't know why. Just did. A bit cheeky but there you are – it were a mag at the dentist's.' She pulled off her plimsoll and picked the sole of her foot. 'Sodding verruca. Anyway facts are it's all written down like a blueprint how you're going to get and they was saying if they could sort of change it, change the clock – something about a *clock* – they could perhaps stop it, not stop it but slow it all down. So that like now when you're eighty is it, you'd go on being fifty.' She pulled the plimsoll on again. The ash was gathering on her cigarette.

When Muff didn't speak, she said: 'Wonder if they'll do it all with drugs?' She got up suddenly, scratching her nose with her thumb. 'Remember that stuff, dopey something – el dopey, that were it, el dopey, for old men with the shakes, and they all jumped out of bed and chased the nurses. Side effects it was. That must have been a carry on – old you-know-whats, hadn't been able to do it for yonks, and then – ' She snorted, laughing, then stopped and looked at Muff. 'Eh.' She raised her eyebrows, 'Gone too far – have I?'

'No place to which you might go could possibly be too far,' Muff said.

Sandy shrugged her shoulders good-humouredly. A few moments later, gathering up her cleaning equipment, she slipped out. Muff, left sitting there, sipped more madeira: dry, it seemed still to taste slightly sweet, cloying. Old age, like a bad taste in the mouth. Sandy's remarks had been in bad taste, as was Sandy herself. (The incredible vulgarity of one of her earliest remarks – it had stayed in Muff's mind over a decade: Sandy washing down the window and saying: 'I was a VE baby. Eighth May 1945 – it come on to rain early in the morning, that's what turned him on see. Better than VD tho', my mum said. VJ Day come and she only just done throwing up . . .')

The same day that saw the beginning of Sandy had seen the end of Cecil. An unfortunate turn of phrase; why should a man's life end at that? As if that were all he was about, as if that were all he existed for. It had not seemed to *him* the end of his life.

She talked so little with women friends, had in fact so few, that the subject scarcely cropped up. 'Thank God,' Madge Goodhart had said once, 'Hugh's past it. Such a relief, my dear – to go to one's bedroom feeling safe, able to plan an early night. To know, my dear, that he can't – although of course it can be awfully *trying* when they're still trying . . .'

But Cecil had not continued trying. That celebration night after a party at Onslow Square: the almost unbelievable length of time in which as he panted and puffed with effort his climax came no nearer (it had not been drink, alcohol was forbidden him now); the incredulity with which, sleep nearly overcoming him, he'd groaned: 'Look, I say, thingie, I can't you know – I don't think, just now . . .' And then two, three minutes later the sound of his heavy snoring.

In the morning he hadn't felt well. Shaking off a headache. He'd said, 'Sorry for the fiasco last night,' and she had replied, not acidly but in a mild rather dry tone, 'not what one might call a performance to remember.' A week later he tried again. Not so much angry as suddenly indifferent, she waited for all to be well. But it wasn't. And that was that. The subject became taboo. Then after an interval was referred to with ease. His remarks were more general than particular: 'time in a man's life, easing off, change of interests, less strenuous activities,

188

wheel coming full circle, food our first pleasure . . .' But he hadn't been old, only just sixty; she'd wondered if it had been a symptom of his illness, an early one, but had never thought to ask. It hadn't been, or needed to be the end of their shared life. They had anyway for so many years allowed each other the maximum of freedom with the minimum of curiosity. It had never occurred to her or fretted her that perhaps with someone else he'd been successful. She was still, and for a long time after, a success herself. For all that it mattered.

All passion spent . . . But it's as clear as yesterday: I know where *my* passion went. In a sudden violence of feeling – and they came now so frequently with her floods of memory as if sometimes she were seeing a film, a play, for the first time: experiencing what seemed to be new emotions – I didn't mind, she thought now, angrily. After all, he was only my husband.

∾

'Lovely,' Polly said, 'it's been such a lovely lovely time. Ten *lovely* days. They just don't come any lovelier – I didn't know.'

'Anyone hearing that, they'd think we'd been having it off in Corfiot olive groves instead of a polluted bit of West London.' His voice was smothered in her hair: 'But that's to come . . .'

'Move your arm, you'll have to move your arm, I can't get at my drink. Oh but it *has* been, it's all been something like never before – and the sun, it's as if the sun is specially shining for us even when it's not out at all – and all the colours are brighter. I just wake up every morning and I don't believe we're real, that it really can have happened. All those things people say: "pinch me, pinch me to show I'm awake" – *ouch*. Taking me literally like that, and pinching me *there* too . . .'

'Christ you do talk rubbish,' he said. 'One thing I remember when you kept turning up everywhere, how you did talk on. You'd have talked all that time in the disco if the music hadn't been so deafening – '

'It was wonderful. I told you I loved you. With all that wonderful noise I could say it out loud in a normal voice – it wasn't like saying it into my pillow – I could actually say it, *to you*.'

'Oh, so. I can't have been watching your mouth moving – '

'No. You were too busy watching your baby dying . . .'

'Oh *that*,' he said. 'What do I have to do to live that down?'

'Just love me. And take care of yourself, always do that, always take care – '

'Will do – if you say. The loving bit, did you want proof of that any particular way?'

'You know how I like it – '

'Go on, get up – into the kitchen where you belong.'

'I don't know my way round it. Wouldn't be able to find a thing.'

'You didn't have X-ray eyes then when you stood outside in the cold?'

'Hey,' she said, 'that's below the belt – '

'Where else would I want to go? . . . No, no, you don't damage my fingers, I need my fingers. Let me go in the kitchen – I'll do something about your voice. Fit for Bach tomorrow – I'll make you a brew Jenny Lind's supposed to have sworn by. Morwen dug it out somewhere. Chicken comes into it but it's mostly eggs and alcohol. According to her, oils the vocal cords.'

'We'll see. What about something to make you blow better? . . . But what's the hurry actually though, are we hungry? We haven't finished our drinks even. Are you hungry?'

'Not to notice.'

'All right, let's?'

'Let's . . . Oh, Polly, Polly darling . . . Pussy, no you can't talk, not now, not when it's – This is how I shut your mouth – like that and like that . . . No, but you see, darling – '

'I make so much noise I know – I know I make a terrible noise, but if you knew, you see – '

'Don't talk so.'

'I'm going to be terribly good. I've got the pill all organized. It's just it doesn't work at first, you've got to be settled or something, give it time. And this is all right, isn't it? Only not so good of course, who says you can't feel it? It was just that first time, only I didn't care, I didn't care – '

'Don't talk so.'

'I don't, I don't . . . it's the smell of your skin, you see, like that and like that – Oh no, oh no, I never thought, my love – no

I can't, I couldn't keep still – you see why I can't – oh I haven't but look . . .'

So much later, so sleepily, she said: 'I only joined that choir to be near you. Just *look* how near I've got . . .'

Chapter 7

It had been quite easy in the end. She had traced Mike through Ampleforth Old Boys. An act of such simplicity and ease that it could have been done any time during the past many many years.

At first, merely thinking about visiting him seemed achievement enough; she was at the moment tired all the time as if drained: as if she had just experienced some great emotion, and since forgotten it.

When Barney went away for two days it came to her suddenly that it was now or never, that *today* was the day. She thought of it at breakfast. There were practical arrangements of course: she had a dentist's appointment first at ten o'clock. And there was Muff . . .

Polly, abstracted, drinking Nescafé standing up, said: 'Oh yes, darling?' when Tessie told her: 'I may be late back. I have to see someone and I don't know how long it will take. There's all that cold stuff in the fridge – can you feed Muff?'

'It sounds like feed the dog or the cat,' said Polly, her mouth full of toast, 'but yes, no trouble at all, of course I'll do that. I'll sit with her a bit too.'

Perhaps she should have written to Mike first? An easy action which she knew would have proved too difficult. It was against all common sense to arrive unannounced: to find him perhaps out, gone away; dead.

For days she had been imagining him. The built-up picture, fitted in here and there over the days and nights, was really only the same Mike, grown older, grown wiser. She couldn't imagine him trendy, excited: Look at me, Mother Church, look – no hands . . . She saw rather a slight rearrangement of priorities, a picking out of the best of modern thought, a quiet holding of principles. Once they had used to discuss religion; it had been, one earnest Easter, the only topic almost. Every moral issue thrashed out: 'But you see, Tessie, the point the Church makes . . .' patiently breaking her down, then coming round to the original position '. . . so you see, the Church *does* know best . . . What they call "hard cases" – they're no good when you're making the rules, Tessie,' coming out with apologetics in instalments, as received at school. Then her saying: 'But if I was dying and I had six children, what would be the good seven of them motherless when it could be six with a mother, loved? I'd love to be a mother. Or, Mike, if I'd married at eighteen and then I realized – and I loved this other man . . .' There had been something called the particular and the general. And always, over and above all, God's grace. Without it she and Mike, everyone, was nothing. With it, even these things would be possible.

Then he would spoil it all, pinching and tickling her, Philomena suddenly coming out in him: 'Oh well, I expect, if it happened to *me* . . .'

In the evenings perhaps they discussed it again, and Philomena would say, 'Oh well now, Mike, and what do the fathers know about it all? Did you ever say to them, "were you ever married at all?" – Mother of God they don't know the first thing, if it was *them* now that was having the babies 'twould be a different story – just wait now till they have women fathers, there'll be less of this "don't this and don't that". . .'

Before leaving she'd meant to have breakfast, but nauseated by the remains of Polly's coffee, the wet toast crumbs, she'd gone without. Sitting in the train now she had no one to blame for the heavy queasiness she felt. The visit to the dentist had passed off all right but her mouth where it had been probed felt sensitive still.

She gazed out of the train window. Glancing at her watch she saw that she was nearly there. The landscape was changing to narrow crowded streets, dark with sooty midweek washing strung along uniformly.

When she got out at the station it had begun to rain a little. She thought: this strange place; for him it is home. There was a map on the platform but she could make little of it, so she asked the first friendly person she saw. She had to take a bus: the first one, she took the wrong way and, getting off too suddenly, feeling foolish, she had to lean against a shop doorway for a few minutes to right herself.

She went into a café until the rain should stop. The cloying

193

taste of the spaghetti on toast: she was assailed by a longing for something savoury. Amongst the assorted cold meats in the fridge at home was some Italian *salsiccia*. In the shop she had picked it ignorantly, at random. '*Piccante*', the man had said impatiently as she dithered between one and the other, '*piccante* then, so? how much, half a pound, one pound?' When out of curiosity she had tried it, it had had a bitter aftertaste, salt and spice so that her mouth burned slightly. She thought of it now with sudden longing – thinking that if she passed a shop with it she would buy it, pull it from the bag, eat it there and then. She was reminded of being carsick once as a child, of wanting above all vinegar on chips, and of being forbidden any solid foot at all, doomed to sipping weak tea and sucking glucose sweets, powdery. She'd argued then, making her mother say tartly: 'Really, if Daddy's patients answered back like that. *They* don't think they know better than the doctor ...' But her inside as if to spite them had rebelled, sending up weak tea and water and something else, unrecognizable, perhaps from the evening before. She would have sold her soul then for vinegar on chips. '*Piccante*,' she said now, lovingly, walking slowly along the damp street.

By the time she reached the address it was already after four o'clock. The road was a quietish one. Some children were roller skating; a black girl with lots of tight little plaits, losing her balance, fell against Tessie and giggled. 'Sorry missus.' Two boys on gleaming Chopper bikes circled round by the entrance to the church. She went in. It was familiar, the scent a longing. She thought she would kneel, pray perhaps, certainly wait a time in the hope not so much that he might just walk in, but that by being here something would come to her, some sort of calming courage.

She looked around her. It was very dark even after the dull light outside. An elderly woman was kneeling several benches in front of her. She thought she might walk about and read the notices; as if they would tell her something about him. To the right of her, not far away, were the confessional boxes. She imagined herself kneeling – his penitent. 'Bless me Father, it is twenty-seven years ... I have – ' Then, oh God, she could think only of one thing that she had done. 'Bless me Father ... Once when I thought you would marry me, when it seemed the most natural thing in the world you came to me with this most unnatural of announcements and told me that you would become a eunuch for Christ's sake and I was so shocked and terrified, so hopeless and broken that I fought with the only weapons I had and I proved to you that you were no eunuch and quite rightly you said that I wasn't being FAIR which is a wonderful public schoolboy word that we go on using all our lives and which puts the other person instantly in their place which is in the wrong. And of course by everything we had both learnt to believe and honour I was in the wrong, and I have been punished. You didn't wish that for me, I can't imagine that you would have wished that for me, but in fact I was punished completely and totally, *I* became the eunuch, if one can say that, the twentieth-century equivalent, a woman with no feeling, so that only in dreams – '

'I don't want to hear of your dreams, my child,' gently said, 'God doesn't hold us responsible for our dreams, just our *wilful* thoughts – '

'For how long does the punishment go on, the more especially as it doesn't come from you, and doesn't come from God, but comes from – who? Shall we lay it all at Barney's door? But I am the door – '

'. . . now thank God for a good confession, and for your penance say – no, wait, something unusual, we are back in the Middle Ages, 300 days – No, better still, what is this, forty years in the wilderness. May you never feel what you caused to feel, may your body punish you. But since it cannot be killed, you may dream. You will be allowed to dream . . .'

So absurd and so fanciful, fancy and horror running away with her. She saw the elderly woman go over and light a candle. She got up and lit one too – she had grown a modern mind now, acquired one: a candle, even when blessed, was no longer just a candle. It was as a symbol that she lit it. Tenderness was what it stood for. It flickered and went out. A second symbol would be too much, so that she laughed, almost out loud, and energetically and sensibly lit it again . . .

She had to ring the bell of the presbytery twice. Rain was dripping from the rhododendron leaves. The woman who opened the door had heavy frown lines between her eyes. 'Which

one is it?' she asked, 'the young one's away – ' Tessie explained.
'He's not in,' the woman said. Would he be in later then?
(Looking at her and thinking, she is the one who has to care for
him, who sees and worries if he catches cold, doesn't eat
enough . . .)

'When he's back it's his tea-time.' She looked at Tessie suspiciously, and as if by rote: 'Is it urgent?'

'I'm a friend you see. I was in the town for a meeting. He's
an old family friend, he – '

'Oh well, if it's *family*. But you'll have to let him have his
tea because he's to go out again, he always goes out Wednesday
evenings – '

She would have liked to look around the room while she
waited. It would have told her something, but she sat shaking,
feeling suddenly sick again. Rain was falling heavily outside
now. A big clock above the fireplace ticked slowly, loudly.
Recovering a little she was about to snoop when the door
banging, voices muttering, sent her scurrying back to her chair.

He was standing in the doorway.

'But it's Tessie! It's my Tessie!' She rushed forward as if
propelled, they clasped hands, both hands, she was clinging
to him or he was clinging to her: 'The *surprise* of it!'

He crossed quickly to a seat, an uncomfortable chair, hard-
backed, leaned forward: 'Tell me everything, all about it, what
became of you. We wondered always what became of you – I
heard you were married – ' His voice was the same, a little
deeper, but as quick although, she thought, perhaps more Irish
than she'd remembered. 'You're married – and you've got
children? What are you doing here? Tell me why you're here,
Tessie, are you staying locally?'

Time for the lie and so she said, 'I came up for this meeting,
you see – and I suddenly remembered that was where someone
had said your parish was. I thought – I'll just look in on the
off-chance.'

She was still trying to get used to the physical shock: because he had changed so much, or rather he was the same but
obscured, overlaid by fat. She could she supposed have just
as well been confronted by a beaky, emaciated, ascetic figure,
voice rasping. At moments she *could* recognize him, but mostly

she struggled to find him somewhere in this altered, thickened man: the fat had given him a high colour so that he looked jolly rather than lively. His neck which had swivelled so agilely looked now too thick to move – and yet she shouldn't have been surprised: this was surely just Philomena's bulk: the big woman she remembered sitting there so cosily . . .

There was a knock at the door. He jumped up, nimbly for his weight. 'A moment,' he said to Tessie. He conferred with the housekeeper at the door, then coming back he said, 'You'll have some too, won't you, Tessie? It's only boiled eggs and tea, a cake or something . . .'

Twenty-five years of accumulated news and it was really quite easy to relate in ten minutes. Some of it of course he'd heard:

'It was great, your marrying one of the Willinghams – although I'd never have thought of it, your marrying a non-Catholic. Was there any trouble with the family? It must have been a great love – I heard about it, I heard, but such a while after. When I think of him, you know – when I think of him now, Tessie – I was thinking, it's a funny thing, only the other day I was thinking of that concert. He'd a fine voice. Remember how he made Miss Thackray race – she was in a terrible fluster and he was saying, "faster Miss T., faster" – I shouldn't think she's ever forgotten it. And Stan, do you remember how shirty he got . . .'

They were launched on that safest sea of all, reminiscence. It could have been dangerous but, ships now passing in the night again, they would not so much as graze against the rocks, the iceberg. A sea so well charted they knew its dangers. The real folly would have been questions of cautious, albeit terrifying immediacy. 'Tell me, has he made you happy? Have you got over me because that was what was wrong, wasn't it? I thought I was bound by childhood ties of easy friendship, that we would merely sadly miss each other, and instead you terrified me with your demands, your explicit declaration that it was something quite other for which you hoped,' and she in reply would say, 'Has it been all right, really, deep down, *really*, or have you woken in the night and longed and thought, even if it wasn't Tessie I would have loved after all, someone to love

197

exclusively I *do* need – this coruscating loneliness, this being everything to everybody and nothing to any person in particular, all things to all men but nothing to any one woman. Only a grey-haired battle-axe to worry about my food and sleep, and that not because I am Mike Kelly the beloved but because I am Father Kelly the parish priest, ordained of God, the holy object . . .'

'I have to be there half past six, quarter to seven – ' he said, 'but it's only just up the road. It would be just the night of the club – can you come along, would you come along? Where are you staying? Far?'

She began to think desperately of alterations, of rearrangements ('Yes, I'm at the Grand, the Metropole, the – ' Surely every town had a small hotel called 'Avonlea'? . . .), but it was too difficult, and to tell him lies too difficult; she had managed just the one, and that not well.

'My train's at eight.' Their meal had been brought in and he was busy arranging everything for her. They ate at a small table in the same room. Outside the rain splashed down still. 'I wonder how many will turn out,' he said. 'Though the young don't usually mind. But you, Tessie, should you order a taxi for the station?'

She asked politely about the club. They were a grand lot, he said. Whoever said there was anything wrong with the youth today? 'They have their problems, Tessie – and in a town like this, with the way the world is today – but it's surprising how easy, how spontaneous they are. And – '

'Have you been happy?' she asked.

As if it were the most natural question in the world, which on the face of it perhaps it was, he said, 'I have, I have. The life has been hard sometimes. You know, once or twice – and then it hasn't been an easy time for anyone in the Church, but no, Tessie, I never questioned it, not really, once I'd decided, gone in for it, I was always sure.'

I am sure of nothing, she was about to say. Help me. Un-attracted by his certainties, desolated with doubts, she changed topics. Philomena, what of Philomena?

Dead: thirteen years ago now; she'd never seen him in a parish. 'She was joking to the end, you know. "I'm sure of heaven," she kept saying, "I've just to say to St Peter, it's

198

Father Kelly's mother and he'll open up, that's my passport . . ."
The ease of it. The *cheek* of it.'

' . . . on mother Kelly's doorstep, down Paradise Row . . .
does she love me like she used to, on mother Kelly's doorstep? . . .'

When she took the top off the egg the sulphurous smell hit
her – it wasn't bad, just an egg. The bread was sliced, spread
she thought with margarine; the cake, which he pressed on
her, was dry and powdery. 'She makes them herself,' he said.
'You know, from these packets. In the bowl and into the oven
in record time. When I think of Ma and all that stirring and
pounding . . .' Imagining the train, she felt sick already. She
thought yearningly again of the *salsiccia*. She wanted to say,
'Have you some pickle, some chutney?' – she thought she would
eat HP sauce on the bread she craved the sour so greatly. The
strong tea she could not touch. I am going to have some
humiliating stomach upset, she thought: be nervously sick,
here in the presbytery.

They had managed to talk for three-quarters of an hour.
He looked up at the clock and she felt the hourglass running
out as if it were in her body. She said wildly, the last resort,
the last link: 'But your dancing, singing, you know – has that
all gone, Mike? Some of the people who get a hearing nowadays – you were *good*, you know.'

His face lit up. 'But I do a lot. Whenever they put on anything, the club you know, I design the routines, coach them.
I have enormous fun, Tessie. And usually I always do a turn
or two – If I had the time now I'd show you – my size, look
at me, so it *is enormous* fun . . .'

Then suddenly time was up. He was saying: 'Look, we
mustn't lose touch. I pray for you of course, you know I always
prayed for you. But I mean, to *see* you, Tessie. The thing is
it's difficult for me to get away. Late in the summer – if you . . .'

A voice from the grave. How do the dead not know that
they are dead? The Mike who moved in my skull, in my guts;
that *homunculus* – where is he?

Mike Kelly is dead. Long live Father Michael!

On the journey home she slept as if she'd been drugged.
Back in the house, queasy, drowsy, she went straight to the

fridge and getting out the *salsiccia* sat at the kitchen table eating it in great greedy mouthfuls. Feeling suddenly better — just immensely, enormously tired. I could sleep for ever, she thought. For ever. Oh God, may I never wake again.

Chapter 8

They sat out in the small walled garden at the back of Bill Bentley's in Beauchamp Place. Polly wore her new Laura Ashley and a creamy floppy hat; her hair trying to burst from it. Happiness, excitement, spilling out in the June evening.

'What's in them?' Sam asked. 'Smoked salmon – honestly. I've got to have a meal later. Sorry about the rosé.'

'Never mind the taste,' she said, 'it's so pretty – the colour, here, now. Can you afford me?'

'Easily. This is a treat – it's not my local on the way home . . .'

'It's some people's – '

'Inside doesn't look exactly stiff with Hatter's. And the people who were out here when we came left at the double. You're the great turn-off – oozing sexy satisfaction and lack of interest in any other male.'

'You make me sick. Who's satisfied now?'

'We both are – '

'Serious,' she said, 'let's both be *serious*. I'm in the middle of exams – I haven't been doing half the work that I should and I wouldn't have done even that if you weren't a night worker – and no, I didn't mean *that*. I said, let's be serious. If I'd been offered a place at some other university, not London – '

'What would you have done?'

'Thrown it all up.'

'That's rash – if flattering. Won't dare mention marriage again though, because I know what happens. From the way you carry on anyone would think I'd seen some lovely bird flying in the sky and wanted to put it in a cage right off.'

'Absolutely. I don't know about the "lovely" though – '

'The cage is reasonably gilded. Free-lance is free-lance, I know – but I trust the living a bit now. It's going the right way.'

'I'm mad, I'm terrible I know – being like that, when I don't want to love anyone else, *ever*, till the end of my life – '

'And that's about me too . . . Drink up so that I can buy

201

you another bottle ... I'll allow you five years for ripening –
makes me a tottering thirty-three-year-old – then I'll ask again.'

'You'll have tired then – '

'We'll be together, we'll be together. For now though, OK,
you're moving in. What's that going to do to them at home?'

'You must be joking – they won't notice. Not so as you'd
notice them noticing. Except Muff. And I've told her so much
that I can't imagine – well, she couldn't pretend to be surprised.
She certainly got around in *her* time, I think anyway. If you'd
seen the photographs – she was absolutely fabulous. She never
holds forth on morals actually, it's much more people's bad
manners or goods in the shops being shoddy. No, I'm just
going to announce it and that's that.'

'You'll bring me back and get me looked over, won't you?
Would I pass with Christopher?'

'Christopher'll be fearfully impressed. But about showing
you off, you won't guess who I've actually heard from at last –
I could hardly do the paper this morning for thinking about
it. Alice ...'

'In one piece?'

'Very much. She's all right, not just well. *Real* all right.
Wait and I'll get it out of my *tagari* – her writing's ghastly and
you can't read a word, but was I glad to see it –

'All these bits first about feeling dreadful not writing, then
a sort of resumé – Alice's Adventures really – I'll show it to
you. The drug bit after the first break-up and all that, then
the Krishna phase and marriage and everything, then the
hitching and busking. Then this bit. She's landed up in France,
in Taizé, as a pilgrim at the monastery. That community
there. "All I could want is for you to be here too. I came at
Easter and I've signed in for six months – I haven't done anything really religious yet, tho' I might do a retreat in a bit,
but I talk and talk and talk, all the things we used to discuss
when we were being serious – there's so many of us here you're
bound to find someone who's been through the same sort of
fire. We're all in it together, we're all searching for meaning
and all in different ways. You can't imagine – when I got here –
it's like being hungry and suddenly being fed, we talk about
everything, it's a most terrific feeling the whole place. All sorts
of us – there were 70,000 came last year – and it's not like

being lost, it's searching. You feel quite *sure* you'll find something even though it mayn't be anything you could imagine ..."
She goes on and on, there's lots and lots, I'll show you it all later. But she's happy – '

'She's found a reason for living.'

'So have I though. That's what it feels like – so happy. I mean, *you're* it, aren't you?'

∞

Waiting for a car to take her to the Home, she felt a sudden surge of irritation. It was towards Teresa – she was worse than ever at the moment. Slow, yawning continually, every movement seemingly an effort. And yet she is not ill, Muff thought.

To think that once it seemed to me that she would *do*. They were the very words I used, quickly, mentally, that day in Harrods. 'She will do.' As if she had been sent, planted there. And looking so well too (she has never looked so well again).

Eldest daughter of a loyal, hardworking, thoroughly *good* man. Accustomed to responsibility, home-loving but with a highly developed sense of duty. And malleable too, surely? She would rid me of Barney. A good Catholic (when they are good they can be trusted not to stray; perhaps), but unlikely to make any difficulties over religion. Socially more or less acceptable – possibly less. (But then did not June née Tripp, singing so charmingly 'Little Boy Blues', become Lady Inverclyde? And all those Gaiety girls . . .)

When then did I see my mistake? (I don't admit mistakes.) It was gradual, I think. Like all unpleasant truths. A poor wife, a poor hostess, a poor mother. A lump of dough, the leaven missing. Why? What went wrong?

But he must live with his mistakes. It is only that *I* must live here too . . . Downstairs, the bell rang loudly. Her car.

On the way to the Home, she decided she would not be visiting Frank again. It was proving too much for her. Now in the summer it was just possible, but as autumn approached . . . Most important of all however she doubted if she was giving any pleasure . . .

It was a long slow walk from the lift to the ward. A nurse accompanied her. Today the next bed but one was occupied:

203

a much younger man, his dark hair only partly greyed, sat up in bed in a maroon cardigan. He was coughing vigorously as Muff was brought in.

The nurse said to Frank, 'Has he been smoking? No tales, but has he? Has Bert been smoking?'

'Sneaky,' said Bert in a surprisingly loud voice. 'Don't you say nothing, Frank – ' Then seeing Muff: 'Lookey, *lookey*!' he said. 'I say, I say, I say, who have we here?'

'Don't mind him,' the nurse said to Muff. '*We* don't.'

'Her,' Bert said, as the nurse left, '*her*. Madame Muck I call her – "has Bert been smoking?" I'll give her *smoking* . . .' Then, 'Here,' he said to Muff, 'watch it,' as she lowered herself into the chair. 'Sure you oughtn't to be tucked up yourself?'

She was about to say something to Frank who was only half sitting up today. He looked very frail, his eyes bloodshot. But Bert called out:

'Frank said you come, I never believed him. I said, "Frank you're having me on – she don't never sit there and *talk* to you – " '

Her chair had been placed, unfortunately, on the side of the bed facing Bert. She looked at Frank: he was pulling at the sheets. 'How are you?' she said slowly, leaning forward a little. 'How have you been?'

'What's that eh?' Bert said. 'Go on, you speak up, Frank. Speak up.' He stopped a moment for a paroxysm of coughing. 'Tell you something,' he said, still coughing, 'I'll tell you – I didn't never believe you came. He's terrible for stories, old Frank – tell you anything, wouldn't you, Frank? I said to him, "Frank, this old duck" – didn't know then, see, you was so la deedah deedah – I said, "she one of your ex'es, Frank? Come out of your fancy past?" He was one for the popsies, Frank. Tell you something, I've heard him call out in the night. "What was you dreaming, Frank?" I ask him, "Oh," he says, "that was a dream. This girl in the Cut – it were when skirts was long – I was with this girl in the Cut . . ." '

'You don't,' Frank said, turning his head, 'I don't, Bert. I – ' He sought for the words. Muff was about to get up: only by going, she thought, could she stop this. Yet it was essential to say that she wouldn't be coming back. How could she say that now? Lifting her hand, she tried to speak as if Bert were

204

not there at all. 'And how is your pain?' she asked. 'Your ears, you had trouble with your ears, I believe?'

'Not so bad,' Frank said. 'Thank you, ma'am.' He looked nervously towards Bert. 'Doctor says it's not my hearing. You've the hearing, a forty-year-old, he said. And I don't see bad – he said, "You'll be sitting watching the coronation of Charles III, hearing and sight like that. Twenty years' telly you've got Frank," he said . . .'

She had to strain to hear him. 'How encouraging,' she replied, 'how very encouraging.'

Bert was rearranging his bed, tucking the sheets round him. 'Hi thank you, hi thank you, ladies and gentlemen, hi thank you . . .'

'Could you be quiet?' she said coldly. 'I find this very trying.'

But his hearing was perhaps not so good as Frank's. Or he chose to ignore her. She asked Frank: 'Have you been able to get out at all, sit out in this lovely weather?'

'You know what I said to Frank? Can you hear me? I said, "If you was in the same war, how come a duchess wants to see you, did you save hubby's life?" What you think of that?' He pulled open his bedside drawer and took out a pack of cigarettes. 'Blow *her*,' he said, lighting up. 'Monty, I was with Monty. You know Monty? You ever meet him? He's old now, older than what Frank is. Took prisoner – that was my lot. Twenty-six I was, lance-corporal. Twenty-sixth birthday when they took me – "here," I said, "you can't, not on my birthday, what would my old mum say" – but they can't take a joke, Jerry could never take a joke – '

Frank, looking embarrassed, did not try to answer at all. His mouth was shaking; there seemed no words, no convenient formula by which she could say that Bert (probably, certainly, for most of the time his friend), could be ignored. That she did not mind – or rather minded only for him.

She persisted. 'This warm weather. Fortunately I have been able to take advantage – '

'You going down for *Softly, Softly*, Frank?'

Frank turned his head away, from both of them. Bert, waving his cigarette, ignoring Muff still, called out: 'You gone deaf sudden? Eh Frank? You was saying doctor said you'd A1 lugholes. You gone deaf?'

205

But she saw that Frank had begun to cry. His face was quite still now but, feebly, tears were flowing down both cheeks. He didn't attempt to brush them away. She watched for a moment as they ran unheeded, then she averted her eyes.

She had somehow got it wrong. She would have to come again, yet how could she? And what to say? Con, help me. As if he could. She saw behind her some great path stretching back, landmarks, accidents: marriage, love affairs, children she didn't really care for, work. All those years of running the village, running people. Grandchildren. Polly. It came back always to Polly.

'Ah yes,' she said, ignoring the tears. 'I forgot to say. My granddaughter has asked to meet you. Polly. Next time I shall bring her.'

∞

Sitting across the desk from the doctor, Tessie swallowed, felt a lurch of her stomach, then again a wave of nausea. She wanted only to lay her head down on the hard wood and drift into sleep. He was turning over some papers with his left hand; his second and third fingers were stained a grubby yellow, the rest of the hand spotless.

'. . . routine tests,' he was saying. 'Haemoglobin, fine, but in the circumstances – as I shall come to the next point – that is, I'd suggest a course of iron, prophylactically. Kidneys, liver. Lungs – we'd looked at those. Waterworks, fine. No infection there. However – ' he cleared his throat, moved a little, 'I did ask for another test, just to be on the safe side, because of, *in spite of* rather, your history.' He paused, smiled a little hollowly. 'What would you say if I told you you were pregnant?'

Behind him a large abstract took up most of the wall: it was wild and tangled, blue, different shades of; violent restless blues. She wanted in spite of the nausea to light a cigarette. Something, anything, to do with her hands.

'Well, let's say, there wasn't, if you remember, I have it here in the notes, no actual *reason*, cause of infertility. Just the facts of infertility. So . . .

'I'm sorry you know, to spring it on you like this. I'd hoped that perhaps – that you yourself would have begun to see how

206

the facts fitted and so on. So – we haven't, aren't dealing with
an early menopause. The position is – of course you'll want to
think. We can't go into it now really. Shock, surprise and so
on – I suggest you discuss it with your husband and come back
in a week. We can – well, look into the whole matter . . . Smoking by the way – I'd try to cut it down. Book another appointment as you go out, would you?'

Chapter 9

She could not believe she could be so happy. She felt weak, quite ill with it. Sam's body was part of her now so that she could feel it, suddenly in the midst of the traffic, sitting in a bus somewhere miles away, or in the middle of the night, in her room which mentally she'd already left.

'You'll come and see us, Muff?' It would depend, Muff said, on whether she liked Sam: 'I shall decide when we have met . . .' Then she said: 'You should have told me before,' and Polly had said, 'I didn't want you to be unhappy for me, because I couldn't have what I wanted. I didn't know how I was going to be able to go on. I didn't realize that for want of one person the world could be meaningless.' Muff had said: 'That *is* a point of view.'

His face now seemed always to be part of her inner vision. Tonight it was beside her: every loved feature, loved line. Lines round the eyes which multiplied with the smile, the hair with such difficulty tamed for public appearances (and not always then). Brown hair to her black.

They sat alongside, a seat near the door. A farewell meal at Anemos in Charlotte Street. The next day she was off to look after Patsy's children for a fortnight – she'd promised back in April. Patsy and Hamish were to go to Mull by themselves. 'I'm going to run the show,' she'd told Sam, 'old bossy boots herself.'

They were eating the last course: yoghourt and Hymettus honey. They hadn't been talking much; the place was very crowded and every now and then people attracted by the loud *bouzoukis* would put their heads round the door, only to move away when they saw how full it was. They sat now, holding hands, she spooning up yoghourt with her left. She looked around her: up on the wall, nestling among the empty *retsina* bottles, was an incongruous Mickey Mouse. 'Look at that . . .'

'It reminds me – I've bought you a present.'

'Not Mickey Mouse?'

208

'Not *exactly* ...'

'Oh my God my love, it's not an engagement ring?'

'It's not – I wouldn't dare.' The waiter came and he ordered coffee. 'About the other sort of ring though – I'll 'phone each evening. Depends on the work of course – tomorrow's the Dettingen *Te Deum*, I'll ring after that. You'll be in surely – buttering bannocks and steaming haggises – '

'You make everything sound faintly filthy. It's baps anyway – their children are always stuffing in baps. They ought to be fat, but they're undersized.' A waiter passing by with a load of plates stopped to do a small dance. 'God. I'm going to be busy. Too busy to think about you ...'

'Good, that's what I like to hear – I never think about you. Have to keep reminding myself there's a bird, sorry a parrot, called Poll around ... There's our coffee and *loukumi* coming – '

Some of the people who were waiting for tables had linked hands, forming a chain, dancing into the body of the restaurant. The record changed: a staccato, slightly haunting tune.

'*Aponi Zoe,*' he said. ' "Life is Callous". That's from my day.'

'You're so happy, feeling all Greek ...'

'Not really – sad rather. We got out before it went wrong. Now I can't think about it. Couldn't go out there.'

'It's bad, I'm bad, oh God,' she said, 'the luxury of having all these silly emotions – fussing about marrying or not marrying, or feeling offended or overworked – when there's *that* going on in the world.'

'That's what my father would say – frequently. But you have them, we all have them just the same. We *should* have them – '

'But when it's all right again, *if* it's all right again, you'll take me out there?'

'When it's all right again – '

The man meant to be grilling the kebabs kept stopping to sound a klaxon. The next tune was very gay. '*Vraho, vraho,*' they were all clapping hands to the rhythm. 'I should bring you here on a Saturday,' he said, 'it really moves. You'd be up dancing, up on your chair – and, yes, the chairs *are* strong enough for me. An act goes on too. A bit of an act.'

Time to go; out into the hot June evening. 'I'm so happy,'

she said, 'so happy. Except about leaving. I just have to live through the fortnight somehow.'

He had his arm round her going out. 'But after that – it's together, isn't it?' He kissed her ear. 'Come live with me and be my love, and we will all the pleasures prove.'

'*All* the pleasures?' She tripped a little on the step going out, 'Oh my love.'

∞

She dreamed that she was back at Corrib. Con wasn't at the house, but they were waiting for him. Cecil seemed to have taken charge: he was walking about, relaxed, jovial. There was a party, some sort of house party. She said to him, 'This is Uncle Barney's place – you are only a *guest*, you know.' But he wasn't listening. No one was. They were all waiting for Con. Waiting and waiting, and all so happy. Only *she* knew something was wrong. But what was it? Such a long long day, such beautiful weather, then suddenly evening coming on. 'How beautiful the catalpa tree is,' she told everyone. But now there seemed to be no one about: she was out on the little island in the middle of the lake. It was sandy near the water but she was in the copse; there were sloes and rose hips and hawthorn; moss too. It was private and dark. In the distance though the persistent sound of guns. Duck shooting. Cecil and Eddie and others. In the confusion of the dream something is wrong. Eddie should not be here. She cried in the dream, 'I haven't thought of you for years.'

There is no time in dreams. A thousand yesterdays ago and it is today. In dreams, I know how thin is the skin time has grown over all the wounds.

She made her protest, willed Eddie away, feeling even in the dream sadness beginning. The shooting could still be heard. 'But you're dead,' she said angrily.

He smiled, he had always such a sweet smile, an extension, facet, of his enormous frightening gaiety. 'But Con's dead too,' he said; and then he laughed.

∞

'I suppose one ought to offer you some sort of holiday,' Barney said. 'Although for the little you do – it might be better to call it a change of scene.'

He came through into the bedroom. He had on only underpants and looked faintly ridiculous.

'France, Italy, Austria, Switzerland? Anyway you could perhaps give some thought to the matter. Polly no doubt will announce what she's doing in the fullness of time. And there's Muff of course to think of – '

'But she's arranged hers,' Tessie said.

'She says nothing to me nowadays. Was it you she told? Hardly – more likely, surely, Polly?'

'It was Polly actually.'

'Obviously.'

She said humbly, 'I should have told you of course. She's off to Russia, believe it or not. Tskhaltubo – I can't say it. It's in the Caucasus. She's going into a sanatorium, for her arthritis. She's evidently always wanted, always meant to go to Russia. I must say I take my hat off to her.'

'I shall take *my* hat off to the staff of the sanatorium when they've had her for – what is it? – a month. They'll all receive the Order of Lenin or the suchlike . . .'

He'd sat down on the edge of the bed.

'Well,' she said. 'I went to the doctor as you said.'

'You don't seem much better,' he said. 'Has he given you any sort of tranquillizer, or pep-up pill or whatever?'

She had been going to tell him, to say: 'I'm going to have a baby if you can believe that.' But it had suddenly become impossible to speak. Her mouth had gone very dry and she licked her lips; a cigarette – she imagined that would cool her. The box lay by the bed and she could feel her hand shake as she reached out.

'I've got a prescription for iron.'

He turned round, looked at her with annoyance as she lit up. 'Well, do get it filled, won't you? Endeavour not to let me find it lying around the bedroom six months hence while you moan and droop with fatigue.' He paused. 'I feel washed out myself – '

'It's the heat,' she said, 'you can't cope with heat, or cold.'

'I must get away,' he said abruptly. He was sitting hunched

now. She noticed that there were tiny freckles all over his back.

'I shall probably go to Corrib – '

'But it's been taken surely? I mean, I remember – '

'One will pay the people off. Whoever has the booking – it's simply a matter of paying for alternative accommodation.'

She thought of saying, but that will be somebody's perfectly good holiday spoilt – you can't. Only to realize that he could; and probably would.

'Where's Polly?' He had changed the subject so suddenly that she was taken by surprise. She said, 'Out.'

'One's reached the stage when one's not certain when one last saw her. What does she *do*, other than play the gramophone and go to parties?'

'Muff says she's very thick with some musician – those weren't her words of course. But that's about all she said. "You can hardly expect me to pass on what Polly has confided," or something like. So Polly has at least spoken to someone – but how much, and what, I don't know.'

She thought he would take this up but he seemed to have lost interest. His mood tired her, angered her too. 'I think I'm going to sleep,' she said.

He spoke, still with his back to her. 'Cigarette finished already? Aren't you going to start another?'

'I'm trying to give it up – '

He said suddenly, turning round, interrupting her: 'I can't go on. Oh my God, *I can't go on.*'

Hatefully she began to feel sick again: a bitter gut memory of – what was it? some frozen lasagne. She sat up to try and fight it: here was the ready delivered moment in which she said the right thing. But she was too sick, too tired to care. The air was full of words and sentences – they jumbled. Only one of them could be right (or did it matter what one said?). She could not believe it when she came out with:

'Doesn't she love you any more?' And when he didn't answer, saying it again: 'Doesn't she love you any more?'

'Didn't you hear me?' he said in a strange voice, 'I said, she's going away – '

But he had not spoken surely? 'What's it all about then?' she asked: suddenly vigorous as if being cruel had given her strength, 'what if she does? Why don't you go with her?'

212

'Hardly – '

'I thought it was all to be such a nice little arrangement. I thought I wasn't to mind, even if I was the laughing stock of everybody – Muff, Polly, any number of people I've never met. Then, being championed by Camilla, just about the worst fate – ' She stopped because she realized that he was crying: his back to her again now, his shoulders shaking.

'Oh no,' she said, 'oh no.' She leaned across the bed, then kneeling, put her hands on his shoulders. 'You've got cold again. Get into bed.'

Oddly, he obeyed her. Climbing in still in his underpants: she could not rid herself of the thought, the recognition, that he looked ridiculous.

He lay on his side at once, turned away from her. Downstairs she heard a door bang and thought: Polly. Then there was silence. She kept looking at his freckled back as if mesmerized. It belonged it seemed to a stranger.

'If you don't talk about it – at all, what am I to do?'

When he didn't answer she said again, 'What am I to do? It's about her, isn't it? You knew I knew it wasn't going right, or something like that – so why can't you say?' She added a little shakily, 'I do have *some* rights.'

'Sarcastic again,' he said, without moving. 'What a weapon you have there.'

She put out a hand and touched his face. It was wet still. 'Where's she going then? Why? And what exactly has she said? Plainly she's said something.'

'Simply, she's going on a tour.' He swallowed. 'She wants me – we both want, need a decision by the time she comes back. It's divorce really – or else finish.'

She felt sudden irrational anger, not for herself, but against anyone who would trap him in this way. She wanted to shout in outrage – no one may do this to you.

'A woman of decision then, how awfully sensible – that's what the magazines say, the sort of advice they give. Call his bluff.' She spoke anxiously fast. 'Well, it should all be easy enough.'

'No – '

'Why not? Give me the push. Push me then.'

He said slowly, 'When it comes to it. When – I don't know

what it is, what weakness it is that one can't take what one wants. One – '

She interrupted, 'You want it then, don't you?' She heard her voice come out gentle: 'Terribly. Both of you?'

He turned over and lay back, his hands behind his head. She realized suddenly that she had forgotten about her body; that for the moment she didn't feel sick.

He said, 'She doesn't in fact think it will work. That's part of it too. She's not exactly father-struck or father-fixed or whatever. And twenty-two years difference – viewed realistically . . .'

'People are always doing it.'

'One doesn't always rate their chances of success very high. She has a point.'

'Oh God, if you really cared – you'd think the world well lost.'

'Whose side are you on?' he asked drily. 'To hear you speak . . . You read too many magazines.'

When he didn't speak again for a few moments, she had to reach for another cigarette; was unable to resist it.

'Keep the smoke on your side,' he said, 'if you would.' Then, as if he'd been thinking about it, he said suddenly: 'All women are much the same, one thought. And when getting married – it would all come to much the same thing. A swift glance around anyway and one would quickly be disabused of any notion that it can matter. One's parents' arrangements – they hardly made it look otherwise – '

Instead of saying, as she wanted to: that is the most terrible thing you have ever said, she remarked casually, pulling on her cigarette before, after: 'What about your parents? I came much too late on to the scene. I always imagine Muff most upright. All my childhood – she was so busy organizing the village. I think of her always in a turban and those beautifully cut slacks or her WVS green, looking absolutely terrific – but too busy-busy to get up to mischief. Was it your father perhaps? Is that what you mean?'

'Both. One never thought of anything being any other way. It's difficult to imagine what she thought – one was not deceived. Those uncle figures of my childhood . . . and the mysterious way it was suddenly found I needed classics coaching two

214

summers running – he was young too, much younger than her – '

'How cynical you are. How cynical everyone is.'

'One was, yes. Until this. I can't – one's not used to talking about emotions perhaps, analysing them, hence this absurd performance.' He got down from the bed. 'I'm going to get a drink – no, just water.'

When he brought a glass through she asked to sip from it too. He kept drinking and swallowing, as if to rid himself of a lump.

'One does have difficulty in talking about it. But – I *recognized* Morwen. I don't know how else to express it. It was immediate – one has to use clichés – when people speak of soul mates – But . . . If I say I fit into her exactly, as if made, the key for the lock,' he shut his eyes, 'can you avoid, can you *resist* the crude, the obvious?'

'Of course.'

'Thank you.' Now, she thought, stubbing out her cigarette, now is when I sit quite still and don't take another.

'You were saying?'

'This is terrible. It was as if one had never felt before – so often there should be feeling, appropriate feeling, but nothing happens, nothing happened. As if a layer, a part of one were missing. But with this it was as if everything were suddenly explained – '

'But you're just talking about being in love! I mean – what else?' She said wildly, 'Anthea, me, other people earlier surely?'

He shook his head. 'Once perhaps. A friend at school – I have spoken of him. But that was very tied up with music – '

'I don't remember.' She tried to think when really he had ever spoken of himself. 'Say his name.'

'Hal Derrick.'

'It rings a faint bell somewhere – '

'He left the Half before me, and went into the Navy. He was washed overboard in the Arctic just after the War ended. It was a friendship, that's all. And a love affair now I look back. Who's to separate these things?'

'Who indeed?'

'It didn't tell me I was homo – if that had crossed your mind.'

215

'I'm so stupid,' she said. 'Stupid little Teresa. It didn't, hadn't I mean. It just never entered my head.'

'No such excitement coming your way. Music was the bond, I don't think I can separate the feeling. One suspects that's where one's feelings go – into music. Then one can say, I *feel* – '

'It's all to do with music, isn't it? You said something about Bach once, when I can't sit through half an hour of him – you said "all of passion is there" – '

'How pretentious of one . . .'

'Why didn't you settle with it, make it your life? Then perhaps we wouldn't all be in this mess.'

He said suddenly, surprisingly, 'She would never have let me.'

'Muff? *She* doesn't decide. What nonsense – '

'The pressures were remarkably subtle. Not even pressures – assumptions. Worse. One would have had to be a hero to question them. Certainly one *should* – one should have taken what one wanted. It was a good voice. I know that – when I had lessons that summer of '42. Probably one could have done more or less what one wanted with it. She was proud of me certainly, and he was to some extent. But she gets very angry with music, very intolerant of the medium. Strange, because they tell me Uncle Con was quite gifted – although it's difficult to tell of course when it's the glorified dead. Neither she nor father would have understood anyway – one should have gone ahead and taken what one wanted.'

She said, feeling faint, 'Well at least you can take this.' Her heart had begun to pound so that for one wild moment she thought of it as the baby: something alive and separate from her. The news and realization came to her in waves; shock waves, she thought. A baby, a baby, a baby. Then she thought that she must be mad that she could say nothing.

'You've got time to think about it though.' (I have not so much time. I will have to decide. And I have no right to do so alone.) 'Age isn't everything – you've done more mileage, true – but if you suit, if it's really like you say . . .'

She felt so sick now that she thought she would have to go down to the kitchen: she craved suddenly sour home-made lemonade. Where would she get it at this hour of night? She imagined herself cutting up lemons, boiling, stirring – and then the bitter, beautiful taste.

'Thank you,' he said. 'For everything.' His voice was unsteady.

They were both silent. He got up and went through to the lavatory. As he was coming back in, she said in a small voice, sensing humiliation as she asked it, 'All that about feeling. About not feeling anything – until *her*. Then what happened that summer? 1953.' Her own voice surprised her. 'You must have felt something. For me, I mean – '

He stood quite still.

'No,' he said after a moment. 'No, not like that. Tenderness, perhaps. You were a funny little thing, Tessie.' He said it very simply; matter of factly almost.

'I can't believe it was some sort of marriage of convenience.' She tried to say it in an offhand voice, mentally shrugging her shoulders. 'I mean – I didn't bring money, I didn't bring breeding – '

'Hardly. But then we had sufficient of both.' He paused. 'Perhaps I thought love would be added unto me? Who knows?'

She said desperately: 'What was I wanted for then?'

'Ah God knows,' he said. 'God knows what you were wanted for.'

∞

In the middle of Princes Street, Polly expected to be thinking about the letter – was surprised when she found music competing with it. Walking along with a list of errands for Patsy's household, and saying to herself: I don't know whether I'm pleased or upset. Then music coming from nowhere, her head suddenly full of it – she could hear it so clearly sometimes that it seemed almost outside her; a great jumble today, from Byrd to Bach to Charpentier to Fauré, one theme vying with another in its richness of texture, all the way along among the crowds of weekday shoppers.

Perhaps it was because she was still so happy. She had not expected to be. Ten days to go before she could be with him again and yet she wasn't impatient. This sudden flowering of peace – quite separate from her daily, hourly ache for his

217

presence. Such confidence, such hope. 'All shall be well and all manner of things shall be well and thou shalt see for thyself . . .'

Back at the house, lolling on the guest bed, was the doll he had bought her – his farewell present. 'That's a terribly 'twenties thing to do,' she'd said, 'I imagine that as *terribly* 'twenties . . .' 'But it's not that sort of doll,' he'd insisted; and indeed it was not. It was a Brontë doll from Yorkshire, wearing a lacy lawn dress and a tiny straw bonnet. He had wanted to buy it for her, he'd said, and that surely was enough – except that something about the doll's expression reminded him . . . 'Oh *you*,' she'd said lovingly; loving it too.

The letter came back to her suddenly. She turned into Rose Street and thought, I'll stop for a cup of coffee, read it again.

It was crowded in the shop. She sat opposite two elderly women who were applying themselves to scones and jam: one had a handkerchief ready to wipe her mouth regularly between sips and bites.

The letter was in her jeans' pocket. She put it on the empty plate beside her coffee cup.

'. . . will I get you one of the cakes, Annie? They look awful good . . .'

'. . . and you're the first to know,' her mother had written. 'I'm not sure why but I just wanted you to know. Of course I'll tell Daddy, it's just that things are rather difficult, I haven't had a chance yet . . .'

'. . . the pink one, you suit it – it's no everyone can wear pink . . .'

'. . . could you though keep it to yourself for the moment anyway? Please. About having it – nothing's settled, in my mind I mean. It's all a bit muddled, you can imagine what a shock . . .'

'. . . if they havna got them at Binn's . . . they were waiting on them at Jenner's they said . . .'

'. . . rather old to have a baby, to start all over again, and then there are other complications . . .'

She paid for her coffee and walked out into the sunshine. The music came flooding back – but she told herself suddenly, sternly, to be practical. She took out the list. Somewhere round here was Patsy's fishmonger. A large lorry was just parking further up the street; as she passed the driver was climbing down. She smiled at him. 'Hallo.'

'And hallo to you,' he said, 'it's good to see the sun. *And* you, pet – you're looking very well.'

She grinned, 'I am,' she said, smiling, laughing, 'I am.'

Patsy had said they were to have fish twice a week so she bought some Finnan haddock; she would make them a kedgeree. When she came out of the shop the lorry was parked still: the friendly driver wasn't there. She felt something flap against her leg and saw that the thonging of her sandal was unwrapping itself. She turned off the pavement into the alley, leant against a door and bent down to fasten it, hearing as she did so the lorry door slam. Her fingers caught in the thonging: oh Lord, she thought, the bread to be collected always by twelve – Patsy said. She tried to hurry the fastening but her fingers felt sticky. The baby, she thought suddenly, I wonder, I wonder what to think of it all? When will it be, because I must work it out. If, suppose, now – the sound of the lorry starting up interfered with her calculations – no, well if she just knows about it now – where are my fingers? – count, seven eight months' time, say about January, February. She must, I think she *ought* to have it, she would love it so. What can I do to help? Sam and I, we could do lots to help. I think that –

The lorry coming nearer didn't seem to be stopping. She got up swiftly, stood back against the wall. She put her hands out before her. 'Oh but stop, STOP,' she cried, pushing the hard warm metal. She opened her mouth again; but the cry was crushed.

'I think you're ever so sensible,' June said. 'It's the best thing for shock really – something like a hair-do. Just to get your mind off it a little. To soothe you, you know.'

'No doubt,' Muff said. 'No doubt that is correct.' It did not seem to her to matter very much – as really it hadn't mattered for so many years now – what she did with her time. As well sit in June's, beneath the dryer, as at home.

'Shall I sit with you? Lesley, get me the blower, love. I'll sit with you shall I and we'll blow-dry it. Then we can have a little talk.'

Her head felt curiously light suddenly, as if her hair were separate from her. She was confused for a moment: why am I here? And then as she began, slowly, to remember, a great throbbing started up – she could not tell if it was her heart or her head.

'My sister's boy,' June said, 'in Belfast. When they shot him – it's six months now but she says – it was the shock you know. Even though he was Army. It was the *shock* – '

Let her talk on. The air, the blow-dryer, they were full of mistaken kindness. They were wasting their time.

'You are wasting your time,' she said.

'What's that – you don't worry. It's a slack day. I was wanting to chat to you anyway.'

Why ever had she bothered to live, except that, perhaps, Polly had been something to do with it? It had all been over long ago. She had known then in 1917 that it was ended. What has it all been about? she thought. What has it all been *for*?

Then, I am confused, she thought again. My mind . . . Seeing through a blur of pain her hair going up, she shut her eyes and then suddenly there it was again, the lightness, the floating. 'I am a little dizzy,' she said, moistening her lips.

But she didn't want the water when they brought it. It was time to go whether June had finished or not. Teresa had said, looking suddenly like Aunt Lettice had once – authoritative: 'You have to promise me you'll take a taxi *straight* back.' Teresa had been going to fetch Christopher. Like shutters going, opening and shutting: memory. Why should Teresa be fetching Christopher, so long before the end of term?

'Some coffee or shall Lesley get you a cab? Lesley you run out – they're terrible just now the cabs . . .'

The air was close outside. It seemed hotter than in June's. It was her whole body now that had become light. She thought that climbing in she was floating: watching this aged woman go slowly up the step. The door was slammed shut. Lesley said, 'I've given the address, don't you bother.'

But she remembered suddenly, and tapped on the partition: 'I am going to Russia,' she announced.

'Not with me – you aren't,' said the driver. She saw his face, his whole head grow small and shrink, a pinpoint. She left the outside window wound down – holding with one hand on to the side lest she float away. Every now and then her head, her mouth shook. Or were they someone else's? She knew now she was watching herself.

This street was familiar: Basil Street. Nearly empty. Why empty? She came nearer to the window. A young man was walking along in morning dress – grey topper, gloves, purposeful walk. Something was wrong; she watched him carefully. As the taxi passed near, she saw that he was Con.

Frantic, she rapped on the glass: 'Stop – at once!'

'My brother,' she said, as the glass slid back. 'My brother – I must get out at once.'

'As you say – you give the orders . . .' She had her hand on the door almost before he had stopped. Fumbling, rushing. It hurt – it didn't matter that it hurt, she had wings. Only hurry, hurry . . . 'Help me,' she cried to the driver, 'help me!' Already Con was nearly out of reach. He was a back view now, about to be lost in Hans Crescent.

She shook off the driver's arm. A hotel doorman had appeared beside her. She pushed at him with her stick. 'There he is!' she cried, pointing desperately.

'Watch it, watch your step,' the driver called.

'Con!' she said loudly, stumbling, her stick falling.

221

But Con, disappearing into the distance, had not heard her.

∞

Barney, standing white-faced at the door of their bedroom: 'You might have told me. I had, I think, a *right* to know.' Then a pause, 'Unless of course it isn't mine . . .'

She felt worse today, colicky with fear and shock and panic. Thinking too, I might lose it and then where should I, we, be? Her mouth wandered, lips wobbled, as she tried to answer calmly.

'I don't know,' she screamed, shouted, 'of *course* it's yours. And Morwen, haven't you fathered something for *her*? Tell me that – '

He surprised her then by taking hold of her arms, gently, firmly. He led her back to the bed. 'You may get ill – or upset yourself. You were in bed, get back.'

When she sat up, the room in the half light seemed to be receding, sloping away endlessly, falling; or she was falling. Coming up the stairs she had moved through some black pall, some thick furry horror. She had been quite alone in it. Groping for the bedrail, she had felt it covered in some dank mould so that she wasn't certain she would ever reach the bed.

'I shall come in too.'

She lay there shaking. To continue living it was only necessary to be; she had merely to lie there and exist.

'She insisted on going to the hairdresser's, did she?'

'Yes. I telephoned them first while she was on the way. I spoke to June. It would have been difficult to stop her.'

'It would indeed. Perhaps some details though? Upset, sedated, yes. But exactly what *happened*?'

'The taxi man was pretty shaken. I didn't get a very good story from him – he wasn't sure whether to go on up to the nearest hospital with her or not. He and a hotel doorman had got her back in again – she seems to have thought she'd seen Theo and stopped the taxi.'

'Why Theo? He hasn't been out of his nursing home for two years – '

'The driver couldn't even see him, whoever it was. He said there was no one about but a boy dressed up for a wedding.'

'Theo couldn't be about. Someone must have looked like him. Oh my God, what a worry.'

They were both silent.

'Christopher's asleep,' he said. 'I looked in on him.'

She said, 'He didn't talk all the way back.'

'Who was she so thick with, this musician – who was he? Did you find anything, did you ask Muff?'

'He's found me – Patsy contacted me. When he'd tried to 'phone her – 'phone Polly – last night. He's coming here tomorrow.'

'What are we going to do?' he said suddenly. 'How are we going to live?' She saw that he was trembling.

'I'm sorry,' she said. 'Not telling you the right things at the right time. My head's – very muddled.'

'Yes.' He got up and went through to the dressing-room. When he came back he climbed in beside her. He was naked. Lying very still, he said: 'One could start again. I could be done with – We could make some sort of fresh start.'

She said: 'Don't make sacrifices for me, don't make decisions you can't keep up, when you're not yourself.' She remembered in the war, in her father's surgery, a couple famous for their slanging matches, their broken crockery, sitting huddled, arms round each other, their only son killed. She remembered too, how it had been a year later.

He got out, switched off the light, then the bedside light. In the darkness he said, 'About the baby.'

'Yes.'

'Please have it,' he said. 'For me.'

She didn't answer.

'Your religion,' he said, 'I thought . . .' Then he added, but very gently, 'Doesn't one have to decide quite soon – medically?'

'Yes. But not tonight. We have to live through some of this first. Please let me live through some of this first.'

She wished only that he would stop talking. She could feel some of his restlessness as he lay rigidly there. She laid her hand on her stomach; it seemed to her that it was still now. Perhaps she had turned to stone.

'A cruise,' he said wildly. 'Shall I take you and Christopher on a cruise? Perhaps – if we were all to go together, in September?'

223

'Muff,' she said. 'What of Muff?' Her skin felt stretched tight over her cheekbones, eyes aching, pulled from their sockets, her mouth dried.

'Or Corrib. Perhaps if we ...'

It's all hopeless, she thought. She was driven into silence as he lay there, seemingly compelled to talk out his pain. His words were like stabs in the darkness.

Like a film unrolling. Stop; quite still; then her heart pounding. *It didn't happen.*

'A cruise might in its way be better. One would – '

'Fat sorrow and lean sorrow,' her father had said, looking round his practice. And indeed money, which solved nothing, could help. Here, like a crutch, he was feeling for it as he fell.

She thought suddenly, irrelevantly, of the trees that Hess and other prisoners had planted at Spandau, that now were full grown.

'It makes no sort of sense, does it?' he said. His head turned on the pillow.

She was in some sort of dark tunnel. It was not possible to see even a little little way ahead. But to get out, to come out, it was only necessary to go on to the end.

She could feel how stiffly he lay. What hope for their two hearts? not bound together, but away wandering. She put out a hand, laid it on his belly. After a while she moved it on, inside his thigh, where the skin was soft.

'Cold,' he said, 'so cold. Warm me, Tessie.'

Pamela Haines

Also available in Fontana
DAUGHTER OF THE NORTHERN FIELDS

Christabel Woodward is the cosseted daughter of a prosperous mill-owner until he discovers her mother's long-held secret: Christabel is not his own child but the natural daughter of Branwell Brontë.

Rejected by her father, and then raped by a man she trusted and admired, Christabel's world is shattered. She is forced to leave her beloved moorland home and suffer the loneliness of exile, a journey leading her, with a final, painful irony, to a court of law where she will stand trial – accused of murder.

A magnificent evocative story set against the wild and beautiful scenery of the Pennines, *Daughter of the Northern Fields* mirrors the heart and pulse of nineteenth-century Yorkshire.

'The nineteenth-century atmosphere is beautifully handled, and the story grippingly told'

YORKSHIRE POST

Pamela Haines

Also available in Fontana

THE KISSING GATE

A grand saga, set in the beauty and pride of Yorkshire, with all the power and excitement of the Victorian era.

The Kissing Gate is at the heart of village life, and marks the beginning of the Squire's land. The rescue of Squire Ingham's son by an Irish servant-girl creates an uneasy bond between Sarah and the Squire's family, which in later generations will explode into forbidden love.

THE GOLDEN LION

Maria Verzotto is in her far-off home in Sicily, Dick Grainger is growing up in Yorkshire when they first hear the legend of the Golden Lion – the story of a heroic prince and how he wins his princess. But there is another Lion who is destined to influence Maria's life – the Lion of the Monteleone, a ruthless mafioso . . .

'Pamela Haines is now undoubtedly in a class all of her own' THE TIMES

'A born writer' Francis King, SPECTATOR

FONTANA PAPERBACKS

Almost Paradise
Susan Isaacs

Jane Cobleigh gave up her ambitions to nurture her husband's rise to stardom. His success brought them glamour and riches, but to her – loneliness, until she began her own career. But could any marriage stand the price of such success?

'Richly textured, gracefully written – a joy to read and remember.' *Cosmopolitan*

'The year's most enchanting novel.' *McCalls*

'The plot is riveting; the characters real.'
New York Daily News

'A wonderful book.' *Danielle Steel*

FONTANA PAPERBACKS

The Hearts and Lives of Men
Fay Weldon

Fay Weldon's stunning new novel is an adventure story in which, you will be glad to hear, love finally triumphs over lust, good will over satanic forces, and sheer kindness over piercing malevolence. The pace never falters; the language glitters. The wit is as ever razor sharp. Yet laughter, tears and a lump in the throat are never far away.

'The sixties background is impeccable and deftly evoked, the style is sharp and the jokes are acidly funny.' *Evening Standard*

'Every word of *The Hearts and Lives of Men* is a delight.' *Spectator*

'I spent a weekend reading *The Hearts and Lives of Men*, and a very good weekend it was too.' *Punch*

'It's unputdownable, of course.' *City Limits*

'Buy it you must.' *Company*

FONTANA PAPERBACKS

The Noonday Devil
Alan Judd

Robert Stevens and Tim Albright are in their final term
at Oxford. Their exams are looming larger and larger
on the horizon. But more important to both of them is
the production of the fierce Jacobean tragedy, *The
Changeling*, which Robert is directing. Along with
them, we follow the fortunes of Gina, the seductive and
enigmatic leading lady in the play; Chetwynd, the
bizarre older student who travels around with a
revolver; and Anne, the gentle wife of Robert's tutor.

In a masterly work of fiction, Alan Judd brings, his
characters closer together until the tension is
unbearable. And all the while, in the background,
international tension mounts to fever pitch.

Alan Judd's previous novels were noted for their
humour and anarchy, and *The Noonday Devil* is spiced
with both, underlying the deadly trap of sloth and
indifference which provides the key to a novel whose
climax is unexpected and unsettling . . .

FONTANA PAPERBACKS

The Green Flash
Winston Graham

David Abden is dangerous. Young, attractive, a baronet's nephew, he is already a convicted felon, and he killed his own father at the age of eleven. Or did he?

The best of everything is David's aim – in his chosen world of perfumery, in fast cars, and in women: Shona, the exotic Russian emigrée; the feline and enchanting Erica; the gentle Alison.

The success he achieves in the shadowy world of business intrigue will lead David eventually to another killing and, finally, to a reckoning with his past . . .

'Defies one not to read on . . . an absorbing, unpredictable chronicle' *Daily Mail*

'Tremendous narrative power' Martyn Goff, *Daily Telegraph*

'Winston Graham keeps a unfailing grip on a narrative that tightens with every page' David Hughes *Mail on Sunday*

FONTANA PAPERBACKS

Fontana Paperbacks: Fiction

Fontana is a leading paperback publisher of fiction.
Below are some recent titles.

- ☐ THE COURTS OF LOVE Jean Plaidy £3.95
- ☐ HERCULE POIROT'S CASEBOOK Agatha Christie £2.95
- ☐ THE FORTUNE TELLER Marsha Norman £3.95
- ☐ TAPESTRY Belva Plain £3.95
- ☐ KING'S EXILE Christine Marion Fraser £3.50
- ☐ HANNAH'S WHARF Connie Monk £3.50
- ☐ GETTING INTO PRACTICE Andrew Linfield £3.50
- ☐ A SOLDIER'S TALE M. K. Joseph £3.50

You can buy Fontana paperbacks at your local bookshop or
newsagent. Or you can order them from Fontana Paperbacks,
Cash Sales Department, Box 29, Douglas, Isle of Man. Please
send a cheque, postal or money order (not currency) worth the
purchase price plus 22p per book for postage (maximum postage
required is £3.00 for orders within the UK).

NAME (Block letters) _____

ADDRESS _____

_____